A Move to Murder

Helena Lamb

A Bride's Bay Mystery

This is a work of fiction. All the characters and events portrayed in the novel are either products of the author's imagination or are used fictitiously. Bride's Bay does not exist, nor does Monkton, but Portsmouth, Southampton, Fareham, Gosport and Winchester can all be found in the county of Hampshire in southern England.

Bride's Bay

Bride's Bay is a small fictitious town in the county of Hampshire on the south coast of England, between the cities of Portsmouth and Southampton. It overlooks the Isle of Wight.

It is loosely based on Lee on the Solent but any similarities to this town are purely co-incidental and are not based on any fact; nor are any of the characters based on any resident, living or dead.

Monkton is based on the nearby area of Hill Head in Stubbington, another town on the south coast of Hampshire.

The fictional Bride's Bay has a population of approximately five thousand and the usual amenities of a small town; a primary school, church, health centre, library, shops, wine bar and small hotel.

The nearest large towns to Bride's Bay and Monkton are Gosport and Fareham.

The beach is shingle and the area is renowned for sailing.
The Isle of Wight is across the Solent and the town overlooks Cowes.

This is the first book in the Bride's Bay series. The second "Deadly Mischief" and the third "Secrets and Skeletons" are available on Amazon.

Copyright 2015 Helena Lamb

All rights reserved

Cast of Characters

Beth Bryson	Part time nursery nurse, lives in Bride's Bay
Nell Collins	Beth's niece, lives and works in Winchester
Will Hayes	Nell's boyfriend
Gina Harris	Beth's close friend, widowed, lives in Monkton
Carol Baker	Beth's close friend, lives in Bride's Bay
Ken Baker	Carol's husband, local Estate Agent
Naomi Pearson	Carol and Ken's daughter, lives in Winchester
Joe Pearson	Naomi's husband, a teacher in Winchester
Florence and Noah	Naomi and Joe's children
Mark Rowlands	Vicar at Saint Andrew's Church
Maggie Rowlands	Mark's wife
April Turner	Manageress of Bride's Bay Charity Shop
Sue Carter	April's assistant
Julian Soames	Owner of Pebbles Gallery and Pottery
Ali Soames	Julian's wife
Robert Salmon	Owner of R. Salmon, Butchers
Barbara Salmon	Robert's wife
Matthew and Hannah	Robert and Barbara's children
Frances Dobinson	In charge of flowers at Saint Andrew's Church
Melissa Harris	A newcomer to Bride's Bay, an artist
Grace Harris	Melissa's sister, a photographer
Tom Callow	A newcomer to Bride's Bay, a retired lecturer

Chapter 1 6
Chapter 2 16
Chapter 3 26
Chapter 4 39
Chapter 5 55
Chapter 6 65
Chapter 7 77
Chapter 8 88
Chapter 9 99
Chapter 10 110
Chapter 11 125
Chapter 12 136
Chapter 13 150
Chapter 14 161
Chapter 15 170
Epilogue 184

CHAPTER 1

Beth's eyes sprang open; her heart thudding as she stared into the darkness, straining her eyes as wide as they could go to peer into the blackness. No, not complete blackness; rather dark shapes against a darker background. Something heavy was pressing against her side and soft snuffling sounds penetrated her consciousness. Her throat closed as she opened her mouth to cry out, muscles tensing, lungs tightening and head dizzy with fear. The room tilted and swayed. She was spinning round, blurred images flashing past, on a roundabout. A wave of nausea hit her, bile burning into her throat. Then the roundabout slowed. Stopped. The black on black began to fade; cracks of light began to show around a door, a window, and shapes became apparent. Relief flooded her whole body as she made sense of her surroundings and realised she was in her bed, in her safe haven of a bedroom, and had been dreaming. The black shapes were furniture; the weight was Charlie, boldly curled up asleep next to her rather than in his dog basket in the kitchen, snoring gently in his sleep and twitching as he also dreamt. Nicer dreams than mine though, thought Beth, as her heart rate slowed and the tension started to drain from her body, leaving her with a dry mouth and a heavy stone of dread in her stomach. Pushing Charlie aside, she rolled over and switched on the bedside lamp, transforming the scene of her nightmare back into her bedroom. She sat up slowly, being careful not to disturb Charlie, though why shouldn't she wake him? He was supposed to be in the kitchen anyway.

She swung her legs out of bed and made her way down the steep stairs, through the hall and into the kitchen, feeling for the light switch and flooding the room with warm, reassuring, safe light. Put the kettle on, she told herself, the cure for all life's dramas and crises. Moments later, she sat at the wooden kitchen table hugging a mug of steaming, comforting tea, absorbing the familiar sights and sounds of the room; the quiet rhythmic ticking of the wall clock, the photo on the dresser of Nell, suntanned in shorts and a skimpy top, her hair the colour of dark honey, tangled and tousled, her teeth white and straight in a huge grin, laughter and joy in her eyes; the photo of Louise with the same hair, the same teeth, but with a faint smile, a cautious look on her eyes as though she already knew of the tragedy that lay ahead; the jug of flowers on the table, deep crimson tulip, their petals studded with yellow and black scattered around it. She should have thrown them out a couple of days before, when they started to wilt, but had wanted another day or two of their vibrant beauty. Gradually the knot of fear and dread in her stomach dissolved and faded away and her grip on the mug eased. A soft padding sound came from the hall and Charlie appeared in the doorway, wagging his tail and eyeing her quizzically, his little hairy head on one side.

"No Charlie, it's not food time, or walk time." Beth leaned forward to scratch the Scottie dog behind his ears and with a sigh he wandered over to his basket, sitting down in it with a thump.

Beth sipped her tea and thought back to the dream, no….. nightmare, flashback, whatever it had been. She hadn't had flashbacks for months now; what had caused it tonight? It didn't take much, she knew; maybe a news item, a throwaway remark someone made, a fleeting glimpse of someone who looked like…. There, now she had done it, brought the memories floating up to the surface when she tried so hard to keep them submerged, hidden in the past where they belonged. Well, be positive, she chided herself, you haven't thought about the past for months now; life is good, so many things to enjoy and look forward to. Concentrate on those things and put the past back in its box, turn the key, throw it away. Think about dinner tomorrow with the girls, about Nell visiting on Saturday for lunch. She was bringing Will too. It would be the first time he and Beth had met. What would he be like? Should she cook or take them out for a meal? She would cook; she'd do Nell's favourite pasta bake and a pavlova to follow. Too early for strawberries but maybe raspberries and kiwi? Though maybe Will was more of an apple crumble and custard man so maybe two desserts? No, that would be overdoing it. She rinsed the mug, placed it on the draining board and smiled down at Charlie, twitching in his sleep as he chased waves or seagulls, then clicked off the light and went back to bed.

The next morning brought sun streaming through the curtains and the promise of a warm, sunny day. And a good job too, thought Beth, as she locked the front door and started the short walk to the school, where fifteen three and four-year olds would soon also be heading for the nursery classroom where Beth was the morning nursery nurse, working alongside the teacher Helen. The previous weekend and the beginning of the week had been wet and windy and the days of enforced indoor play had made the children fractious. At least they could play outside today and relieve some of that energy. Well, today should be good; Wednesday meant a music session with Tim, always good fun; then this afternoon was her stint in the charity shop and a chance to catch up with Gina then this evening she was calling round to Carol's to help her with a dress her friend was trying, and failing, to make. A job she loved, good friends, Nell, and a lovely place to live, thought Beth as she glanced down the road towards the beach, where the sun sparkled on the sea and the island was clear in the bright morning light, before turning in through the school gates.

"So, have you met either of them yet?" Gina asked as she passed a fragile tea set to Beth, one cup at a time, to arrange in the charity shop window. "No, not there, you need that big space for the tea pot". Beth rearranged the cups to make space for the errant tea pot.
"There, how's that looking? And who are you talking about? Who am I supposed to have met? Or is that whom?" Gina was a stickler for correct grammar.
"Your two newcomers; Carol said there are two people who have just moved here, one to Addison Crescent and one to Bay Road East." Gina handed up the last piece of the set and stood back to gather up paper and boxes.
"Why two houses? Don't they live together?" Beth stepped carefully off the step. It was only one small step but she didn't like heights, not even thirty centimetres. Gina frowned, turning back to Beth, her silvery blonde hair swinging in a perfect arc.
"Why would they live together?"
"You said there were two people" Beth explained patiently.
"Yes, but I didn't say they were together! He is a retired lecturer from Reading University apparently and she has moved from Bristol. They're not a couple!"
"Ah, I see. But no, I haven't met them yet. Tell me more about them. I assume Carol knows about them through Ken?"

Gina and Beth moved back into the stock room at the rear of the shop to resume emptying boxes and wash the crockery and glassware they contained, ready to display.
"Yes, the man can't remember his name, has just completed on that big house at the end of your road, your main road at least, on the corner. What's it called?"
"Alma House? I didn't realise it had been sold, I know it was on the market for a while after Mr Simons died but I didn't know anyone had moved in."
"Well, he moved in on Monday apparently. I'm surprised you didn't see the removal van."

"We're not all as nosey as you!" Beth grinned, knowing how untrue it was of her friend, who was actually very discreet and sensitive to people's privacy. Now, if it had been Carol...

"But I know the woman's name, Melissa, and according to Carol she is as glamorous as her name. Tall, amazing figure, glossy dark hair. Amazing bone structure. Carol said she's a Nigella Lawson lookalike. Designer clothes, stunning jewellery."

"So she only got a quick look then!"

Gina smiled. "She's rented the Thomson's house for a year, while they are in Brussels."

"How old is she? What does she do?"

"Late forties Carol thought, and I don't know about her work, Carol hasn't found out yet but..."

"Beth? Could you come and serve please?" Gina was interrupted by the call from the shop and Beth hurried through to where April Turner, the manageress, was dealing with a queue of people waiting to pay.

The rest of the afternoon passed quickly and business was good; although it usually was, thanks mainly to the double act that was April and her assistant, Sue Carter. Both women were extrovert and friendly; Sue in particular knowing most people who came through the door and if she didn't, possessing an innate ability to gauge their personality and hone in on their likes and dislikes. Before they knew it, customers would be leaving the shop clutching a carrier bag containing a purchase they hadn't realised they wanted or needed. April was more subtle; finding out what the customer was looking for and patiently helping them to find it. She also knew who was in genuine need, discreetly ensuring they received what was required for what they could afford. Between them the two women ran the shop efficiently and happily, along with a band of volunteers. Again, April and Sue knew their volunteers' strengths and weaknesses and made sure the lonely felt befriended and the low had support. Beth always finished her stint feeling tired but happy and upbeat and knew the other volunteers did too.

As she and Gina walked down the High Street, leaving April and Sue to lock up, Gina resumed the discussion the newcomers.

"Anyway, you'll meet Melissa on Friday because Carol has roped her in to come along to flower arranging to see if she wants to volunteer."

"Carol has? What will Frances have to say about that?" queried Beth, thinking of the touchy women in charge of the church flower arranging.

"She will want to vet her first and make sure she is up to the job! I'm always amazed she lets me arrange the flowers, I belong to the "bung 'em in a vase" school of flower arranging."

Gina laughed. "No you don't, you always arrange them beautifully. Stop putting yourself down."

She touched Beth's arm briefly and gave her a quick hug before kissing her on the cheek.

"Anyway, bye for now. See you tomorrow evening?"

"Of course. Take care."

Beth continued walking down the High Street, stopping suddenly as a figure rushed out of the Co-op and collided with her.

"Oh! Sorry! Oh Beth, sorry, sorry." A small blonde woman pulled herself up short and gave Beth a harassed smile. "I'm in a hurry as usual".

"It's okay." Beth looked at the woman. "Are you okay, Barbara? You look a bit fraught."

"No, I'm fine, just hurrying to get some milk before they close. Matthew was supposed to get some, but he's helping James and Joe. And Robert is not pleased" a grimace "he's supposed to be helping him."

"Oh." Beth wasn't sure what to say. This particular battle had been going on for some months now, seventeen year old Matthew doing odd jobs for James Lamb's building company after school, rather than helping his father in his butcher's shop.

"I don't want him to be working for either of them; I'd rather he was at home doing his homework, he's got exams coming up…." Barbara's voice trailed off and she pushed her blonde curls out of her eyes as she spotted her husband beckoning to her from his shop across the road. With a hurried goodbye she was off, dodging a cyclist as she ran across to him

Beth strolled on down to the end of the High Street and across to George Road, looking ahead at the splash of colour in the small front garden of her little terraced cottage. Even from here she could see the rich red and sunshine yellow of the tulips and the splash of mauve of the grape hyacinths underneath them. She had moved to this cottage with Nell mainly to provide the young girl with a garden. Nell had loved growing things, from sunflowers to herbs and vegetables. When other young girls had been saving up to buy clothes and make up, Nell had been saving for plants and seeds. The flat they had lived in when Beth had first moved to Bride's Bay had been spacious and comfortable but had no private outdoor space. Beth had bought this cottage mainly for its garden; although the front had been a small, paved area full of weeds and cracked slabs; the back had been over 100 feet long, mainly lawn with a central path running down it to a shed and greenhouse at the end. When she had first brought Nell to see it, the young girl's eyes had sparkled with delight; she had run down the path, excitedly making plans for the garden before she had even seen inside the house. It was the first sign of happiness Beth had seen since the young girl's mother had died and she vowed to afford the little cottage somehow.

Over the years she and Nell had worked hard until now neither garden bore any resemblance to its original appearance. The front had been gravelled and filled with seasonal tubs, planters and hanging baskets, ablaze with seasonal colour, while the back garden had been transformed into a series of "rooms" with seating areas; a terrace for meals, a secret garden through a willow arch and a small vegetable patch hidden behind a trellis over which tumbled a clematis and winter jasmine. The shed and greenhouse remained but an arbour with a swing seat had also been added and Nell and Beth had both spent many a contented hour chatting and swinging, a glass of juice in Nell's hand and a glass of wine in Beth's. Buying this little cottage had been the right thing to do, reflected Beth, as she let herself into the hall and greeted Charlie. It had provided the teenage Nell with security and the cosy home plus the miracle of nature transforming the garden had helped heal the young girl after the death of her mother when she was only twelve. It had also helped to heal her, reflected Beth, as she sat on the garden swing with a mug of coffee before taking Charlie for a walk. Moving to Bride's Bay to care for Nell had changed her life dramatically; but the years here by the ever changing sea, in her own little house, with her work and friends, had also helped her to recover from the shock of Louise's accident and she was proud of the beautiful young woman her niece had become and the lives they had both made. Every time she spoke to Nell, she was bubbling with excitement over her job at a large horticultural firm near Winchester, her rented flat and, more recently, Will, a young man she worked with and who now seemed to be mentioned more than the job or the flat. Beth suppressed a pang of anxiety at the thought of meeting the young man. She just had to trust in Nell's judgement. Surely if Nell liked him, so would she? Stop worrying, Beth reproached herself; Nell has sound judgement, stop looking for problems!

She kept Charlie on his lead while they strolled down to the beach, glancing at Alma House as they walked past. Signs of life were apparent;

windows were open upstairs and downstairs and the sound of a power drill drifted out. On the driveway was an old estate car, in need of a clean. So he has a dog, Beth thought, registering a dog guard in the back of the car, then smiled to herself at the thought she was turning into Carol, hunting for clues. He must also be about sixty, if he was retired. Gina had not mentioned a wife or partner. Divorced, widowed? mused Beth. Or maybe just single? Though it was a large house for one person; maybe someone was following him down? His house certainly had stunning views, straight across the Solent to the Isle of Wight and round the bay to Portsmouth, the Spinnaker tower shining brightly in the sun. The house itself was also a treasure, Beth knew, never having been inside but having seen the photographs when it had first been marketed by Ken, Carol's estate agent husband. An impressive late Victorian detached house, it had most of its original features and succeeded in being spacious and full of character as well as comfortable, thanks to its previous owners, Mr and Mrs Simons, who had installed secondary glazing, a new heating system and good quality bathrooms and kitchen. Harry Simons had also been a keen gardener and Beth knew Frances Dobinson had greatly admired his garden and the variety of plants he had grown. Harry had generously allowed Frances to cut flowers and foliage from his garden to use in church and since his death, Frances had frequently bemoaned the fact she could no longer visit his garden, even going so far as to ask Ken Baker if he could let her into the garden to cut them. Ken had told her bluntly she could not trespass but it grieved Frances to know the flowers were there but unattainable. Perhaps the new owner would let her pick them? Frances lived in a similar cottage to Beth's, but with a much smaller back garden. Despite the size, Beth knew her garden was a riot of plants and flowers, Frances having no time or inclination for grass or vegetables. Her garden was one subject guaranteed to put a smile on the disapproving face of the other woman, and the only thing Beth really had in common with her.

  The sun was still high in the sky but not so intense now and the island was a haze of soft greens. The sea was calm, highlighted by flashes of silver, and small waves bubbled and whispered as they crawled onto the shingle beach. Beth sat down near the water's edge and gazed at the water, while Charlie ran backwards and forwards, sprinting into the sea then immediately running out to shake vigorously. Sailing boats glided silently back and forth, their sails colourful against the silvery blue water. Out of habit, Beth sifted the shingle around her through her fingers, searching out interesting shells and pebbles to take home and then maybe into school for the children to use for art and craft sessions. Today's search proved fairly fruitless and Beth glanced at her watch and straightened up, calling Charlie, to head home for a quick snack before going to Carol's.

"I can see what you've done, those marks are for the shoulder pleats, not those" Beth pointed to the tiny black marks on the paper pattern and Carol peered over her shoulder.
"Ugh, I knew I should have picked a pattern for a sleeveless dress".
"I'll pin it for you, then you'll be fine".
The two women sat down and Beth began unpicking the stitches Carol had made in error.

"So I hear we have two newcomers? One bombshell and one useful man?"
"Well, certainly a bombshell. I don't know how useful he will be, I haven't met him yet. But he's a retired lecturer so probably not very practical, a dusty, dry academic I expect."
"Carol! That's a bit of a generalisation! He might have lectured in car mechanics, or engineering or carpentry or something."
"Do they have degrees in carpentry? If they do, I don't suppose it's called that these days" doubtfully. "Anyway, I have a feeling Ken said it was economics, or business or something, so equally boring."
"When I walked past today, someone was drilling in there, so he must be quite practical" Beth reasoned.
"How do you know it was him? It could have been a workman, or a friend, or anyone."
"Poor man!" laughed Beth. "You've got a down on him already!"
"No I haven't, I'm just reserving judgement until I meet him and get to know him." Carol was at her dignified best.
"Huh. When did you ever wait to form a judgement? There, all done. Now, tell me about Sunday, how are Florence and Noah?"

Beth handed the half-finished dress to Carol who folded it away on her sewing table and led the way downstairs. The evening sun was shining through the stained glass window on the landing, throwing blue, red and yellow patches on the white wall. The oak flooring glowed a deep honey colour as Beth followed her friend through the light, airy sitting room and the original French doors into the conservatory. Worn wicker chairs and sofas looked out over the garden, a pile of magazines was scattered over the small table and an impressive tower of Duplo bricks adorned the floor. Beth stepped carefully around it to avoid knocking it down, to reach the sofa. Carol's home was like her, thought Beth; warm, welcoming, comfortable. She and Ken had lived in the house for over thirty years, bringing up two children. Now their granddaughter skated on the oak flooring, played on the swing hanging from the apple tree and made dens in the shrubs and borders. Noah at only six months was content to lie and gurgle at the shadows cast by the sun through the trees. Lucky children, mused Beth, having Carol and Ken for grandparents.

Carol had been the first friend Beth had made when she had moved to Bride's Bay; the first person to call round and talk openly about the accident that had taken Beth there, wrapping her in her arms and rocking her back and forth when the grief of it all had been too much. She had called round every day with meals for Beth and her niece; had washed and ironed, kept the fridge stocked and helped Beth with Nell, when the young girl, still a child, had refused to go to school or leave the flat. How she would have got through that time without Carol, Beth had no idea; or without Reverend Mark and his wife Maggie, who had also been there with emotional and practical support, helping her to plan the funeral when her mind screamed it shouldn't be happening. Later, Carol's husband Ken had been a rock helping her find a small house to buy and sorting out the builders, decorators and various tradesmen needed to get the little house ready for her and Nell. What a time that had been, and how weak and helpless she had felt. Now, ten years later, Nell was a happy, confident young woman and Beth was content, but she would never forget those dark days and how Carol had helped her get through them.

An hour passed comfortably with a bottle of wine and chat about grandchildren, church business and town affairs until Beth glanced at her watch and stood up.
"Do you want Ken to run you home?"
Beth shook her head. "No, thanks all the same, it's a nice evening to walk. See you tomorrow."

She went out through the garden gate and began the ten minute walk home. The sun had set and the air was warm and scented. Voices drifted to her on the air, the hum of lawn mowers and chink of dishes. She strolled back along the seafront, making out the bobbing lights of fishing boats and the fuzzy glow over on the island, Charlie padding along beside her. Lights were also blazing from every window in Alma House and Beth smiled as she remembered Carol's character analysis.

"I hope the poor man knows what he's doing, moving to a small town like this, he'll have no privacy. But I wouldn't have it any other way!"

CHAPTER 2

"So unfortunately the poor man used to get confused between which bodies were for his work and which were for pleasure!"

Melissa raised her glass with long, slim fingers immaculately tipped with a rich coral polish. Her nails perfectly matched the stunning silver and coral necklace and earring that swung from her ear, the other hidden, at least Beth presumed it was, behind a cascade of rich brown waves. Carol was right; Melissa certainly was a bombshell, and funny and friendly with it. Beth had received a text that morning from Carol asking if it would be alright if she invited Melissa to join them at their usual Thursday evening get together at the local restaurant, as a way for Melissa to get to know some people. Beth had read it, understanding immediately the sub context, as a way for Carol to get to know Melissa! But so far the evening had been fun; Melissa had been pleased to accept the invitation and had been sitting at the bar when the others arrived. To Beth, who was still uncomfortable waiting at a bar on her own and always tried to arrive after the others, Melissa had been the epitome of confidence and elegance; perched on a bar stool in a simple white shift dress, long tanned legs ending in strappy white sandals, her chestnut hair thick and glossy around her shoulders. When she had turned round to greet Beth, her deep brown eyes had been warm and friendly, fringed with long black lashes and framed by perfect arched brows. And yes she did have perfect cheek bones, thought Beth, reflecting on her own cheekbones which presumably she had, albeit well hidden beneath softly padded cheeks.

The four women had moved to their table in the window and conversation had flowed easily, Melissa exhibiting an ease of conversation and a wicked sense of humour. Within an hour, the three women had found out enough about the newcomer to satisfy even Carol; where she had moved from (Clifton), what she did (a trained nurse but had given that up to pursue her painting), how she had lived with Neville, a surgeon in Bristol, for six years, until his wandering eye wandered one time too many. Why on earth would someone with Melissa for a partner drift elsewhere? wondered Beth.

"So he promised it would stop, he would never stray again....ha ha, as if! So I decided on a fresh start, a move to somewhere new."
"What made you pick Bride's Bay?" Gina asked curiously.

"Location." Melissa poured herself more wine. "I wanted somewhere with a fast train to London, I go there quite regularly to promote my work. Plus an airport and you're spoilt for choice here with three, but I also wanted to be near water; I love rivers, lakes, sea, you name it. I can work anywhere so this seemed to tick the boxes."

"But you haven't bought?" queried Beth.

Melissa shook her head. "No, I'm renting for a year then who knows? If I decide to settle here, I will look for something to buy, if not, I shall move on. It's an adventure, who knows what may happen!"

"Well, I think a toast is in order" Carol raised her glass and the others followed suit.

"Welcome, Melissa! And here's to adventures!"

Melissa left before coffee, pleading unpacking still to do but Beth suspected it was the woman's tactful way of giving the three friends time on their own.

"Phew she's a whirlwind" Gina leaned back in her chair. "But a nice whirlwind!"

"She certainly is." Carol agreed. "Lots of energy there to get involved…."

"Carol! Give the poor woman a chance and let her settle in before you drag her onto this and that committee!" exclaimed Gina.

"I will! But if you want something done, ask a busy person, and she looks as though she would be efficient and reliable."

"She'll certainly raise a few pulses! Can you imagine her nursing?" marvelled Beth.

"Actually I can" Gina looked thoughtful. "She's very glamorous but she's kind and cheerful. All those funny tales of people she has worked with and so on, but she never once said anything spiteful or catty about them, not even about Neville."

"I wonder if she's on the lookout for another man" Carol began, to be immediately interrupted.

"No! Carol. Stop it, leave the poor girl alone" laughed Gina. "You've tried with me, you've tried with Beth, can't you accept some of us are happy on our own?"

"Well! I only try to help."

"We know, and we love you for it" Beth patted her hand, "But I think Melissa can find her own man, without any help from you!"

Beth glanced at her watch. "Time I made a move." They stood to gather up their belongings and pay.

"I wonder what the new man Tom looks like?" queried Carol as they made their way outside.

"He might be a George Clooney lookalike, or Daniel Craig!" teased Gina.

"Daniel Craig!" Carol stopped, closing her eyes and clasping her hands to her chest. "Be still, my beating heart!"

"You've got your own James Bond at home!" Beth nudged her.

"So I have! And not much difference between the two!" The three women burst out laughing, each thinking of short, stocky Ken, with his balding head and glasses.

"He'll do for me, though!" She hugged Beth, then Gina, and turned to walk the short distance home.

"See you Sunday" Gina kissed Beth's cheek and slid elegantly into her sports car, waving as she drove away.

Beth walked quickly home, the day had been warm but now the air had a coolness to it and she wished she had brought a warmer jacket. Lights twinkled on the island and on the beach where the evening fishermen sat and the moon was almost full, shining down on the sea. A line of Shelley popped into Beth's head, "and the moonbeams kiss the sea." They certainly were tonight.

He didn't look like George Clooney. Nor Daniel Craig.

Beth had woken up later than usual on Sunday morning, stirred from sleep by Charlie pawing her arm and looking at her quizzically, his little black head on one side. Saturday had been busy, cooking in the morning for Nell and Will's visit, a long walk at the nature reserve in the afternoon and an evening of food, wine and chat, hearing all about Nell's job as well as getting to know Will. The young man had been quiet, content to sit and relax while Nell chattered on and Beth saw to the food and drink. But he was polite and at ease, sitting with his long legs stretched out and a warm expression in his brown eyes as he listened to the conversation between Nell and her aunt. He was also quick to jump up and help Beth and Nell clear the dishes and tidy up. Well brought up, thought Beth, good for you Will's mum, whoever you are. It had been late when they had left and Beth still had to finish the tidying and take Charlie out for a quick walk. So this morning she had washed and dressed quickly, pulling on a white cotton top and simple blue cotton skirt that she realised to her dismay had a stain on it, as she hurried along the High Street. Even her sandals looked scruffy. The navy nubuck sandals with Velcro straps had looked smart when she had bought them, and were certainly comfortable, but had not worn well and looked shabby. Not like Melissa's sandals last night. Melissa wouldn't be seen in velcro, Beth was certain, recalling the high heels and thin white straps encasing Melissa's perfect feet. Oh well, Melissa wasn't running around after fifteen young children every morning, or walking a dog three times a day. For now she would tuck her feet out of sight and hide the stain on her skirt with her bag. She quietly let herself into church and sat near the back, only greeting people in the queue for coffee after the service.

"Beth, Beth." She turned at the sound of Carol's voice to see her friend beckoning her to a table across the hall. Balancing her cup and saucer and bag, imagining everyone's eyes on her crumpled top and stained skirt, Beth weaved her way through tables, acknowledging greetings, until she reached Carol's table and saw a tall, sturdily built man standing up to pull a chair out for her.
"Thank you." She smiled up into the unfamiliar face, realising Carol was talking.
"Beth, this is Tom Callow. Tom, my good friend Beth Bryson."
"Hello, Beth." The man smiled down at her, hazel eyes crinkling at the corners, holding out his hand. Beth put her cup and saucer and bag down and felt her hand gripped in a strong, warm handshake.
"Hello, nice to meet you, and welcome to Bride's Bay." Beth had to look up to make eye contact, her eyes being on a level with the pocket on his light blue cotton shirt.
"And welcome to St Andrews, Tom'" chimed in Frances, seated on Tom's other side.
"What parish have you come from? Were you involved there? I do the flowers here and of course we always need side's men and church wardens and…."

Tom managed to stem the flow with a smile, turning to Frances. "I was admiring the flowers, they're stunning. And now I know who is responsible."
"Well" preened Frances, patting her short silver hair. "I do my best…. and I do have some help" she added reluctantly, catching Carol's eye. "Some of the other ladies are on the rota, we take it in turns, but I have the overall responsibility, you know."
"The garden with my new house is a real plantsman's garden, you are very welcome to call round if you want to see if there's anything you can use in church" offered Tom, unwittingly saying exactly what Frances had been

desperate to hear and being rewarded with profuse thanks and a smile that transformed Frances's usually stern face. She really did have beautiful skin, Beth thought, and lovely pale blue eyes, but her mouth was usually grim and her movements quick and impatient.
"That's very kind, Tom. Mr Simons, the previous owner, let me cut some for the church and it would be wonderful to do so again. May I call round tomorrow?"

The conversation became more general and Beth had the opportunity to study the newcomer, noticing with a small smile that Carol was doing the same, though not so discreetly. He wasn't as old as Beth had assumed, mid-fifties maybe, and had thick sandy reddish hair, flopping slightly over his forehead, faded to a peppery blonde around the temples. Tall, well over six feet, not overweight, but broad shoulders and solid. As he leaned forward to take a programme of church events from Ken, Beth saw his eyelashes were thick, reddish brown and his hands were large and tanned. No, not George Clooney, she thought, but nice looking and he and Melissa would make an attractive couple, then chided herself for being as bad as Carol.

"Sorry." Beth blinked and realised a question had been addressed to her. Flustered, she picked up her cup and it dripped coffee on to her skirt from where it had slopped into her saucer during her slalom through the hall. Bother, another stain.
"Beth! Here." Carol handed her a tissue and Beth mopped at the underneath of the cup and the patch on her skirt. Carol diverted attention from her friend, seeing her blushing with mortification and biting her lip.
"Tom was asking if dogs are allowed on the beach. I said yes, up until the end of May. You walk Charlie on the beach every day, don't you?"
Beth nodded. "The main part of the beach is dog free from the end of May until the end of September, but you can walk them on Pebble beach all year round, that's the part from the sailing club round to Stern Head. If you go over the road from your house onto the beach and go left to the sailing club you can walk all the way along to the headland. That's where I usually walk Charlie." She had regained her composure now although her face still felt red and sticky. How warm it was in here. She wished someone would open a window or the doors to the gardens.
"I'll have to explore with Tess. We'll soon find our favourite walks."
"Tess? Your wife?" Carol's innocent expression didn't fool Beth.
Tom laughed. "No, no. Tess is a beautiful blonde, but a beautiful blonde

Labrador. She's nearly twelve now and slowing down, but that suits me. Gentle strolls along the beach sound just about right. And that's my cue to go and take her for a walk before lunch. Many thanks for your company, good to meet you all."

He stood and smiled around, raising his hand in farewell and walking across the hall to the door with long, easy strides, seemingly unaware of the several pairs of eyes watching his progress.

"Coming back for another coffee, Beth?"
"No thanks, Carol" Beth shook her head. "Poor Charlie hasn't had a walk yet today and I've got some chores to do."

At home she stripped off the top and skirt, throwing them into the laundry basket and opening the wardrobe door. Not normally over fussy about her clothes, she rummaged through the wardrobe rejecting everything. How long had she had that skirt? And that dress? The style had been popular ten years ago and she knew she would never wear it again, providing it even fitted, knowing her chest was larger than ever before and her hips curvier now than one year ago, never mind ten. At just five feet four, Beth had been most comfortable when she was a size twelve, but knew she was now easily a fourteen, sometimes a sixteen, depending on the style. Her waist was smaller in proportion to her hips and chest, giving her a very feminine figure that she would have preferred to be less curvy. Now most of her clothes seems to strain across the hips and bust, as well as being worn out. Time for a shopping spree. She would see if Gina could go with her. Admittedly Gina would look good in anything, being so tall and slim, but she could also pick out shapes and colours that would flatter Beth's shorter, curvier figure and her colouring. A sharp bark from downstairs reminded her poor old Charlie was waiting for his walk. She grabbed a pair of white cotton trousers and a blue tee shirt and a minute later ran downstairs to collect Charlie. Forget her appearance; Melissa's cool glamour had unsettled her but she was clean and usually tidy and was never going to be as stylish as Melissa or Gina. What did it matter anyway? But she would go shopping and buy a few new bits, and definitely some new sandals, a pair that were comfortable and stylish.

Monday afternoon. Beth pushed open the door into the church hall, balancing a cake in one hand. The hall was almost full, just a few empty chairs around the tables set out in squares. She made her way to the serving hatch and handed the cake to Gina.
"Just a lemon drizzle, easiest to make in a hurry."

"And always popular, thanks Beth. Are you coming round here or circulating?"

"I'll circulate….but what's going on over there?" Beth nodded towards the table by the French doors, where the vicar's wife Maggie Rowland's had her arm around Mary Wren while various people hovered around, looking concerned.

"Haven't you heard? The Wrens had a burglary, sometime over the weekend." Gina broke off as she was nudged to fill the tea pot from the urn.

"That's awful. Poor Mary and Bill. I'll go and see them when they're on their own."

She picked up a cup of tea and gazed around the hall, spotting Melissa at a table with two women and a toddler and made her way towards them.

"Hello. Alright if I join you?"

"Hi Beth. Here, just let me brush the crumbs off" Becky Smith pulled a chair out, removing a toy car along with the crumbs and handing the car to the little boy looking solemnly at Beth. Becky was a short, lively, vivacious young woman with dark curly hair and large brown eyes beneath strong arched brows.

"Heaven help you when this one joins your class. Looks angelic but…" Becky rolled her eyes. "Have you got children, Melissa?"

Melissa shook her head. "No, never happened, though it would have been nice."

Melissa was as well turned out as before, in tight fitting jeans today with a beautifully cut white jersey top, modern silver – or white gold? – jewellery at her wrists and ears. Her nails were tipped with a crimson red. Did she do them every day? Beth wondered, marvelling that anyone would have the time, or the inclination, to give themselves a manicure more than once a week, even once a month. Or did she have them done at a salon?

Beth turned her attention to the third woman sitting at the table. "Ali, how are you?"

The thin, nervous looking woman twisted awkwardly to answer Beth, her long light brown hair swinging round her face, pale blue eyes watery and anxious.

"I'm fine, thanks Beth. The shop's busy so that's good. In fact, I've been telling Melissa here about it, she's going to call round and have a look and meet Julian."

Beth remembered Melissa saying she painted and was about to ask her about it when Becky leaned forward. "Wasn't that awful about Mary and Bill? The burglary?"
"I only just heard." Beth turned round to look at Mary, who was now composed and sitting close to Bill. "What happened?"
"They'd been away for the weekend; they got back last night to find the house turned over, all her jewellery gone, laptops, Kindles...the kitchen door had been forced open."

"Oh poor Mary and Bill." Beth thought of the gentle, grey-haired couple, imagining the shock of coming home to find someone had been in your house. Horrible. Her car had been broken into once and that had been bad enough, the thought of someone rummaging through the car, but to have that happen in your home, your sanctuary...no wonder Mary and Bill looked shattered.
"Do the police have any idea who did it?"
Becky shook her head. "No, and Mary can't bear to go back yet so they are staying at the vicarage until the police are finished and Christine has been down to tidy it all up for them. She'll be here this afternoon."

Mary and Bill's daughter Christine lived in Sheffield; Beth remembered her as a nice woman and was relieved to think she was on her way. Becky got to her feet to go, picking up toy cars and dinosaurs, and Ali and Melissa resumed talking about the gallery and Julian's pottery. Beth excused herself and spent the next hour in the kitchen, loading the dishwasher and wiping down the worktops.

"Fifty three people today" announced Maggie, bustling into the kitchen. "A good turnout, thank you for your help, ladies."
"It's been nice." Carol finished putting the tea and coffee jars away and gathered up wet dishcloths to take home to wash. "Well, apart from poor Mary and Bill. I'm glad they're staying with you and Mark, Maggie."
"I think Christine will persuade them to go home as soon as possible. The longer they leave it, the harder it will be, but they are welcome for as long as they need."
And they would be, Beth knew. Maggie, small, slight, with her mid-brown wispy hair and sherry brown eyes was like a little brown mouse and had a heart of gold. So did Mark, their vicar; only he was more of a St Bernard, wiry brown hair going grey, kind blue eyes, solid and dependable. The Wrens would be supported and cared for until they were ready to look after

themselves again.

"Come on, Beth." Gina picked up her handbag and took Beth's arm. "I'll give you a lift and scrounge a cup of coffee before I go home."

"Of course I'll go shopping with you." Gina leaned back in the garden chair, crossing her long shapely legs. "But what's brought this on? You only ever shop for stuff for the house, or Nell."
Beth wriggled her bare toes in the grass, comparing them with Gina's pretty pale pink toenails.
"I don't know, maybe it was seeing Melissa so simply but beautifully dressed on Thursday. Or church yesterday when I felt so scruffy....honestly Gina, I had coffee stains all over my skirt, I was so embarrassed! Everyone else makes an effort and I just make sure I'm clean! All my clothes are old, out of date. Of course I can't wear anything too good for work but it would be nice to have some practical but stylish clothes."
"And so you shall Cinderella" laughed Gina. "You've got a good figure, lovely colouring. Yes you have" as Beth started to protest. "You're very soft and feminine. You're not the tall, tailored type but in soft colours, floaty fabrics, heels."
"I can't wear heels; I just fall over on them!"
"Not vamp high heels, just medium, kitten heels, that sort of thing. So, when are we going and where?"

Gina's eyes sparkled and Beth felt a rush of affection for her friend. Carol had been her first friend in Bride's Bay and would always be close. She was outspoken, energetic, a natural born organiser and had a heart of gold. Gina was reserved; to people who didn't know her she came across as aloof and unapproachable, but Beth and Carol knew her to be compassionate, thoughtful, sensitive and generous. Carol had introduced her to Beth five years before, when she had become friendly with Gina through the choir they both sang with. Beth had immediately recognised a sadness in the other woman and a sense of caution with people that she herself shared. She and Gina had gradually formed a close friendship and Beth ached for her friend at times; knowing Gina still grieved for the daughter she had lost at four days old and her husband who had died eight years ago. Her only child, Robert, lived in Scotland and Gina missed him terribly. To the outsider, Gina in her beautiful house with her looks, her sports car and no money worries seemed to have it all. But Beth knew she would have sacrificed everything in a second to have her family back. Gina was the one person she could share her worries and problems with, knowing she would understand and be supportive. Carol was practical, energetic, but black and white. Gina had more empathy and patience, understanding Beth's insecurities and weaknesses. But both women were very dear to her and Beth couldn't imagine her life in Bride's Bay without either of them.

Bringing her attention back to the present, she answered Gina's question.
"Tomorrow?" Or are you busy? Any day is fine really. Apart from Wednesday."
Gina shook her head. "No, not at all, tomorrow is fine. Portsmouth, Southampton or Winchester?"
"Southampton." Beth decided. "Then we can go to John Lewis. And Ikea" she added as an afterthought.
"No" Gina tapped her arm. "We're buying you clothes, not things for the house, or Nell's flat!"
They made arrangements to meet at Gina's as soon as Beth finished work and have a late lunch in Southampton. Gina got up to go, laughingly saying she hoped Beth's bank balance was healthy. Which it was. Beth wasn't extravagant and lived well within her means.

Closing the bedroom curtains that night, she looked down the road to the lights still glowing fuzzily on the island, the pinpricks of light on the beach where the fishermen sat silently in their tents and the shimmer of moonlight on the sea. Charlie sat quietly by the bed, ready to jump up as soon as Beth was settled.

"Come on boy, I give up!" Charlie wagged his tail and scrambled up, Beth catching him and stroking his warm, hairy little body as he burrowed down with a sigh.

CHAPTER 3

Tuesday morning was busy. The first lesson was PE, involving changing fifteen wriggling, unco-operative three and four year olds into their shorts and tee-shirts. Then at snack time one of the children began to choke on a piece of apple, leaving both Helen and Beth shaken. Just before lunch Mrs Fielding, the head teacher, brought a couple in to the classroom to view the nursery. They had had a thorough look round before commandeering Helen to ask questions, leaving Beth to work alone with the children. By the time they had left it was gone twenty past twelve, causing Helen and Beth to rush to get the children ready to be collected at half past. Parents and guardians were waiting impatiently in the playground and Beth felt flustered as she tried to match book bags and art work to pupils as quickly as she could.

"Beth, I'm so sorry to ask, but there's an early years' meeting this lunchtime. Could you…?"
Beth anticipated Helen's request, smiling at her
"Of course. Leave it all to me. Just go" shooing the teacher out of the door, knowing Helen would barely have time to go to the toilet let alone eat before the afternoon nursery children arrived. It was all very well people making derogatory comments about the short working day of teachers and the long holidays, but Beth knew her colleagues were in school long before school started officially and didn't go home until well after the last child had left, even then taking marking and preparation home with them. She also knew their days were filled not just with lessons but with duties, meetings, phone calls. Helen rarely, if ever, had a proper lunch break, working non-stop from when the children arrived at eight forty five to when they left at three fifteen, then carrying on with paperwork. She had no desire to be a teacher, Beth reflected, as she tidied away toys and washed up the beakers and plates from snack time. She loved being with the children but it was Helen who did all the planning, the assessments, attended the meetings and training courses. No, the pay might be poor but the job suited her. She swilled out the sink, put the tea towel to dry and picked up her bag.

"Sorry I'm late" she apologised fifteen minutes later as Gina opened the door, well-groomed as ever in white linen trousers and a pale blue and white patterned top.
"Bad morning?" queried Gina. Beth shook her head.

"Just busy. So I feel a bit hot and scruffy."
"Do you want to relax a bit before we go, have a drink and sandwich here?"
"No, it's fine. Let's go and find somewhere and have a nice cool drink."

Gina drove them into Southampton with the roof of her car down. It was still only April but the sun was warm, the sky cloudless. The breeze tossed Beth's hair around but it was cool and refreshing and by the time they arrived at the car park she was feeling much less fraught. Gina led the way to a small Italian restaurant she knew and Beth sank onto the leather bench seat with a contented sigh. She felt even more relaxed an hour later, after a glass of chilled white wine and a large bowl of chicken Caesar salad.
"That's better." She sighed happily. "Come on then, my personal shopper, sort me out."

Gina needed no encouragement, rushing Beth from one store to another, darting between lingerie, casual wear and the shoe department until Beth's head was spinning and she was worn out with undressing and trying on different outfits, spinning round for her friend to inspect, then starting all over again. She sat on the stool in a shoe department with a sigh and begged her friend to stop.
"Gina! I've never bought so many things! Take pity on my bank account!"
Gina looked stricken.
"Have you spent too much? Do we need to put something back? Or will you let me treat you to something?"
"No, no, it's fine" Beth laughed, squeezing her friends arm. "But I've got enough, honestly. I don't go anywhere to wear all these things. Besides, I can't carry anymore! Now, let's go and have a cup of tea."

They made their way to the coffee shop and sat down with relief, smiling at each other.
"That was fun" Gina grinned, pouring the tea. "Are you pleased with what we bought?"
"Oh yes. How could I not be?" Beth thought briefly of the tops and trousers, dresses, shoes and sandals, the lacy underwear.
"Well, you're kitted out for the summer. And we can do this again in September, choose you a new winter coat, boots, woollens…"
"Stop! Let me get over this trip first! And save up for next time!"

Gina paused, putting her cup down. She had got so carried away choosing outfits for her friend she hadn't even considered the cost. When

Malcolm had died he had left her very comfortably off, she didn't need to work and filled her days with her hobbies and voluntary work. But Beth's circumstances were very different.

"Beth" she hesitated "are you alright for money? Because if not…you know I would always help you out."
She picked her cup up again and took a sip of tea, embarrassed. Beth felt a lump in her throat. She put out her hand and squeezed Gina's.
"Gina, honestly, I'm fine." Gina's lovely blue eyes looked up at her, troubled.
"But I know teaching assistants don't earn much, and you've got your house to run, and Nell. You would tell me if you … if you were ever in difficulty?"
"You're right, my pay isn't great. But it's my choice to work part time. I like to be able to help at the shop, do the flowers and Tea and Chat. I could get more hours if I needed to, but while I can manage, I'd rather be part time. And I couldn't leave Charlie all day. But remember I don't have a mortgage now; I paid that off last year. And my outgoings are quite low, I'm not extravagant." They both glanced down at the sea of carrier bags around their feet and burst out laughing.
"Well, not usually! I can't remember the last time I bought new clothes, and never this amount! But I don't spend anything on Nell now she is working, apart from the odd treat of course. So honestly Gina, I'm fine. But thank you for being so concerned." She swallowed the lump in her throat. Gina looked happier.
"But you would tell me if you needed anything?" she persisted.
"Yes Gina. I promise. Now, shall we make a move before the traffic builds up?" She needed to change the subject, eyes watering at the thoughtfulness and generosity of the woman sitting opposite.
"Too late for that." Gina glanced out of the window at the steady stream of traffic on the road below.
"But yes, let's go. Can you stay for a bit when you get back or are you busy?"
Beth shook her head. "I've time for a quick cup of coffee. Charlie will be fine. He can get out into the garden."

They drove back to Monkton and Beth felt the rush of pleasure she always had when she sat in Gina's kitchen, gazing out of the window at the long garden sloping down to the beach, at the waves splashing frills of white lace onto the browns, greys and yellows of the shingle. Gina and her husband Malcolm had bought the plot of land over twenty years before, designing the house themselves. It was a perfect location, with woodland to the front and a view over Titchfield Haven; the beach and sea behind. Osborne House and Carisbrooke Castle nestled amongst soft greenery across the water and the usual cluster of brightly coloured sails fluttered in front of the lively little town of Cowes. The houses either side of Gina's were older; one a large gloomy Victorian building, the other an Arts and Crafts beauty. Gina's house sat between them, strikingly crisp and modern. The interior was also contemporary and minimalistic but managed to be comfortable and homely at the same time. Beth knew Gina and Malcolm had made the decision to move to Monkton soon after the death of their baby daughter, Gina finding it unbearable to stay in the house they had imagined to be a home for the little girl; with the pale pink nursery and the pram in the hall way. Planning a new house so close to the beach and moving in with their young son Robert had given them a fresh start but Beth knew the pain of losing her daughter had never gone. It would never go. How could it?

An hour later Beth pushed open her own front door, laden with glossy bags. She was tired but happy, feeling a bubble of excitement at the thought of all her purchases. She couldn't remember ever buying so many new clothes before but Gina had been right, it had been fun. She greeted Charlie, placing the bags on the floor and checking the answer phone for messages then glanced at the clock, realising with a start it was just gone seven. Oh well, she didn't need anything to eat after that late lunch. She only had to take Charlie for a walk and put the new clothes away. Clipping Charlie's lead on they went out of the front door and down the path, turning right to the park rather than left to the sea front. She was too tired for a long walk along the beach tonight; a couple of turns around the park would be fine for once.

Later, she unpacked all the purchases and laid them out on her bed, feeling a glow of pleasure at the sight of the colourful dresses, the pretty tops, the skirts and trousers. Next to the trousers was a pile of frothy lace and silk underwear. She suppressed a smile at the thought that she would be the only one to see them but at least if she had an accident and ended up in hospital she needn't worry about being seen in old tatty underwear. Did the nursing staff notice underwear, she wondered? Probably not, but it was still a nicer thought that she would be wearing decent undies. She glanced down at the floor where three pairs of sandals sat squarely on the cream carpet, no nubuck to be seen. Carefully packing the sandals back up in the tissue paper, she placed the boxes in the bottom of the wardrobe then found hangers for all the new clothes, having to raid Nell's wardrobe when she ran out. Now for a shower and bed. It had been a busy day but good. Very good.

The next day was not so good. There had been another burglary. Beth heard about it from April and Sue when she arrived at the charity shop.

"Reynard's House, you know it, Beth, a few houses along from Gina's. That's why she's not here yet. She phoned to say she would be a bit late, she's been round to see if she can do anything."

Beth felt cold. Reynard's House was in fact two houses along from Gina's, a stunning Art Deco home with a long garden running down to the sea. Anyone could access the gardens from the beach. How would her friend be feeling? Gina had a good burglar alarm but so presumably did Russell and Francesca Dean, the owners of Reynard's House. Beth racked her brains for what she knew of the couple. Both doctors, at Portsmouth hospital. Two teenage children at private school somewhere. Monkton was a desirable place to live, all the houses large and secluded and the lane overlooking the sea where Gina's house was situated was particularly in demand. Anyone would see at a glance there would be rich pickings from the homes there. Gina was bound to be feeling very vulnerable, alone in that large house.

She rushed in twenty minutes later. "Sorry, sorry April." Her hair was still immaculate, kept back from her face with a narrow velvet band, but she had no lipstick on and her hands shook slightly as she hurriedly put her bag down and picked up her apron.

"That doesn't matter love, calm down." April pushed Gina onto a chair and turned to Beth, ordering her to make a cup of tea "strong, with sugar." Beth made the tea, omitting the sugar. Shock or not, Gina would grimace at sweet tea.

Gina sat on the chair, cradling a mug of strong tea. Her hands were no longer shaking but her face was still pale. The other three women stood around, waiting for her to fill them in.

"So Francesca came home early, she didn't feel well at work this morning. She usually works Wednesday afternoons but got someone to cover for her and came home after her morning appointments. She knew something was wrong straight away when the burglar alarm didn't go off. But she went in and went through the house. They could have still been there."

Gina's voice shook and Beth clasped her cold hand as she shook her head to clear it and continued.
"The place was a mess, everything thrown around, but no graffiti or anything thank God. Her jewellery box was empty but they had a safe and although they found it, they couldn't break into it. Then the usual iPads, kindles, laptops etc. The children's computer games, small items they could carry. Oh, and some silver and a couple of small sculptures and paintings. Fran and Russell had some lovely things."
Tears trickled down her smooth cheeks and she hastily brushed them away.
"Sorry, it's just the shock and..." She broke off; Beth, April and Sue guessing she was thinking it could have been her house.

Just then a group entered the shop and April and Sue hurried to serve them, April telling Beth to stay in the store room with Gina and sort out bags of contributions.
"Sorry!" Gina tried to smile. "Come on, let's get busy and take our minds off it." She wiped her cheeks, looking at Beth and frowning as she noticed her jeans and tee-shirt. "Why aren't you wearing your new clothes?"
"They're much too nice to wear here, when I'm just sorting all this stuff out and...." Beth's voice trailed off at the expression on Gina's face.
"Alright. Alright I know! I'll start wearing them tomorrow, I promise."
"You'll wish you had worn them today. I met Melissa on my way here, and she wanted to know what was wrong. She's invited us round for a coffee after this." Gina gave a shaky laugh at Beth's horrified face.
"Serves you right for not getting rid all your old clothes straight away! You could have washed and pressed them and brought them with you today."
"No one would want my old clothes." Beth made a face. "They've been well loved and worn to death. I'll put them in the clothes recycling." Or maybe just keep them for cleaning and gardening, she thought to herself. The two women started to empty and sort out bags and the afternoon passed quickly, Gina calming down with the routine of sorting and organising donations.

"I've never been in this house before." Beth looked round the kitchen curiously, at the glossy units and island at one end, the elegant glass table in the centre surrounded by black leather and chrome chairs and the two large sofas at the end overlooking the garden. Melissa handed her a cup of tea. "It's stunning."

And very different from her own; thinking of her cluttered kitchen with its old cream painted units, wooden worktops, the oak table and farmhouse chairs and the dresser she was always meaning to clear of random objects. Everything always seemed to find its way to the dresser, but at least it meant she knew where to look for items. Homes reflected their owners and Beth knew she wouldn't relax so much in this kitchen, no matter how stylish it might be. A bit like the kitchens on Grand Designs, she reflected, beautiful but not homely, not her sort of homely anyway. She always meant to have a colour scheme in the kitchen but the reality was a kaleidoscope of colour; pale blue storage jars, red saucepans, cream kettle and toaster. But the overall effect was warm and cosy and suited Beth. This kitchen was minimalist to the extreme, the worktops empty apart from a chrome toaster, kettle and state of the art coffee maker. Elegant but too clinical.
"It is" agreed Melissa "and I know what you're going to say, it's way too big for one person, but come and see this" picking up her own tea cup and ushering the two women ahead of her back through the hall and into another room through double doors.

Beth gasped. The room stretched from the front of the house to the back with a large round bay window overlooking the road at one end and another square bay with French doors at the other, leading onto the terraced garden. The walls were painted white with curved, silver light fittings along them and two fireplaces, both original, flanked the outside wall. There was no furniture; instead the whole room had been turned into a studio with tables holding paints, jars and still life arrangements. Canvasses were propped against the walls and three easels filled the space. The only incongruous note was the wood effect vinyl on the floor and Melissa laughed as she caught Gina looking down at it.
"There's the most beautiful parquet floor underneath but I couldn't risk ruining it, so I had this put down on the top while I'm here. This is why I rented it. The Thomson's put all their furniture in store which meant I could use these rooms as I wanted. The light in here is amazing, so is the space. I live in the kitchen and work in here. Have a look." She gestured towards a small pile of finished canvasses and some framed paintings and the two women walked over to see.

Beth caught her breath. "They're beautiful, Melissa" and they were, mostly paintings of plants and flowers, so skilfully executed they could almost be touched and smelt. Some were of animals, people's pets maybe?

Beth was in no doubt that they captured the animals as closely as photographs would have done. A still life painting of some terracotta pots caught her eye. She could almost smell the sun baked clay and feel the texture and curves of the pots. Gina was examining the flower paintings with awe; staring at a painting of a glass vase of roses, the crystal vase transparent and sparkling, the petals soft as velvet.

"Melissa! You're so talented! Where do you sell them? Do you take commissions?"
Melissa pushed her shiny chestnut waves back from her face and laughed. "Yes I do, in fact I do a lot. I advertise on the internet and have photos sent to me of pets, gardens, houses. But I like painting flowers best; I like the detail in petals and leaves and of course the colours."
"I would love a painting of my garden. Do you sell through galleries? We have one here, Pebbles. Julian Soames runs it, his wife Ali helps as well. I think you met her at Tea and Chat, didn't you? He's a potter really but he sells local artist's work. You should call in."
"Yes I know Ali and I've already called into Pebbles, it's a good gallery. Julian was very helpful, he's coming round to see my work to decide if it's the sort of thing he could sell. And I sell to galleries all over the place, a couple back in Bristol, some in London, Brighton. Now I'm by the coast I'm planning to do some seascapes too."
Beth and Gina were in no doubt that Julian would jump at the chance to sell Melissa's paintings and the three women went back to the kitchen.

"Now, enough of me. Gina, what happened today? Why were you so upset? Tell me while I cut this cake, it's from Bread and Buns, which I'm assured is the place to buy cakes round here. Though I expect all the worthy ladies bake their own?" lifting perfect arched brows towards Beth and Gina.
"Some do, they enjoy baking. I do if I have the time. But bought ones can be just as good, this one is delicious". Beth contentedly licked the cream cheese frosting off her fingers and accepted another cup of tea. The talk switched to the burglary, then to the local area and it was gone half past six before Beth stood up to leave.

She checked the answer phone and wandered into the kitchen, patted Charlie's head where he lay in his basket, resting his hairy head on his paws, one eye open watching her. Ten to seven, supper time. But the thought of supper didn't appeal, she was too full. The carrot cake had been supplemented by scones with jam and clotted cream and both Gina and

Beth had indulged. Melissa had munched her way through a large slice of cake and two scones piled high with cream. How on earth did she stay so slim? wondered Beth, who only had to sniff cake to put on weight. Life wasn't fair. Well, at least she could walk off the calories now by giving Charlie a long walk to make up for the fact it was later than usual.

It was still sunny but the wind had blown up and white froth bubbled over the shingle at the water's edge, looking like frills of lace on a wedding dress. A few children were still playing on the beach; their shouts high and clear as they ran off their last bit of energy before bed. Charlie also ran off his energy as Beth sat on the shingle, throwing bits of driftwood down into the water's edge for him to retrieve.

Footsteps scrunched behind her then stopped and Beth looked up, squinting into the lowering sun, as a voice asked "Can I join you? Or is this space taken?" Beth recognised her new neighbour, Tom Callow, and looked around at the expanse of empty shingle, laughing.

"I think there's room for one more." Tom squatted next to her, then sat down on the shingle and stretched his long legs out, looking at her and smiling. His mouth was well-shaped with straight white teeth and his skin was tanned, rough around his chin. Beth couldn't see his eyes, behind the dark lenses of his sunglasses, but could make out laughter lines and a few more lines under his thick, sandy coloured hair, where it fell over his forehead. His jeans were almost as disreputable as hers, she saw; even worse, being ripped at the knees. His short sleeved cotton Polo shirt revealed muscled tanned arms, and a patch of gold hair curled at the neck. She was suddenly aware of her old jeans and the tee-shirt that had been washed so many times it had lost its shape and hung unevenly, being lower on one side than the other. It also clung a little too snuggly to her curves. Oh well, nothing she could do about it now.

"Hello Tess." Beth held her hand out to the gentle looking dog who stood by her master, slowly wagging her tail. "Oh, aren't you a lovely girl." Charlie bounded up with his stick, dropped it and started circling the Golden Labrador, barking excitedly.
"Charlie! Stop!" Tess slowly sank down next to Tom, rested her heavy head on his knees and gazed at the little Scottie dog as Beth picked up the stick and threw it again. Charlie stood, tail wagging, torn between staying with his new friend to continue their acquaintance, or chasing his stick; but his usual exuberance won out and he hared off back over the shingle into the water.

"So, how are you settling in? I expect you're still unpacking?"
"Good, thanks. And yes to the unpacking, it's going to take ages. I've unpacked the kitchen boxes, and the bedding and towels and so on. Now I'm on the books and CD's, that kind of stuff. Though I haven't got enough bookshelves or storage so I should get that sorted first, really. The living room looks alright, it's just got the furniture in it as yet but the curtains are up now, lampshades fitted and so on. And the kitchen is done. But the large spare bedroom is full to the ceiling; anything I wasn't sure about, I just told the removal men to put in there. But it will all get sorted one day, there's no hurry."

"What brought you here? Do you know the area?" A few people moved to Bride's Bay but the majority of residents were locals who had lived in the area all their lives.
"Slightly. We had all our family holidays on the Isle of Wight when I was a child so I have fond memories of it." Lucky man, thought Beth, thinking back to her own childhood; not many fond memories there, and certainly no holidays.

Tom gazed at the island just a couple of miles across the water from them and continued.
"I always wanted to retire to the coast, that old cliché" grinning at her "so I looked all along from Eastbourne to Poole. This seemed a real town, all the facilities I wanted, good transport links and so on. And the house prices were good, better than Brighton or Bournemouth. So here I am."
"Where were you before?" Beth felt a qualm of unease at her nosiness but he didn't seem to mind.
"Reading. I taught at the university. I've been there for nearly fifteen years, in the same flat. So I'd accumulated quite a lot of …well, rubbish really! Things I didn't need, anyway. So I had a good clear out before I moved, a good declutter. It's very therapeutic." Another grin. His face was open, friendly. He obviously had no problems with her questions. Beth nodded, her dark blonde hair whipping around her face in the breeze.
"I should do that. I've collected too much stuff over the years."
"It's easily done. Accumulating stuff I mean. Getting rid of it isn't quite so easy. You have to be ruthless."

"So what do you want to do; now you're here? Do you sail?"
He shook his head. "No, but I'd quite like to take it up. I like walking, and Tess here needs that, though not so much these days." He stroked the dog's smooth head gently. "And I like reading, visiting old towns, buildings,

that sort of thing. Music. Plus I write a bit so the plan is to semi retire and do some writing. I lectured in politics and economics, that's what I write about" in response to Beth's quizzical look.

"Ah." Beth didn't know what to say. Not exactly two subjects she could discuss for long, for any amount of time, come to that. She had no interest in economics and although she was interested in current affairs, she didn't know or understand enough to discuss politics in any great depth; didn't trust what she read in the newspapers so gleaned all her views and information from the news on television and radio but was doubtful they would stand up to debate with an expert.

Tom laughed. "I know. That's a conversation killer, like saying I'm from Inland Revenue or a traffic warden. Though come to think of, that doesn't stop conversation, it usually stirs it up! But I'm beginning to wonder if I did the right thing moving here, two burglaries in a week! Is it a sink town of crime and depravity?" His grin told her he was joking.
Beth smiled. "No, it's a very law abiding little town. Usually the worst thing that happens is when the local youths pull flowers out of the hanging baskets! Though actually that is a crime of major importance, in Frances's eyes."
"Ah Frances, flower arranger in chief. She's coming round tomorrow to cut some of the flowers in the garden. I must say, it's a lovely garden, some really unusual plants. I'm looking forward to working in it. The house is good too; it's still got a separate living room and dining room, but I'm making the dining room into a library cum study. I can eat in the kitchen, it's plenty big enough. And the location! Those living room windows just frame the sea and being able to step out of the front door and walk over the road to the beach is wonderful! Now, your turn, I know you live over the road from me, Carol said. What do you do? How long have you lived here? Are you from here originally?"

Beth shook her head. "No. I was born in London, I grew up there. Then I moved to Bournemouth for work. And you're right, it is expensive! But I worked in a small family run hotel and had accommodation provided. I went to college there, to do nursery nursing, and worked shifts in the hotel around my lectures. Then I moved here ten years ago." The memory of that time hit her like a wave, causing her throat to tighten.
"Was that for work?" Tom was looking at her with interest.
"No. My sister lived here..." she swallowed. "She moved her after a divorce, with her little girl. But she was killed in an accident, a car accident,

ten years ago. Nell was twelve by then. Her father lives in Australia and didn't really want to know, so I moved here to take care of her." She blinked hard to stop the tears falling, her throat aching.

Tom shifted and put his large hand over hers, speaking quietly. "I'm so sorry, I shouldn't have pried." She looked down at his tanned hand covering hers, waiting to tense, but his skin was soft and his fingers warm and firm, pressing comfortingly against hers. She swallowed hard.
"No, it's okay. But that's how I ended up here. Nell's home was here, her friends were here, she was happy at school. She'd just started secondary school. I couldn't uproot her to Bournemouth. So I left Bournemouth and we lived in Louise's flat at first and I got my job at the primary school. We moved to my little cottage just over a year later. And I've been there ever since."

Her voice trailed off but Tom still kept his warm hand on hers. "And Nell? I don't think I've seen her, have I?" Beth shook her head. "She went to university in Hertfordshire and now has a job near Winchester, in horticulture. She rents a flat there." The thought of her happy niece chased the dark memories away.
"Do you have any other family?" Tom shifted slightly, releasing her hand to rub Tess's smooth golden head where it lay on his knee. She shook her head.
"No, there's just me and Nell. And Charlie of course" rubbing the little dog's head, as he lay panting next to her on the shingle.

"So tell me about your job. You work at the local school, don't you?" They talked companionably about Beth's job, her voluntary work in the charity shop and involvement in church and local affairs until the sun sank over the island and Beth shivered slightly.

"Are you ready to go?" Tom unfolded his long length to stand up and put a hand down to help her up. Thanking him, she brushed her jeans down, calling to Charlie. They walked companionably along the shingle, crossing the main road opposite his house. Pausing, he smiled down at her. "Same time tomorrow? Nicer than walking alone. Or do you prefer to do that?"
"No, it's fine. We're happy to meet up, if poor Tess can put up with Charlie."

Tom walked down the driveway, waving goodbye, followed slowly by Tess while Beth crossed the road to take a few steps up the side street to her house, Charlie trotting alongside. The sun had set and she shivered as she walked down the path in the shade. She was so used to walking Charlie alone; enjoying the peace and quiet after a busy day, but it had been nice walking along with Tom. He was good company, easy to chat to, and it was good too to have new people to get to know in the little town.

She unlocked the door, nudging Charlie ahead of her and yawned. "Come on boy, we've had quite enough excitement for one day. Supper and bed."

CHAPTER 4

As April moved into May the weather continued warm and sunny and Beth spent every morning the following week outdoors; the teacher she assisted keen to take sessions outside to make the most of the fine days. She had also got into the habit of walking along the beach with Tom and Tess in the evening; spending an hour or so strolling along the water's edge while Charlie ran in and out of the waves and Tess padded along contentedly behind Tom. Chat was easy; Tom talked mainly about his work at the university, the flat he had lived in, his family of a sister and brother-in-law in Norfolk, a niece in London and a nephew in Kent. He didn't ask many questions, for which Beth was grateful, except those regarding the local area; shops, train times, dentists and doctors, all the information needed but unknown when moving to a new area.

In return, Beth told him more about her job as nursery nurse and about Nell, her love of plants that had led to her career in horticulture, the shared interest they had in history and visiting old towns and cities, their love of the sea and the sea shore. Tom talked about his love of books, music, also of historical buildings. He had a dry sense of humour and was easy to talk to and Beth found herself relaxing more and more in his company as they strolled along the beach, Tom deliberately slowing down as his long legs covered the beach far more quickly than hers, both content to chat or be silent, enjoying the warm evenings and the sun setting over the island.

The fine weather had a mellow effect on the whole town and people strolled along the beach path, chatted outside shops, queued for ice creams and generally enjoyed the warm sunshine. The police were no further on with their investigations into the burglaries but general opinion was that it had been youths, or opportunists, even gangs from London. But it was in the past and people stopped talking about them and began to plan for the summer instead; the school fete, an auction of promises at church, Cowes Week.

That was until the third burglary.

Beth heard about it when she went into work on the Friday morning. Helen looked up as she walked into the nursery classroom,

smiling a greeting and handing her a mug of tea.
"Hi Beth. Isn't it awful about Mandy?" Beth was confused for a moment. "Mandy? You mean our Mandy? Dinner lady Mandy? Why, what's happened?" Helen put down the paintings she had been hanging on a string across the classroom and perched on the edge of a tiny table.
"She went home yesterday after shopping with a friend, and they'd been burgled. She got in literally five minutes before Ella got home from school. The house was wrecked. Luckily her neighbour was in and Ella went round there so she didn't see the mess but Mandy was distraught. She kept saying what if Ella had got home first and seen the mess? Or even disturbed the burglars? And Paul is furious. Ranting and raving."
Beth felt sick. "Oh Helen that's awful. I thought the other two were one offs, but to happen again. How did they get in?"
"Smashed a window at the back. Usual stuff taken, jewellery, iPads, laptops and so on. Even the kids' video computer games. Small stuff they could carry easily."

 The children started to arrive and put an end to the conversation, though Helen and Beth were aware of the parents discussing it as they dropped their children off. Three burglaries in two weeks. What was going on? Who was doing this? And why hadn't they been caught? Beth walked slowly home that afternoon, wondering if she should have a burglar alarm fitted. Everyone knew her house was empty every morning; most afternoons too come to that. And she always walked Charlie at around half past six in the evenings. She was a creature of habit. It would be easy for anyone to work out when her house would be empty and break in. But she didn't have anything worth stealing, did she? But then, would that make a difference? The three houses broken into were all very different. Admittedly Fran and Russell Dean had a beautiful home, plenty of money, expensive belongings. But Bill and Mary were an ordinary couple in a modest bungalow and Mandy and Paul lived in an ex- council house with a young daughter, a teenage son and not much money. There was no pattern to these break ins. Even the areas were different; exclusive Monkton being two miles from Bride's Bay and the Wren's bungalow on the opposite sides of the small town to Mandy's house. It seemed everyone was vulnerable. Beth shivered. Of course she had Charlie but he was more likely to welcome an intruder with a wet tongue and a wagging tail than deter them. Perhaps she would have some more locks fitted? But then they said burglars could get into any house if they were determined enough. Oh dear, it was so hard to know what to do. Perhaps she would talk to Ken about it.

She would go back to Carol's after flower arranging and talk to him when he got back from work.

It was Saturday afternoon. Beth put the cheeses and chutney back in the fridge and tidied away her lunch dishes. The fridge looked alarmingly bare, certainly not enough milk or yoghurt to last until Monday and the salad tray contained a single tomato and some wilted celery. A supermarket visit was needed this afternoon; it didn't open on Sunday and Beth wasn't keen on the choice or prices in the corner shop that would be the only option the next day.

"Come on Charlie, another walk, you lucky boy!" They would stroll along the sea front; have a cup of tea at the Cake Stand, then walk home along the High Street, stopping at the greengrocers and Co-op on the way.

She glanced in the hall mirror before leaving the house, pulling a brush through her thick wavy hair and sliding on a peachy lip gloss, noticing to her surprise her arms and face had developed a pale golden tan over the past couple of weeks and the blonde streaks in her hair were more pronounced, her hair looking more blonde than the usual mix of blonde and light brown. To Gina's delight she had finally thrown out the old clothes, surprising herself daily with how much nicer the new ones looked when she looked in the mirror before going to work.

"Afternoon Beth, you're looking very cheerful". With a start Beth realised she was approaching the parade of shops and there was June Jacobs sitting at a table outside The Cake Stand tea rooms.
"June! Sorry, I'm miles away. Are you on your own?" The older woman shook her head, grey curls sticking rigidly to her head. "Rose is inside, ordering our tea. Sit down" gesturing to a metal chair.
"I'll just go and order." Beth joined the queue and ordered her drink then followed Rose back outside.

"Phew it's warm." Rose fanned herself with her newspaper. "So how are you, Beth? How's Nell?" Beth filled the two women in on Nell's news and in return heard about their children and grandchildren before conversation turned naturally to the burglaries. Mary and Bill Wren earned sympathy from June and Rose, their age making them vulnerable and deserving of concern. Anyone who had served in the Second World War automatically earned their respect and what was the world coming to, when decent people like the Wrens were the targets of crime? Mandy and Paul Davis were also discussed with shock and dismay, Rose recalling how hard

Mandy had worked when she had done a spell of cleaning with them at a local care home. "She was a good worker" grudgingly from Rose. Neither she nor June liked to give much credit. "And she keeps her house spotless. And those children. Well brought up they are, always polite, never any trouble on that estate." Beth was amused. She made the estate sound like a troubled inner city slum, rather than a small estate of tidy little houses further along the main road from Beth's.

But neither woman was so sympathetic towards Fran and Russell Dean. "Just asking for trouble, the Deans." June pursed her lips. "Those huge windows in that great big house and no nets, anyone can look in and see all their belongings and see they've got money. Who needs a house that size, anyway?"

"But they don't deserve to be burgled!" exclaimed Beth.

"I'm not saying that, just that they could have taken more care. If you have so many valuables on display, well, it's too tempting for some people. Apparently the alarm wasn't even on! I mean, why have an alarm if you don't set it? I hope your friend Mrs Harris puts her alarm on when she goes out."

Beth waited uncomfortably for a comment that Gina was asking to be burgled too, alone in her large house. A change of subject was needed.

She started to talk about the forthcoming school summer fete, knowing both women had grandchildren at the local primary school, but Rose got there first, mind obviously still on the burglaries.

"And of course you know who the police suspect?" Her face loomed closer to Beth's, watery blue eyes magnified by thick lenses. "James Lamb, that's who." Beth's first impulse was to laugh. Rose looked affronted.

"Oh yes! Whose building firm has done work on all three houses? His!" Rose sat back and folded her arms, satisfaction all over her thin, lined face. "He altered the bathroom at Mary's house, when they decided not to move. Then he knocked down the wall between the dining room and kitchen at Mandy's to make one big room." A sniff expressed her opinion of open plan kitchen/diners. "And apparently he did some work at the Dean's house. Though what could possibly have needed doing there, I have no idea."

Beth looked at the complacent face of the woman sitting opposite with a sick feeling in her stomach. How could people be so smug when discussing traumatic events? Was it just relief that they hadn't been the victims? Or was it a distasteful pleasure in someone else's misfortune?

"It's true." June patted Beth's hand. "He's the common denominator, they called it. Becky told my Sandra; in floods of tears she was. Of course no one suspects James, but those lads he has working for him? What do we know about them? They go round all these houses, see how secure they are, lay their plans. Or some of Joe's mates? You have to admit, Joe Lamb mixes with some, well, questionable characters. Meets them down the pubs after work every night. And I have heard James himself mixed with a rough lot when he was a lad." She gave a sniff and wiped her nose.

Beth looked from one face to the other and felt a wave of revulsion. James Lamb had worked so hard to build up his firm and had a reputation for reliability and high quality work. He had faced bankruptcy twice; once when a developer had failed to pay him and again when a spell of bad health had prevented him working for a year. He didn't deserve this gossip. She had to get away before she said something she would regret.
"Well, I must get on with my shopping." She couldn't bear to look at them, their faces smug at someone else's misfortune, and bent down to pat Charlie before leading him away, hardly hearing their good byes.

She managed a few steps and stopped to look in the window of Pebbles Art Gallery and Pottery to compose herself. Julian had changed the window. Two containers of flowers; tulips, freesias and lisianthus were flanked by three paintings, each one reproducing the flowers in the vases. It took Beth a minute to realise she recognised the style of paintings. They were Melissa's. She tied Charlie's lead to the hook outside the shop and went in, greeting Julian and his young Saturday assistant.
"You admiring my new artist?" Julian nodded towards the window.
"Stunning, aren't they? There were five but two sold straight away."
"They're beautiful. I was at her house last Wednesday; she was showing her work to me and Gina."
"I shall take as much as she wants to sell. Nice to have a new artist locally."

Beth stayed chatting for a few more minutes but was still unsettled by the news about James. She was anxious also in case Julian brought up the subject with similar glee, though she didn't think he would; Julian was generous, always giving people the benefit of the doubt. Long-legged and broad shouldered with floppy dark brown curls, Julian was as good looking as he was charming and extrovert. Even so, she didn't want to discuss it.

Fortunately she completed her shopping with no further encounters. At least weekend shopping meant young Saturday staff and not the usual chatty workers. But church tomorrow would be a hurdle. Maybe she would miss for once and go to Winchester to see Nell?

In the event Nell had plans for the day so Beth went to church but offered to help serve teas and coffees to avoid the chat. Though if Reverend Mark or Maggie heard any gossip, they would soon stamp on it. Maybe the new week would bring more developments and James would be eliminated from enquiries? Goodness, television crime series had a lot to answer for, everyone knew the jargon, Beth thought ruefully. She hurried home after, pleading a busy afternoon; the reality of which was half an hour's gardening and two hours on the swing seat with a magazine. And a doze.

There had been no Tom to walk with that weekend. Beth tried to remember if he had said he wouldn't be around. Now she thought of it, he had mentioned his sister in Norfolk was visiting his nephew in Kent. Maybe he had gone to see them? Oh well, another weekend had come and gone. Not a great one really, she just hoped the week ahead would be better.

No, it wasn't.

The weather continued to be good but the sole topic of conversation at school, at Tea and Chat and in the local shops was the sudden crime wave of burglaries and who could be responsible. Few people were brazen enough to come out and say they suspected James Lamb or his companions; but speculation and discussion were rife. Popping into the butcher's on Tuesday afternoon, Beth had been served by Barbara, her usual sparkle markedly lacking as she weighed and counted Beth's order. Beth was determined not to gossip but found herself asking how the other woman was, suspecting the answer would involve Matthew, then James Lamb. Sure enough it did.

"Oh Beth." Barbara rubbed her hand over her forehead, ruffling her blonde curls. "The rows, you wouldn't believe. Robert has banned Matthew from working at James's. Matthew says he has to as he has already promised, then he gets on his high horse that James and Joe can't possibly have anything to do with the burglaries and Robert says, how does he know? Is he working part time for the police as well as the building firm as well as here? Then Matthew says he doesn't want to work here, he's made to, but as soon as he can he'll leave school and get an apprenticeship and work full time with James. Honestly, I can't stand it. Nor can Hannah, she spends all her time at Amy's these days."

Beth put her parcels away and patted Barbara's hand. "It will settle down; we all know James and Joe had nothing to do with it. I suppose the police have to investigate all sorts of avenues, to eliminate people. As for Matthew..." She hesitated, wanting to say he had to make his own career choices but unwilling to upset Barbara further. But it seemed the other woman thought the same.

"I tell Robert Matthew has to do what he wants, not what we tell him to do. Robert wanted to follow his father into the business but if Matthew doesn't, we can't make him." Barbara's round blue eyes were swimming with tears as she looked up at Beth. Beth felt so sorry for the woman. What a dilemma, and she knew Barbara would be caught in the middle. Robert could be a difficult man. Beth was well aware locals preferred to be served by the cheerful Barbara rather than her quiet, moody husband. He was also very stubborn. Matthew took after his father in looks as well as temperament and Beth was unsure who would win a battle of wills between the father and son. Fourteen year old Hannah was so like her mother; blonde, bubbly, extrovert. Beth remembered her from her primary school days when Hannah and her best friend Amy had been known by the school staff as the "giggly girls." But Hannah was as stubborn as her father. She just had such charm that she almost always gained her own way through that rather than confrontation.
"Perhaps Hannah will go into the business?" Beth suggested hopefully.
"I don't think so! Last I heard, she and Amy were undecided as to become human rights lawyers or open a nail bar together!" At least Barbara was smiling and Beth left as another customer came in.

Wednesday afternoon was no better. A Chinese whisper went around school that someone knew someone who claimed one of James's workers did know something about the burglaries. Conversation in the charity shop grew heated when a customer was firmly told by Sue to keep her offensive opinions to herself, retaliating there was no smoke without fire as she flounced out, indignation in every muscle.

By Wednesday evening Beth was tired and uptight as she walked over the road to call for Tom. The day had been fraught; everyone irritable, gossipy, nervous. Even the children seemed to have picked up on the tension and were loud and argumentative. But the soothing scent of honeysuckle washed over her as she walked up the path and Tom came out of his house, hazel eyes crinkling as he looked at her, his easy grin warm and friendly as he put his hand under her elbow as they crossed the road, his fingers warm and firm. They walked along the beach and sat down by the water's edge in the evening sunshine. The air was warm and still, white frills rolled over the shingle and yachts sailed quietly past. The Isle of Wight ferry could be seen in the distance and a large cruise ship was making its stately way out of Southampton.

Charlie was chasing seagulls and Tess curled up by Tom, calmly watching Charlie. For the first time all day Beth felt her tenseness ease as the sights and sounds around her soothed and calmed. She kicked off her sandals and stretched out her legs, noticing white stripes on her small feet where straps had been. She gave a contented sigh and closed her eyes to relax. Tom looked at her quizzically.
"Bad day?"
"Mmmm. Everyone gossiping about the burglaries, about James and Joe. Even the children are talking about it." Tom was quiet. "Are you worried about the break - ins? Your house is quite secure, isn't it?"
Beth nodded. "Yes. But don't they say anyone can get in of they are determined to?"
"I'll come round and put some extra locks on for you, if you want." Tom offered.
"I think I've got plenty. But thank you." Beth was quiet, hugging her knees and gazing out to sea.

Tom changed the subject, beginning to tell Beth about his progress with the garden. He had plans for it, wanting to replace some of the borders that held annuals with perennials, plant more shrubs. But he needed to go carefully, he added ruefully. Frances liked the annuals, she kept telling him he needed a balance between annuals, perennials and evergreen shrubs.
"I wonder whose garden it is sometimes! But there's no point upsetting her, she knows her stuff and is keen to advise." Frances had convinced him, no; make that ordered him, to leave well alone for the rest of the year so he could see what flowered where. It was sensible, really. At least she showed no interest in the house and he was ready to go ahead with some alterations.

Beth was still gazing out to sea, half listening to his deep voice explaining about the garden, the alterations, half dreaming, when she registered a name.

"So I was going to get a quote from James Lamb, everyone seems to use him. But is that wise, do you think, with the current situation?"

"The current situation? What current situation?" Beth shook herself to full consciousness, turning to look at him.

"Well, all the talk about his firm being involved somehow with the burglaries." Tom hesitated, seeing Beth tense. She sat up straight, staring at him in astonishment, her eyes wide.

"Don't say you believe all the tittle tattle too? Poor James, he would never be involved in anything like that but the poor man is considered guilty already." To her dismay her voice shook and her eyes filled. She turned her head away to hide it, staring intently at the white ferry making its way between Portsmouth and Ryde.

"Whoa! Stop! I'm sorry! I didn't mean to sound as though I think he's guilty. I don't know any of these people, remember. But I'm sorry I've upset you." Tom moved to put a warm hand on hers. "Please, let's start again."

Beth shuddered, looked down and pulled her hand away, swallowing hard and blinking.

"I'm sorry." She took a deep breath. "I overreacted. It's just been such a horrid week; everyone talking about it and convinced they know. But I've known James and Becky for years, and Joe, and they would do anything for anyone. James has done work for lots of people I know and hasn't even charged them the going rate, to help them out. There's no way he would ever rob anyone. When I first moved to my house with Nell he was so helpful, he did work for me, waited until I could afford to pay him, never rushed me. I trust him completely..." Her voice shook and she stopped to compose herself, pushing her hair back behind her ears, staring intently out to sea and willing her eyes not to fill up again.

"Then I really am sorry." Tom's voice was quiet. "I shouldn't have been so suspicious. I'll phone him tomorrow and ask him to come and quote." Beth swallowed and blinked. She forced herself to breathe slowly and reminded herself Tom was right, he didn't know any of these people like she did. Gradually she began to feel in control again.

She got to her feet and called Charlie. The air was getting humid and muggy; maybe a storm was brewing after the fine weather. That would be about right, stormy weather to match the stormy atmosphere in the town. Tom patted Tess and got to his feet. Beth started walking along the beach up to the road and Tom registered her tense back and silence. As they crossed and approached his house, he put a hand under her elbow again, forcing her to stop.

"Come in for a coffee? Please? So I know I'm forgiven?" His voice was quiet, gentle. His sunglasses had lightened to clear lenses and Beth looked up at warm, concerned hazel eyes, fringed by thick lashes, a slight frown on his forehead. His sandy hair flopped down and she felt a sudden urge to push it back, out of his eyes. The knot in her stomach eased a little and she nodded.

"Alright. But I prefer tea."

"Tea it is." He found himself letting out a sigh of relief, leading the way down the drive and round to the back of the house.

Tom led the way into the kitchen at the back of the house. Beth had calmed down and looked around with interest. The previous owners had replaced the kitchen a couple of years before with modern units but in a warm solid wood. Granite worktops flecked with greens and golds were mixed with solid wood worktops. An island in the centre had the hob on it with stools facing and Tom gestured her to one of these before turning to fill the kettle. Tess padded quietly over to her basket by the French doors and Charlie followed, climbing in with her. Beth wasn't keen on bar stools, her legs were too short to climb on as elegantly as Gina or Melissa, but Tom was facing the sink and didn't see her lack of grace. "Did you want to sit here or there?" motioning to a sofa on the side wall.

"The sofa, please." Beth climbed gratefully down and perched on the edge of the sofa, tugging her skirt over her knees. Tom put the tray down on a side table, asking if she took milk and sugar before looking at her.

"I am sorry, you know. I wouldn't have upset you for the world." He still looked so concerned, Beth knew he was genuinely apologetic and felt silly and guilty for her outburst.

"I'm sorry too; I shouldn't have had a go. It wasn't just you. I've been anxious about it all week and that was just the final straw. Let's forget about it."

She took her tea from him, gazing around the kitchen with its long wooden table covered in clutter.

"This is a nice room. Have you any plans for any changes in here?"

"No, it's fine. It's a really lovely room. I love the fact I can eat in here, or just sit and look out at the garden. The living room is good too. When you've finished your tea I'll show you the dining room; I want to make it into a library and study. I kept wondering which room was best as a study, but it has to be the dining room. I would never get any work done if it was in the living room."

It was obvious why. The living room windows were high and wide, with the original shutters. The view through them was stunning; the white wood surrounds framing the island and out to sea, past the Spinnaker tower and Gunwharf Quays, the three forts visible in the distance.
"See" Tom grinned, his eyes crinkling at the corners. "How would I ever concentrate enough to do any work, looking at that view all the time?"
"But surely you've got a nice view from the dining room?"
"Yes, but not as distracting as this, come and see."

The dining room had doors on to the garden, framing a view of greenery and splashes of colour, mature trees and shrubs; but as Tom said, although it was pleasant it lacked the movement and constant change of the view of the sea. It was a large square room, at present filled with boxes and stacks of books.
"I want bookshelves put in both these alcoves" Tom explained "with cupboards built underneath, then I can keep all my files and so on in them. My desk will go here and an armchair and reading lamp here."
Piles of books balanced precariously on the floor and Beth twisted her head to read some of the titles. There were reference books, autobiographies, travel books. And piles and piles of fiction, mostly psychological thrillers and crime. Many were by authors Beth liked and she craned her neck more to read the titles.
"What sort of books do you read?" Tom asked curiously.
"These" sweeping an arm towards the pile of novels by Elizabeth George, Reginald Hill, Jo Nesbo, Ann Cleve. "Though nothing too gory, Jo Nesbo can make me cringe a bit." Tom laughed.
"That one with the spiked apple thing was particularly gruesome."
"I haven't read this Ian Rankin, The Beat Goes On."
"Ah yes. I love his books. That one is short stories. I thought I'd feel a bit cheated by it, not being a full length novel, but I was engrossed." He crouched down to ease it from the pile without causing an avalanche of books. "I was so scared Rebus would be no more, after Exit Music, but thank goodness he came back."
"That was a great book, though, wasn't it?" Tom straightened up. "There's a new Rebus coming out later this year, in November, Even Dogs in the

Wild. I've pre ordered it. But do you want to borrow this?" He held it out to her. "Now, another cup of tea?"

They discussed books and authors while they had a fresh drink, then Beth stood up to go, patting Charlie awake. He opened his eyes reluctantly, stretching and yawning before climbing out of the basket.
"Thanks for the tea. And the book. I must be going."
"And I'm forgiven?" an eyebrow was raised as Tom followed her to the door.
"You're forgiven!" Beth laughed. "And I'm feeling much better now, thanks to the restorative powers of tea! "Good." Tom looked down at her, hesitating as though wanting to add something, but simply raised his hand in farewell. "Beach at seven tomorrow then?" Beth nodded her agreement and walked down the path, down to the corner and over the road to her own house. She felt exhausted. And low. Maybe a good night's sleep was what she needed and things would be better in the morning.

There was no thunder storm but Beth woke on Thursday morning to dark, oppressive clouds. By lunchtime it was raining and six hours later it still showed no sign of abating. She phoned Tom to check he wasn't expecting to meet up for a walk but it went straight to the answer machine. Unreasonably relieved that she wouldn't have to chat, despite the truce reached the night before, Beth left a brief message to say she would see him the following evening, weather permitting. She changed into one of her new dresses, the fitted waist and flared skirt emphasising her waist and the soft curves of her hips. The narrow straps were perfect for a warm evening but not for tonight. She shrugged on an off white crochet cardigan Gina had picked out and slipped her feet into a pair of smart cream sandals with low heels. Usually she would walk to the wine bar to meet Gina and Carol for dinner, but tonight transport was called for and she drove the short distance in her old blue Golf.

Gina was already seated at a table by the window, watching the rain streaming down the glass.
"Summer's over!" Beth dumped her bag on the floor and slid onto the bench opposite Gina. She had only walked from the car park into the restaurant but her hair felt flat and damp. Gina's hair was immaculate as usual, a golden bell swinging around her perfect oval face. She wore a mid-blue linen tunic that perfectly matched her eyes, over white linen trousers. White gold jewellery with diamonds and sapphires flashed at her ears and on her long fingers. Beth knew her husband had bought her beautiful

jewellery and would bet that all Gina's earrings were in pairs, none going missing as hers frequently did. Gina smiled at her.
"It's not supposed to last, sun again tomorrow".
"Good. No Carol yet? Not like her to be late." Beth looked around but there was no sign of her and it wasn't until both women had ordered drinks and caught up with news that Carol came through the door, shrugging off her raincoat.

It was obvious something was wrong. Her short, layered hair needed brushing and her grey eyes were anxious, her mouth tense.
"Carol? Carol, are you alright?" Beth started to stand up but Carol waved her down and sank onto the bench next to her.
"Don't take any notice, I'll be alright." She picked up the bottle of wine and poured herself a large glass, drinking half in one gulp.
"No you're not." Gina frowned. "Come on, what's happened?" Carol was silent, putting down the glass then picking it up again, her eyes strained and her mouth tense.
"Well, do you want to know about me first, or Ken?"
"Either! Just tell us, what's happened?" Beth was starting to feel alarmed, a knot of tension tightening in her stomach.
"Okay, Ken first" Carol took a deep breath. "The good news is the suspicion should be off James Lamb now. The bad news is, it's now on Ken." There was a shocked silence.
"But why? How?" Gina leaned across; clasping Carol's hand but Carol shrugged it away.
"No, no. No sympathy or I really will fall apart."
Now Beth really was worried. Carol was the sensible one, always calm, always rational. To see her like this was dreadful.

The waitress arrived to take their orders. She left and there was silence until Carol looked up and broke it, her usually composed face ravaged with worry.
"It seems that Ken's estate agency handled all three house sales. So the police are investigating wrong doing at the office, keys kept, that sort of thing."
"What?" Beth was incredulous. "But the Wrens' have lived there for thirty years! Is he supposed to have kept the key for thirty years?!" Carol shook her head, eyes worried.
"No, but a year ago they thought of moving to a retirement apartment and put it on the market. Ken did the marketing and there were some viewings

but then they changed their minds. They altered the garden, did up the bathroom and so on. And the Deans' only bought their house less than two years ago, through the agency. Ken handled the sale for the people who used to live there. Then the Davis's bought their house ten months ago, again through Ken. So you see, now Ken is the common denominator." She gave a wobbly smile. Gina poured her more wine.
"But Ken's had his agency for over thirty years, it's ridiculous!"
Beth agreed. "It will be alright Carol; they'll find they're barking up the wrong tree."

Another thought occurred to her.
"But you said you and Ken. What about you?" She looked anxiously at the woman sitting opposite.
"Oh I'm sure it's something and nothing" Carol paused, to be prompted by Gina.
"What is? Come on, tell us." Gina looked as worried as Beth felt.
"Only... oh I've had a bit of bleeding, well quite a lot actually, and I'm through the menopause, I haven't had a period for over two years. But it happens, doesn't it?" looking at the two women "Doesn't it?"
Beth nodded her head. "Yes, it happens, but it shouldn't. You need to get it checked out, Carol."
Carol's chin wobbled, silent tears sliding down her face. "But I can't, not while poor Ken is so stressed..."
"He'll be even more stressed if he thinks there's something wrong with you and you're not doing anything about it."
There was silence while the waitress brought their food and Carol composed herself. She looked at the two women, speaking defeatedly.
"I know, I know. I'll make an appointment with Doctor Clarke tomorrow."

None of the women had much appetite. Carol picked at her food and Gina and Beth ate but with no enjoyment. I need another drink, thought Beth, but she had to order tonic water, remembering her car outside. Poor Carol and Ken. How on earth would he prove he had no connection with it all? And Carol, there could be an innocent explanation or... no, stop, don't start thinking like that. It would all get sorted out and life could get back to normal. But she felt sick, thinking of Carol's face, the worry in her eyes, the tears. She had never known Carol cry, which made this evening's behaviour even more alarming. Carol was always so strong, such a rock. But she was human, worried sick about Ken and about herself, no wonder she was tearful and anxious. The three women finished their

meal in silence, each lost in their own thoughts. It was still raining when they left. Carol accepted a lift in Beth's car and sat silently beside her for the short drive to her house. She gave Beth a brief hug, looking anxiously at her house where the lights shone out from the living room.
"I'll see you tomorrow. Thanks for the lift." Then she was gone, hurrying up the path. Beth drove slowly home, windscreen wipers on full, her heart heavy.

One more person in Brides Bay was also worried. Ali Soames sat googling holiday cottages in Cornwall, seemingly intent on her task. But the images flashed by on the screen without her seeing them. Her greyish blue eyes stared at the idyllic stone cottages, the sandy beaches, turquoise sea and crashing waves, but her ears were sharply attuned to the phone conversation going on behind her. She could only hear one side of it but it was enough to know her husband was talking to Melissa and arranging to show her the historic dockyard in Portsmouth. Julian was animated and loud; no, he was saying, Ali wouldn't want to go with them, she had been many times before. Yes of course he would drive, or they could get the ferry over to Gunwharf Quays. Ali would take them to Gosport. They'd make a day of it. Ali would watch the gallery, and there were good places to eat. What did she like? Thai, Italian? Julian paced as he talked, limbs loose and relaxed, dark curls flopping over his forehead, a smile evident in his deep voice. Ali clenched her fists and clicked off the travel website. Somehow, she wasn't in the mood to plan holidays with Julian. Her head ached and her eyes stung as a feeling of dread flooded her stomach. It was happening all over again.

At least there was one happy person in Bride's Bay. Beth watched Frances whisking dead flowers out of the large pedestal by the altar in amazement. The other woman was actually smiling. And Beth obviously wasn't the only one who had been clothes shopping; Frances was wearing a flowery blue and white skirt with a pretty white top, rather than her uniform of beige and brown. The blues complemented her silvery hair and pale blue eyes. The shorter skirt showed her legs, usually hidden beneath long shapeless beige skirts, to be surprisingly good. But even more surprising was her manner. Usually sharp and critical, Frances hummed as she worked, pausing now and then to comment favourably on the other women's efforts.

Ali and Gina looked equally bemused; used to their efforts being criticised and modified. Well well, thought Beth? What has brought about this new, improved Frances?

It wasn't a what, it was a who, she realised a while later as they sat over a cup of tea before leaving.
"And I got those from Tom's garden" nodding to the delicate Lily of the Valley. "Such a helpful man. He said I could go round anytime to help myself. Of course, he has no idea what the plants even are." She smiled indulgently. Not exactly true, thought Beth, remembering Tom's account of his garden and knowing he knew more than Frances was giving him credit for. But she wasn't about to disagree.

The other woman was still talking happily.
"I said I will help him out when he wants to do his garden. I can advise him on what plants are already there and what he needs to do. He was so grateful." She sipped her tea happily.

Gina caught Beth's eye and grinned. Lucky Tom, Beth could read her face. But he would be well able to manage Frances and it was nice to see someone happy at least.

Beth herself cheered up when she arrived home after flower arranging. The phone was flashing and she pressed the button to hear Nell's light voice. "Hello Aunty Beth. Sorry to miss you. Just wondered if you are doing anything tomorrow? I know it's short notice but I wondered if you wanted to meet for lunch in town? Will is off cycling for the day and I need some things. Let me know, byee."
She deleted the message, smiling. A day out with bubbly, lively Nell away from Bride's Bay was just what the doctor ordered!

CHAPTER 5

Beth woke early to sun streaming through the windows. Charlie snored beside her, his hairy chest rising and falling and his small pink tongue hanging out. He opened one eye as she turned over, looking at her as she sat up and stretched, then he jumped off the bed, waiting expectantly. She quickly washed and dressed, slipping her feet into flat sandals. They were the most comfortable and she guessed they would be doing a lot of walking today, knowing her niece's propensity for shopping. She and Gina were well matched, she mused. Possibly Nell was even more enthusiastic, but she had youth on her side and a smaller bank balance, consequently she had to search more carefully than Gina who could afford to buy as she saw. She took Charlie for a walk to the park then sat down for a quick cup of tea and piece of toast, while Charlie munched his way through his bowl of food. By ten o' clock she had tidied the kitchen and living room, checked she had everything she needed for the day, then put Charlie in the car and climbed into the driving seat.

The journey to Winchester usually only took half an hour but today the traffic was heavy and it was nearly eleven before she pulled up in the small car park attached to Nell's block of flats. Walking up the path to the entrance, she glanced at the well-tended flower beds and the trim lawns. Nell's flat was small, just one bedroom, a tiny wet room and a combined living/dining/kitchen but Beth knew her niece had chosen it for of its proximity to the town centre as well as the quiet residential area. It was also secure and well maintained. "I'd rather have less space" her niece had explained earnestly "and live somewhere safe, than a bigger flat somewhere not so nice." Beth wholeheartedly agreed. The block was modern with a state of the art entry system and she was happier knowing her niece had a comfortable, secure and warm home. The rent was horrendous but Nell seemed to be managing all right financially, though Beth decided she would quiz her about the state of her finances later.

Nell threw open the door and hugged her aunt. "It's so nice to see you!" Her eyes sparkled, smile wide.
"You only saw me recently!" Beth laughed, kissing the young woman's cheek.
"I know! But it's still nice to see you now." Nell danced ahead into the kitchen area and put the kettle on.
"Now. A quick cup of coffee before we hit the shops?" Beth nodded.

"And I need to take Charlie for a walk before we leave him here. You're not allowed dogs in your grounds, are you? "
Nell shook her head. "No. But we can take him to the park round the corner."

Half an hour later they were walking into the town centre, arm in arm. Nell made a beeline for her favourite shop and Beth watched indulgently as she flew from one rack to another, picking up a dress here, a top there, bright blue eyes shining and hair tumbling round her shoulders, a mass of untidy curls. She was pleased when Nell finally decided it was time for a coffee and sandwich and they sat squashed in the corner of a coffee shop, raising their voices above the hisses and gurgles of the coffee machine and the chatter of the other customers.
"So is there anything you really need?" Beth asked as she picked up a steaming panini and caught some cheese as it dripped out, wincing at the heat on her finger.
"Well." Nell considered, her head on one side. "I could do with a new skirt for work, or a dress."
"Okay, you buy one and I'll treat you to the other."

Choosing a skirt and dress took up the rest of the afternoon, Beth eventually sitting to wait on an uncomfortable leather cube while Nell waltzed in and out of the fitting room, twirling happily in front of Beth.
"That's lovely." Beth looked at the slim figure in front of her in a charcoal grey short fitted jersey skirt with black panels down the side. Nell was blessed with long shapely legs and the skirt was the perfect length.
"Yes, it's just right for work." Nell smoothed the skirt over her narrow hips. "I'll take this one and that dress." Beth handed her the hanger she had been holding and they made their way over to pay.

"Come on, we should choose some bits for you, to go with all your new clothes." Nell tugged Beth's arm, leading her to a display of silver necklaces. She had been suitably impressed with Beth's new clothes, making Beth spin round to show off the well-fitting trousers and the beautifully cut top.
"No, I don't need anything." But Beth found herself picking up a delicate silver chain with a ring hanging off it containing a tiny pearl.
"You may not need anything, but that's not to say you shouldn't buy something."
Giving in, Beth joined her niece in studying the selection of jewellery on offer. How like her mother she was, she thought with a pang as she

watched the young woman's face light up at the sight of a delicate silver chain punctuated with coral beads. Louise had been a magpie, loving scarves and hats, jewellery and bags. A shortage of money had never hampered her; she would trawl charity shops, gleefully bringing home an eclectic collection of items then put them together and dance around like a vibrant butterfly.

"Aunty Beth! I said what do you think?" Beth forced herself back to the present and looked at the necklace.

"That's beautiful. I've got a top in just that colour. But Nell, I've already chosen this one."

"So now you've got two!" Nell weaved her way to the pay desk, ignoring Beth's half-hearted protestations.

It was ten o'clock and Beth stretched out along the sofa. Nell sat opposite her on the floor, hugging her jean clad knees, her back to a battered armchair. Her blonde curls tumbled around her soft pink cheeks and her vivid blue eyes looked up at her aunt. Beth had planned to go home but Nell had persuaded her to stay the night, overriding her protests by blithely stating they could stop off at the corner shop to buy dog food for Charlie, and she had a nightie and toothbrush Beth could use. Now they sat in the cosy living room, Nell with a glass of juice and Beth a mug of tea.

"It's been a lovely day. Are you pleased with what you bought?" Nell's clear gaze searched her face.

"Oh yes. And it was fun, wasn't it?"

Nell nodded. "And dinner was good. The food is always good there." They had been to Nell's favourite Italian restaurant where a very attentive young waiter had served them, his liquid brown eyes gazing at Nell in admiration.

"But their penne pasta with pesto is still nowhere as near as good as yours! Will loved it too."

Nell was quiet, absentmindedly rubbing Charlie behind the ears as he lay on the floor by her side.

"So? What did you think of him?" Her clear eyes held an uncharacteristic expression of concern.

"Who? The waiter?" Beth laughed at Nell's face. "No, I know. He's very nice Nell, I liked him a lot."

"He is, isn't he? I really like him Aunty Beth, he's so..." Nell screwed her face up, thinking of the word.

"Calm?" Beth offered, thinking of the young man's quiet composed manner.
"Yes, calm, but not boring. Definitely not boring. He's so funny, but in a quiet way, you know?" Beth nodded, silently amused at the earnest expression on Nell's young face.
"And he's so thoughtful and considerate. And clever. He wants to do a PhD. But he's not arrogant or full of himself." She sat, gazing into space.

"And nice looking." Beth added. She had never seen Nell like this over a boy and suppressed a smile.
"Mmm. He is, isn't he? But he's not flash, not like some of the boys at uni. I don't think I could go out with anyone vainer than me!" She laughed. "Some of them used to spend more than me on hair and skin products! Will just likes to be clean! He doesn't even like cologne or after shave. And he's not an alpha male, but he's …I don't know…" she hesitated "he's strong, and trustworthy, honest… I know I can always rely on him."
Nell was thoughtful, twirling a curl around her finger and absentmindedly putting it in her mouth.
Beth looked at her affectionately.
"Well, as long as he's kind to you, he gets my vote. And stop chewing your hair!"

Nell looked up grinning, but obediently released the lock of hair, twirling it round her finger instead.
"I wish you would meet someone." Her clear blue eyes met Beth's with a question in them.
"No, no, I'm quite happy as I am, thank you. I'll leave the dates and flowers and chocolates to you."
"Some chance! Will came round with a present for me the other day, some energy saving light bulbs he had seen on offer!" The two women laughed and the moment was gone. Nell assumed Beth had never met anyone special before she had taken over caring for her, and Beth was happy to keep it that way. There were some things her niece was never going to know.

They both slept in the next morning, Beth waking only when Charlie whined softly, nudging her arm with his head. For a moment she was disorientated, before realising she was on the sofa bed in Nell's living room. She stretched and sat up. "Come on Charlie, I'll take you for a quick walk before I shower." She dressed quickly and quietly, not wanting to disturb Nell. Letting herself out of the ground floor flat she and Charlie walked down the road, into the small park at the end. Gina had been right, it was sunny again and the sky was a clear pale blue, with the promise of brighter skies to come. Once back, she had a quick shower and dressed again in yesterday's clothes. Nell had lent her underwear, Beth squeezing into knickers that were two sizes too small as well as being half the size of the ones she wore. Oh well, they would be fine until she got home. Nell was awake and sitting yawning at the small table in the living room. "You will stay for the day, won't you?" she asked. "Will is coming round this afternoon. We could go for a walk, have a picnic maybe?"

So that was what they had done, walking down the road to buy the Sunday papers; then croissants, fresh bread, cooked meat and peaches at the deli. They sat quietly together enjoying a lazy brunch while they read the papers and waited for Will. Beth drove the three of them into the New Forest, parking in Lyndhurst. They walked for over an hour in the dappled shade of the ancient trees of the forest, inhaling the pungent perfume of wild garlic, while Charlie ran ahead then back over and over again, then sat at a picnic table as Nell spread the food out on paper napkins. She had forgotten a knife but they pulled the bread apart with their fingers and popped pieces of chorizo and Italian ham onto it.

Biting into a succulent peach, the juice dripping over her fingers, Beth watched the young couple. Will was obviously as smitten with Nell as her niece was with him. Nell had been popular at university, with both boys and girls, but had not had a serious boyfriend there. Watching her niece's face as she laughed and chatted with Will, Beth felt a fleeting pang that she wasn't the only important person in Nell's life any more. Stop that, she told herself firmly. Be happy for her. And she was, really. Will was funny, thoughtful and kind. He treated Nell well and that was all that mattered.

Beth drove home late that evening feeling rested and happy from the change of scene. It had done her good. She hadn't mentioned the burglaries to Nell, or the suspicions raging around the little town. Now after nearly two days of not talking about it, even thinking about it, she felt more relaxed than she had since the spate of burglaries had begun. But as she pulled up in front her cottage she felt a pang of unease and wished there was someone with her. Only there wasn't and she had to get on with it. She walked up the path, unlocked the door and went in, letting out the breath she hadn't even realised she was holding as she saw everything exactly as she had left it.

The answer machine was flashing and Beth pressed the button, expecting to hear Gina's voice or Carol's. But it was Tom's. "Beth, hi, it's Tom. Just to say hope you've had a good weekend. I've got to go into Salisbury tomorrow, I won't be back until late so won't be walking Tess. But see you Tuesday? Call for me? Bye now."

Beth shivered, but it was a pleasant shiver. His voice was deep, warm and rumbling, seeming to fill the small hallway. His voice was like him, comfortable, safe, solid. She felt a pang of disappointment that he wouldn't be walking Tess the next day, immediately snuffing it out. She always used to walk Charlie alone, what was wrong with doing that again? What difference did it make? She went to put the kettle on and feed Charlie, avoiding thinking of the answer.

Monday afternoon. Tea and Chat was going well and the presence of Carol, who was very well liked, prevented any gossip about the latest "common denominator." She was busy circulating, smiling and chatting as though everything in her life was rosy. Gina and Beth, watching from the kitchen serving hatch, marvelled.
"I'm glad she's here though, better than staying indoors worrying." Gina topped up the teapot from the urn.
"Hmmm. Definitely. How was she yesterday after church?"
Gina shrugged. "Same as now, chatting, smiling. We asked her if she and Ken wanted to come out with us but she said Naomi was calling over."
Beth raised her eyebrows inquisitively.
"Tom and I went to the haven for some lunch and a walk."
"Aah." Beth's stomach lurched.
"There is no aah! He just mentioned the other day he wanted to visit it and as it was dry and sunny yesterday, we decided after church to go. It was a spur of the moment thing." Gina lived opposite Titchfield Haven and Beth knew she frequently walked there.

Gina turned away to stack some crockery in the dishwasher and Beth gazed at her straight back. If Gina and Tom formed a friendship, then how nice. And if it developed into something more? Her friend had been on her own a long time; Malcom had died over eight years previously. It would be lovely for her to meet someone special. And it wouldn't make any difference to their friendship, would it? Why then did the thought of it make her feel so low?

The next day Beth called into the gallery to buy some birthday cards. Julian was perched on his stool as usual. Melissa was leaning against the counter, in a short red linen skirt and white clinging jersey tee-shirt, the top of her perfect breasts showing above the tight fabric, her long legs tanned and bare, red sandals exposing matching red tipped toes. Her chestnut waves shone with health and her lips were full and a glossy crimson.

"Beth, hi. I missed you on Sunday." A wide smile showed perfect white teeth and high cheek bones. Of course. "I was at my niece's, in Winchester." Beth explained.
"Winchester. Now that's somewhere I've never been, but I hear it's beautiful."
"It is" agreed Julian. "I have an artist there; I'm due to visit him if you want to come along?"
"Lovely. Just tell me when." Melissa eased herself away from the counter and picked up her bag. "Well, duty calls. Back to the paintbrushes. Thanks for the coffee, Julian, bye Beth." She walked to the door, back straight, hips swaying, glossy dark hair hanging over her shoulders.

Beth smiled her goodbye, turning to Julian to explain she needed some cards and her heart sank at the blatant admiration in his eyes as he gazed after Melissa. His brown hair curled around his face, falling over his collar; his deep brown eyes, as rich and sultry as Melissa's, were liquid, shining. He looked like a man in love. Or lust. Whichever, it was Melissa who was the cause of his expression.

Ali soon discovered Julian was visiting his artist in Winchester. He needed her to cover the shop and announced he would be taking Melissa with him as she was keen to see the artist's work. Ali's narrow shoulders hunched and her throat felt tight, aching with tears. How could she compete with Melissa? What woman could compete with Melissa? She certainly couldn't, aware she lacked the other woman's confidence, charisma, sex appeal. She knew she had been attractive once; her ethereal looks attracting boys, especially the artistic, sensitive ones who saw her as a Lizzie Siddal, a pre Raphaelite angel with a delicate, sensitive beauty. Her personality had reflected her looks; she had been quiet, sensitive, reserved. Maybe it was true that opposites attracted. Certainly her fair looks, her shy personality and lack of confidence had been the opposite of Julian's sultry dark good looks, his charismatic extrovert personality. But they had been madly in love once. He had treated her like a fragile doll, loving her helplessness, her delicacy. And how she had loved being looked after, cherished. So what had changed? And when? When did he stop seeing her as a fragile beauty to love and protect and start seeing her as a weak, characterless, helpless female? When had he started to despise her?

But she had never stopped loving him; never stopped seeing him as her strong, passionate, caring partner for life. She had quietly supported him, keeping their home warm and clean and comfortable, cooking, shopping, making sure he had everything he needed. Or had she? Maybe what he had needed was a vibrant, passionate, confident partner, not the shy, boring, colourless person she actually was, no more than a cleaner or housekeeper. Maybe if they had had children.... how she had yearned for them, praying and hoping every month it would happen. But it never did. Julian had said he was happy as they were, just the two of them. But she had felt even more useless, even more colourless, weak and invisible. She had never found it easy to talk to anyone. She had very few friends in the town, even though they had lived there for nearly twenty years. Everyone was friendly; Maggie, Carol, Barbara, Beth, they all chatted to her, but the only person she really spoke to was Frances, recognising the same loneliness and awkwardness in the other woman. And she couldn't even talk to Julian now, she thought with an ache in her chest. If she tried to explain to Julian how she felt about Melissa he would laugh, say she was imagining things. He was married to her, wasn't he? But he had been married to her before, when a bubbly young redhead had appeared, another artist who had found Julian attentive, attractive, ignored the fact he should have been unavailable. It hadn't stopped him then and it wouldn't now. Last time she had sat tight, pretended she didn't know what was happening, hoped and prayed it would fizzle out. And it had. So she would do the same again, be patient and supportive and maybe, just maybe, it would all go away and Julian would settle down again.

Ali wasn't the only one disturbed by Melissa. In the vicarage Maggie sat at the kitchen table picking at a bowl of pasta. Mark was at a deanery meeting and wouldn't be home until late. He could microwave his dinner or it could be frozen if he had already eaten. Maggie put down her fork and put her head in her hands, running her fingers through her soft, wispy brown hair. The house was so quiet and empty these days. Rachel and James were both at university and how she missed their noise and mess and company. She was pleased they were so happy at university, of course she was, but Mark was so busy and always seemed to be needed. Well, she needed him too. But by the time he had finished his duties for the day he was tired and drained, content to eat his meal and watch some mindless television before turning in for the night then starting all over again a few short hours later. Yet for other people he was a rock, emotionally and practically. Melissa, for example. She had turned up for the family service on Sunday and had cornered him after, talking quietly and seriously. Then she had called at the vicarage on Monday and he had been closeted in his study with her for over an hour; just poking his head round the kitchen door to ask if Maggie could possibly make them some coffee.

Maggie felt miserable. Who supported her? When did anyone ask her if she was alright? But would she be feeling like this if Melissa was old and faded and grey? No, she wouldn't. Yet she trusted Mark completely, so why was she so unsettled? Mark just saw people in need. The effect Melissa had on people, especially men, would have passed him by completely. His blue eyes would be puzzled and disconcerted if she mentioned any of this to him. Yet they had always discussed everything; so why was she feeling this constraint now? Was she just feeling inadequate, compared to beautiful, vibrant Melissa?

She caught her reflection in the mirror on the dresser, feeling a jolt at the face staring back at her, old and tired and grey. She had never been a beauty, she was just normal looking. Average height, average size, brown hair, not thick and not thin, small brown eyes. Everything about her was ordinary. She wasn't plain, she wasn't pretty, she was just…ordinary. But it had always been enough for her and enough for Mark too, or so she had always thought. He never told her she was lovely, attractive, the love of his life. But he had always seemed happy with her. Had she given too much time and energy to bringing up the twins? Should she have made more of an effort, been more of a lover than just a partner, a mother? Should she have worn nicer clothes, make up, had her hair dyed? But she doubted that Mark would have noticed; he didn't notice when she had her hair cut, hadn't even noticed the time she had radically changed the style after Rachel had encouraged her to try something new. To him she was just Maggie. And he was never home anyway. What difference would it have made if she had done more for herself, rather than building her whole life around the twins, the house, the parish? But just as she felt lonely and empty without the twins, Mark didn't even seem to have noticed they had gone. He was livelier, more cheerful. His appearance was the same, his hair was showing more grey, his face more wrinkles. But he was happy. Happier than her. Was it Melissa making him happy? She felt sick. Her head throbbed and her chest felt heavy.

A whine at her feet brought her back to the present and she looked down at Pippin, his soft faded brown eyes gazing up at her as he struggled to put a paw on her knee. Poor old boy. They had got him when the twins were four and he was showing his age. She leaned forward to stroke his wiry grey hair. "What a misery I am, I have nothing to be fed up about really, yet here I am feeling sorry for myself. Come on, this won't do, let's go for a walk."

Pippin whined agreement and followed her out of the room, but his slow, stiff movements echoed those of his mistress.

CHAPTER 6

The week was passing quietly. Police investigations were continuing but there had been no more burglaries and thoughts began to turn to the summer and the holiday season. Not that Bride's Bay was a popular destination for holidaymakers; most preferring to bypass the small town as quickly as possible and continue west in search of sandy beaches and amusements. The shingle beach deterred tourists, as well as the lack of funfairs, water parks and celebrity restaurants. There were no campsites, no caravan parks, not even a hotel. The little town boasted two bed and breakfasts' but even they only had two and three guest rooms, respectively. There were plenty of places to visit nearby; the Isle of Wight, the New Forest, Chichester and Winchester as well as the sights and museums of Southampton and Portsmouth, but most people preferred to stay elsewhere.

The little seaside town was popular, however, with day trippers who drove from inland towns and villages for a day at the seaside when the weather was good. It was also a popular place to sail, windsurf and jet-ski and weekends in particular saw the sea full of colour and activity as people came out to play. But the visitors and water sports enthusiasts needed places to eat and drink, to spend their money. Several local shops and cafes would gear up for an increase in trade; in particular Julian's gallery, Maisie's Gifts and Bryn Cards and Gifts, the ebullient Welsh owner extending his shop out onto the pavement to provide visitors with buckets and spades, beach balls, postcards, sunscreen, sunhats, rock and all the paraphernalia required for a day on the beach. The tea and coffee shops also spruced up for the visitors, employing extra staff for the season.

The influx of day trippers provoked mixed feelings amongst the population of the small town. Beth herself enjoyed the extra life brought to the town; the excited children and indulgent grandparents. But many locals complained at the longer queues in the shops, the litter, the difficulty parking and the inconvenience. But it was a fact of life and no-one complained at the increased revenue the town received. As well as the businesses preparing for the visitors, the school's plans for the summer fete gained momentum with the Friends of Bride's Bay Primary School busy organising the stalls they would have, the displays the children would put on, the refreshments that would be provided and, most importantly, persuading parents to help on the day.

The PCC continued with the arrangements for an auction of promises to raise funds and Mark was delighted to report to Maggie they had been promised meals at local pubs and restaurants, a helicopter ride, cleaning and gardening services, tickets for theme parks, theatres and cinemas, a weekend at a hotel on the island and, most bizarrely, a tattoo of choice at a local tattoo parlour. The burglaries were forgotten by most and life returned to normal.

Beth found herself providing Tom with a history lesson during one of their evening dog walks. Tom was looking for a weekly cleaner and had been recommended one in Milton Avenue, querying the literary naming of the avenue and the surrounding roads. He counted them on his fingers.
"There's Milton Avenue, Chaucer Avenue, Wordsworth Court, Byron Road..." he frowned.
"Keats Road" added Beth, sinking down to sit on the shingle near the water's edge.
"Yes of course. And Yeats Road."
"I'm impressed! You've only been here a few weeks and already you know the roads so well. Are you doing the knowledge?" He looked blank.
"You know, the training course taxi drivers have to do to get licensed." His face cleared.
"Of course. But where you a cab driver in a previous life? You sound so ....I'd say knowledgeable if that wasn't such an awful pun!"
Beth laughed, looking at him, her green eyes clear and sparkling in her suntanned face.
"No! But I grew up in north London. And there were loads of taxi drivers in our neighbourhood! I woke up to the sound of diesel engines warming up rather than an alarm clock."

She fell silent, the smile fading. Tom looked at her curiously. Her pink curved lips of just a few moments ago were set in a tense line and her eyes were bleak. He wanted to ask why but hesitated, sensing the barrier she had erected. Better to change the subject

"So go on then. Why all the poets' names? Was someone a fan of 19th century poetry?"
Beth shook herself back to the present, forcing the memories away.
"Not a fan. But there is a connection with them" she explained.
"Percy Shelley. His nephew bought the land behind the sea front in 1885. He was a landowner in north Hampshire but spent a lot of time on the Isle of Wight. His father, Percy Shelley's brother, was a keen sailor and William

Shelley, the son, also sailed. The family had a house over in Cowes. So he knew this area and when he married, he decided to build a house here for his new bride. It's the Island View Hotel now, the oldest building here. But he also thought he could make the area into a seaside town to rival Brighton and Cowes, combining seaside attractions and sailing. So houses were built for the gentry along the sea front. Then the church and some shops and a school, that's the library now in School Road? Cottages were built for the workers on the east side of the town, like mine. A pier was built and apparently there were plans for a railway but that never happened. But he lived here with his wife until they died."

"Hence the name Bride's Bay? And I assume the town developed gradually, judging by the mix of housing?"

Beth nodded. "More houses were built in the late 1800's, early 1900's, including yours, then a few in the 1920's and 30's; the art deco ones in Bentley Road and the flats on the sea front. You know the two blocks just down from you? And some of the shops as well. Then it was quiet until housing was needed after the second world war and the council houses, sorry, social housing now, were built behind me, on the Innings Estate. The Poet's Estate as we call it was built in the 1950's, all the little square bungalows. Some town planner had the idea to name the roads after Shelley the poet and his cohorts, even though Shelley had died before our William Shelley was even born! The latest of course is the Grove Road estate, all the big executive houses. That estate caused a stir when it was built, taking open space but not providing any affordable housing. Though it's all settled down now. People never like change, do they? Or green space built on."

"So youngsters and young families need to live further out in Fareham or Gosport?"

"Or even further, Portchester, Whitely. It's a shame when they have to leave, but hasn't that always been the way? I grew up in London but couldn't have afforded to buy there, not that I wanted to."

"I grew up in Oxford but my first flat, that I bought, I mean, was in Hoxton, when I got my first lecturing post in London. A bit different from here."

"Did you like living and working in London?" Beth asked curiously. Tom thought, frowning .

"At first I did. The buzz and the novelty of being able to go out and shop at three in the morning for halloumi or hummus."

"Did you often do that?" she teased.
The shadows had gone from her face and Tom was relieved to see her relaxed and smiling again.
"Never!" with a laugh. "But I liked the fact there were loads of coffee shops and restaurants…..and pubs! And public transport was good, I didn't need a car. Then of course the theatres and concert halls, museums…you're spoilt for choice there. I went to loads of exhibitions, concerts, it was good. I liked the job, I was doing what I had studied for and it was nice to have some money at last, after being a poor student for years."

He gazed at the view ahead of them; the sun still sparkling on the sea, turning it pinkish gold, patches of colour from boat sails, the buildings in the distance on the island, surrounded by hazy green.
"But it soon lost its novelty. The noise, the dirt and the crowds. My flat was nice but the area wasn't great. And commuting was a pain. I missed the countryside too, there are no seasons really in London. Well, summer and winter obviously, but no spring or autumn, at least not many signs of them in central London."
He turned to Beth. "But you grew up in north London you said? Which part?"

"Mill Hill. Well, between Edgware and Mill Hill. We did have seasons there; it was quite leafy and green. You know, daffodils in the parks and autumn leaves on the trees. But we went into Central London a lot, our nearest shops; big shops anyway, were in Oxford Street. Until they built Brent Cross at least, but I was almost grown up by then."

She was silent, thinking back to the years growing up. She tried not to think about her childhood home, the modest semi-detached in a quiet tree lined street.
"Did you like growing up in London?"
Beth shrugged. "You don't know any different, do you? You just accept where you're born as normal."
Just keep the conversation centred on where she was born. No need to talk about the move from the scruffy semi, or the reasons for it. "I wouldn't want to go back though. I love it here, the sea, the beach, the fresh air."
"Mmm. I can understand that. It's special. It's always different, with the weather and the boats. And there's always something going on but so easy to find somewhere quiet and peaceful."

They were silent as they each gazed at the view ahead of them; at the small frills of lace as the waves crawled onto the shingle, the sun glinting on the water and the muted greens of the countryside opposite.

"What church is that, do you know? The one with the tall spire." Tom was looking over at the middle of the island. Beth took her sunglasses off to see more clearly.
"Which one? I can see two."
He shifted, putting his hands on her shoulders and turning her to the left. For a second she froze, then forced herself to breathe slowly and relax. He was very close. She could feel the strength and warmth of his hands though her blouse and smell his skin, slightly tangy and musky.
"There, the one with trees all around, not the one to the right with the buildings round it."

He was leaning closer to her now and his chest was pressed against her back. She could feel and hear him breathing, felt soft breath against her hair. It would be too awkward to pull away but she knew her spine and shoulders were rigid and tense against his chest and arms. He must have felt it too, pulling away and releasing his hold on her shoulders as she answered shakily.
"I think it's All Saints. It's in Ryde, the ferry goes there from Portsmouth."

She put her sunglasses back on to avoid looking at him, edging away slightly and missing his curious glance.
"Anyway, you'll have to get the ferry over there one day and explore. Just go as a foot passenger; you can get a ticket that includes buses and trains and it's easy to get around, probably easier than driving on the narrow roads and parking." Beth knew she was gabbling and jumped to her feet, calling Charlie.
"I am" he answered easily, patting Tess. "Melissa and I are going on Friday. Neither of us has ever been so we shall explore together."

They walked back up the beach and Tom looked down at the top of her dark blond head as they paused outside his house.
"Same time tomorrow for another history lesson, Miss?" Beth laughed.
"No, I won't inflict any more facts on you. But you listened very patiently!"
"Ah, but do I remember any of it? You can test me sometime." With a wave he walked up the path and Beth continued to her house.

The answer phone was flashing as she let herself in. It was Carol, sounding a little more cheerful than she had earlier in the week. "Only me. Just to say I saw Doctor Clarke and she's referring me to QA in Portsmouth. But I'll tell you about it tomorrow."

Carol and Gina were already seated when Beth arrived on Thursday evening. A bottle of wine was on the table and Beth poured herself a glass after greeting the other two.
"So, tell us what he said, now Beth is here" urged Gina. Carol put down her glass and took a breath.
"She felt my tummy and said it all felt fine, but any post-menopausal bleeding is always followed up so she has referred me to the post-menopause clinic at Queen Alexandra's. It's within the government's two week guideline but that's routine."

Carol looked and sounded a lot more like her usual self, to Beth's relief.
"And what about Ken? What's happening there?" enquired Gina.
"Well, as you can image, Ken is not taking it lying down." Carol grimaced. "He's instructed our solicitor Jerome Caswell to deal with it all. Jerome is in discussions with the police while they investigate but so far there's been nothing; no evidence of any wrongdoing or cracks in security, data, privacy, what have you."
"But that's good; much better to be proactive than to do nothing and worry" stated Beth, failing to see the irony that she was far better at worrying than facing up to things and tackling them. Carol nodded, her eyes brighter than they had been the previous Thursday.
"And apparently nothing has been found with James Lamb or his lads either. It all seems to have gone quiet."
"So maybe it's all outsiders after all?" suggested Gina and the three women sat back to enjoy their meal and put all the worries and suspicions on to the back burner.

Beth squeezed her way between chairs, trying not to spill her cup of tea, making her way over to the table in the far corner where Melissa and Gina, their backs to her, were looking at something and laughing. Ali motioned her to an empty seat beside her and Beth sat down thankfully, smiling at the other woman. Julian on Ali's left was deep in conversation with Tom. Ali must have been a stunner as a young girl, Beth thought, not for the first time.

Her long, fair hair still fell either side of her face in a centre parting and her silvery blue eyes were large and expressive. She was blessed with high cheekbones and long dark eyelashes and delicate brows. Beth had seen their wedding photo; a nineteen year old Ali in a long white lace dress, feet bare, a circlet of white flowers in silvery blonde ringlets that fell softly almost to her waist. She had had perfect luminous skin, huge innocent eyes. Everything about her had been delicate, her slight frame, her air of fragility. She really had been an ethereal beauty. No wonder the young art student Julian had been captivated. But now that same slenderness had aged her, giving her a sharp brittleness. Time had aged her skin, and her hair and eyes had lost their shine, their delicate colour fading. Age had not been kind to her. But Julian, she wondered what he had been like as a youth. Gangling and awkward? Or confident and charismatic? He was certainly charming now; his dark curls soft and silky and his rich brown eyes intense. He had a habit of staring deep into the eyes of whoever he was talking to, listening intently, although Carol had once remarked tartly he probably just needed glasses and hearing aids but was too vain to wear them. Men as well as women got the same treatment and Julian was currently hanging on Tom's every word as the older man emphasised something with his hands and laughed, lines creasing around his eyes and mouth. Laughter lines, thought Beth cynically, wrinkles on us. Melissa was also laughing and passing her iPhone from Gina to Frances.

"See, that's Tom, trying to hide his ice cream from the eagle eyed waitress, and managing to get it all over his jeans! Apparently, only drinks bought there were allowed to be consumed on the premises, not cones from the ice-cream kiosk next door." Frances sniffed and passed the phone to Beth.
"I don't hold with all these photos on phones. Whatever happened to taking your picture on a camera and having it printed?"
"But it's just another way, Frances. You can take photos on a digital camera, or a tablet or iPad, or a phone. Then you can play around with them and create wonderful pictures. Look at David Hockney. His Big Picture exhibition had wonderful work he had produced on his iPad." Melissa sought for further incentives to persuade Frances. "Think of the photos you could take of your garden! They would be wonderful."
Another sniff. "I'd rather see the real thing, thank you very much. Nature is the best artist."

There was no answer to that. Frances's good mood had obviously been short lived. Beth diplomatically commented on how good it was to have all these options these days and looked at the photo.

Tom was laughing, holding an ice cream cone below the table. His thick reddish sandy hair flopped over his forehead and his jeans emphasised long, muscular legs. His arms were tanned and strong, covered with sandy hairs. He really was a very good looking man; the pair of them must have turned a few heads as they strolled around Ryde.

The phone had reached Julian who looked at the photo and laughed.

"A 99 in a cone! Tom man, you need to ask for New Forest ice cream here, not that muck from a machine! Melissa, when we go to Winchester on Friday remind me to take you to Dolby's. Now they do proper ice cream and you don't have to eat it under the table!"

Beth stood up to go and looked round the table to say goodbye, catching Ali's expression with a shock; a look of part desperation and part fury on the other woman's face.

"So the appointment is this Friday, 28th, 10.30. I see the consultant and have a scan." Carol grimaced.

"Do you want me to take you?" Gina offered, knowing Beth would be at work.

"No, thank you for offering, but Ken is taking the morning off to come with me, Harriet can cope."

The three women were in the kitchen; Ali, Melissa and Maggie circulating, ensuring everyone had a drink and someone to chat to. Maggie appeared and passed a tray of dirty crockery to Beth.

"I'll come round and help, those two can cope now."

Beth began to wash the dishes that couldn't go in the dishwasher and Maggie dried them. They had just about finished and were putting them back in the cupboards when Mark appeared, rubbing his hands.

"Wonderful news" he beamed. "Melissa has just offered to give one of her paintings for the auction of promises next month. She says she will either donate one, or the winner can chose one or even commission one. Isn't that so generous?" He was bouncing up and down on his toes with excitement.

"That should make some money, it will be very popular." Gina smiled at the vicar's obvious excitement.

"I'm going to pop round later to look at some of the pictures, see if we think it's best to offer one or let the winner choose. I'm not sure about commissions" frowning "it could put her in an awkward situation. Anyway my love" a kiss was dropped on the approximate area of Maggie's right cheek "I'll see you later. Go ahead and have dinner if I'm not back, I'll heat mine up." He almost danced out of the kitchen.

"He'll already be thinking of how best he can use the money, who he can help," smiled Carol. "Honestly, he would do anything for this church and congregation, wouldn't he?"
"Unfortunately, yes." Maggie angrily snatched up the cleaning materials from the worktop and tidied them away under the sink, slamming the cupboard door, her face red and her eyes watering as the three women stared at her in astonishment. Then she walked stiffly out of the kitchen and they watched as she walked over the lawn towards the vicarage.

"Do you think we should follow her?" Beth asked uneasily. Carol shook her head.
"No. Just leave her. I'll give her a ring later, after she's calmed down."
They finished clearing away in uneasy silence then left, to go their separate ways.

Carol phoned Beth later, just as she returned from walking Charlie. "She said she was just tired and to ignore her, and that she and Mark had been more affected by the burglaries and gossip than people realised."
"Do you think that's true?"
"It could be." Carol sounded unsure. "The Wrens' stayed with them for over a week, then they've done a lot to support James and Becky as well as checking up on me and Ken... but I don't know, she seemed so bitter."
"I know she's missing the twins. Maybe she's a bit depressed?"
"Maybe." Carol paused. "But I get the impression it's more between her and Mark."
The call ended suddenly as Carol's doorbell went and Beth looked at the clock, realising it was nearly time for her favourite television programme.

"So he used to sail down here?" Tom was fascinated by the history of his new town.
"Was Cowes Week an event then, when he bought the land and developed the town?"
They sat on the shingle in the evening sun, looking over to Cowes on the island.

"Well, Cowes Week as such began in 1826, though there were races there from the beginning of the 1800's, but the first cups were presented at the 1826 regatta and that's the date Cowes Week is taken from. So our William's father would have raced in the first Cowes Week and then William sailed here from childhood. Of course, the sailing and the area became even more popular after Queen Victoria leased Osborne House in 1844."

"I'm impressed." Tom grinned at her. "You know so much, you should write a book on the history of Bride's Bay."

"You're the writer! Have a change from economics or whatever and write history instead. I might read it then!" "Cheek!" Tom jumped up and pulled Beth to her feet, smiling down into her face. "I'll have you know my books are very popular – amongst economics undergrads who don't have any choice!"

Beth laughed, the wind whipping a strand of hair across her face and into her eyes. Tom reached down and pushed it aside, tucking it gently behind her ear. His fingers were soft and warm. A jolt of electricity shot through her and her eyes widened as they met his. His fingers lingered on the soft skin behind her ear and his face seemed very close, so close she felt breathless. For a moment she gazed into his eyes, seeing the black pupils, the hazel irises with specks of golden amber, the thick lashes and the wrinkles at the corners. Then she jerked back, turning away to pick up her bag, her hands trembling. Tom watched her quietly while he called to Tess and clipped her lead on. Beth couldn't bear the silence.

"I've got a book on Osborne House if you want to borrow it. I'll bring it tomorrow."

"Yes, please. That would be good. Melissa and I want to go back sometime and the house and Carisbrooke Castle are on our list of places to see. We were going to go this Friday but Julian has arranged to see his artist in Winchester, so she blew me out for that!" Tom was back to his relaxed self, striding easily along but stopping every now and then to wait for Tess, and the walk home was made in the usual companionable way.

The wind had dropped and the air that night was still and humid. Beth tossed and turned, getting up to open the window, then to close it as moths flew in. One flew close to her head and Beth had a vivid memory of Tom's warm eyes and his gentle fingers in her hair, followed by an image of Melissa and her laughing, beautiful face. She wouldn't have jumped like a scalded cat. The memory was painfully embarrassing. But so what? Tom wasn't interested in her; he was out and about with Melissa. Or Gina. Gina had been out for dinner with him a couple of times before going to local concerts together. She hadn't said much about the evenings, simply that they had been pleasant and he was good company. Beth was reluctant to quiz her friend about it and Carol had been too preoccupied worrying about her doctor's appointment to exhibit her usual curiosity. What difference did it make anyway? Beth could never let him get close, even if he wanted to. Her last jumbled thought before she went to sleep was that he wouldn't want to and she didn't want him to, and even if she did, or he did, she couldn't, could she?

Julian dressed carefully for his day in Winchester. Ali watched him bleakly as he brushed his hair and splashed cologne on his face. He hadn't shaved for a day or so and his jaw displayed dark designer stubble against his tanned skin. He was wearing his best summer suit; linen, in a pale biscuit colour, with a sage green shirt open just enough to reveal the dark curls on his chest. His well-shaped lips curved in a smile as he thought of the day ahead. He planned to introduce Melissa to his artist in the morning then take her out for a good lunch and spend a leisurely afternoon showing her around Winchester. He knew a small hotel that was very discreet and the smile widened at the thought they may end up there. He had already told Matt Brett that he couldn't take him for lunch this time, pressure of work and all that, he would make up for it on the next visit. He gave a few last minute instructions to Ali and bounded out of the door, grabbing his keys and briefcase on the way.

But he wasn't going to take Melissa to Winchester that day. Or any other day.

Parking the car outside her house he strolled down the front path, following it round to the back garden, hands in his pockets. The kitchen door was open, sunlight streaming in. He stepped into the empty kitchen and called out hello. There was no answer. Walking through into the large airy hall he called again. Silence. Frowning, he glanced around. Was she upstairs, still getting ready? Or maybe she was in her studio. Trust her to still be working when they were due to leave!

She wasn't working.

She was lying on the floor; face turned away from him. Her long legs were stretched out, in her short red linen skirt. She wore a matching red blouse. And a red hat. Why on earth was she wearing a hat in this weather?

He slumped against the wall and opened his mouth in a silent scream as his brain processed what his eyes were seeing. It wasn't a hat. Or a red blouse. Melissa lay in a pool of blood.

CHAPTER 7

Of course the news spread like wild fire.

The sirens were heard first by the visitors strolling along the beach path then police cars and an ambulance were seen racing along Bay Road West before turning into a side street. People stopped what they were doing to watch the screaming procession, with mingled expressions of excitement and concern.
Shop owners appeared at their doorways to peer along the road, before shrugging and returning to serving their queues of customers. The trio of noisy vehicles screeched to a halt at the same time outside the unremarkable detached house halfway along Addison Crescent.

Two paramedics and several police ran round to the back of the house and entered the Kitchen, stopping at the sight ahead of a crumpled figure on the hall floor. Julian sat huddled against the wall, shaking and sobbing, his head on his knees. His arms were clasped tightly around his skull, shaking fingers plucking and flattening the dark curls. Tears poured down his cheeks and off his chin to soak his trousers. His legs shook violently, his shoes drumming a rhythm on the wooden floorboards. A paramedic squatted down beside him as the police disappeared into the studio. The uniformed figure called to him, asking him his name, but Julian didn't answer, tearing at his head, his hair, his skull. Somehow he was aware of the figure alongside while his head pounded and his legs vibrated as his feet drummed.

He was underwater; he could see faces and bodies swimming close to him then floating silently away, their mouths moving but making no sound. But yes there was a sound; a roaring in his ears that came and went in time with the pounding and pulsing in his skull. He tried to lower his arms to release his grasp on his head, opening his mouth to speak to the faces swimming past but he couldn't make them hear. They were staring at him but not listening. Why wouldn't they listen? He opened his mouth wider and shouted at them. Get her up. Make her talk to me. We're going out. Tell her to wake up. He yelled louder, louder and louder until he was roaring at them but still no one listened. Then he was screaming, saliva flying out of his mouth, teeth bared and rigid.

A face swam right up to his, opening and closing its mouth like a goldfish. Julian could see pockmarks in the skin, black pupils in bulging eyes, gold teeth, but still no sound except the roaring of the waves and his screams. He felt his arm picked up and held but it was heavy, too heavy, and he dropped it to fall into his lap. The waves were pounding in his skull, pulling and pushing at anything in their way. Then the waves crashed over his head and he was swept away, floating, floating.

A small crowd had gathered along the pavement near the house. Neighbours from the surrounding houses and passers-by, united in their gawping. They stood together, heads close and eyes and mouths wide with delicious horror. This was Melissa's house. What had happened? Hushed voices speculated in suppressed excitement. Had there been an accident, had she been taken ill? But why the police cars? A communal gasp went up as two paramedics appeared in the front door and pushed a stretcher down the path. A sheet covered the figure up to the neck but black curls spilled out against the white cotton. The eyes were closed and the skin grey but they recognised him at once. Julian, not Melissa. So where was Melissa?

Someone broke away from the crowd and ran down the street, hair and heels flying. Moments passed as the stretcher was wheeled to the back of the ambulance and there was silence as the crowd watched and waited, breath held. Then they turned as one at the sound of footsteps and rasping breath.

Ali came running along the street, hair wild and eyes huge with fear.

"What's happened? Tell me what's happened?" Her voice wailed as she grabbed the paramedic's arm, giving a low moan when she saw the body on the stretcher, her legs giving way. Arms caught her and a faraway voice called "it's her husband." A policeman had come down to the pavement and gently took her arm, murmuring "alright now Miss, come with me" as he led her down the path and round to the side of the house. Another policeman started putting tape around the front garden and moving people along. The crowd shuffled back, over to the other side of the road, as the siren started again and the ambulance drove off. Mark Rowlands pushed his way through the crowd, ignoring the voices calling to him.

"Please, I'm the vicar. What's happened? Ali, my dear!" catching sight of the small figure stumbling along the path, a uniformed officer supporting her. He hurried to her other side and the three figures disappeared from sight into the back garden.

It was quiet. There was nothing to see. Nothing to hear. People looked at each other and whispered, shrugged, then began to move away down the silent street to the main road and the shops and cafes, where people chatted and laughed, children cried and shrieked, and life went on.

It was afternoon before the news broke that Melissa was dead. After the initial excitement of the emergency vehicles and the sight of Julian being stretchered out of Melissa's house, it was assumed he had been taken ill while visiting her. The less charitable in town speculated maliciously on what he had been doing when he was taken ill. The kinder ones stated it could have been anything; maybe he had simply had an accident. The vicar had appeared after half an hour, leading Ali out of the house to be hugged by Maggie who had driven their car round. The three had climbed in, driving away in the direction of Fareham. It was a quiet road so no one noticed the van that drove up later, or the stretcher with the body bag that was removed from the house. But the arrival of further police cars and white clad figures didn't go unnoticed and by two o clock rumours were spreading that Melissa was dead.

Beth heard the rumours when she arrived to do the church flowers with Gina. The news that Julian had been taken to hospital by ambulance from Melissa's had reached school in the morning but Beth had been too busy to spare more than a fleeting moment of concern for the man. She had gone straight home after work to walk Charlie and make a sandwich, eating it quickly while she flicked through the day's post. As she walked into the church car park Gina was just parking and she waited for her, smiling a greeting, before they stepped from the bright sunshine into the cool gloom of the church.

Frances was hovering in the entrance, eyes gleaming wetly, an excited smile on her face, her always nervous movements even more erratic. She grabbed Beth's arm and thrust her face close.
"Did you know Julian was taken to hospital from Melissa's this morning? But something else is going on! Addison Crescent is full of police cars, four of them, and there's tape all round Melissa's front garden."

Beth was reminded of June and Rose in the cafe and her stomach lurched at the other woman's evident pleasure in what was obviously bad news.

"Do you think she's been burgled as well?" Beth's mouth was dry. "There wouldn't be that many police cars for a burglary, surely?"
Gina looked pale and her voice trembled.
The three women looked at each other.

"Well, we'll find out soon enough." Gina felt a wave of nausea at the excitement in Frances's pale blue eyes and briskly put down her bag, moving over to a flower arrangement in the Lady Chapel.
"Beth, do you want to start this one with me? Frances, are you doing the altar arrangement as usual?"

"Of course." Any suggestion someone else would do it jerked Frances from her enjoyable speculation and she scuttled over to the tall pedestal with her flower arranging basket. But her noisy, jerky movements and heavy breathing told the other two she was pondering on the events at Melissa's.

No one spoke. Beth didn't know what to say; it seemed wrong to chat happily when something had happened at Melissa's. Not knowing was awful and it was human nature to think the worst. She just wished she knew exactly what had happened. As she and Gina removed dead flowers and replaced them with fresh ones, they glanced at each other worriedly.

They found out half an hour later when Mark and Maggie returned. The couple walked into the church stiffly, in silence. Maggie's eyes were red and tears trickled silently down her face. Mark's skin was a greenish grey and he had aged ten years. Beth watched them, ice cold dread washing over her. She had seen them like that just once before; the night she had been driven to the vicarage after hearing the news about Louise.

Her knees buckled and she grabbed hold of the cold stone of the altar, heart racing.
"Tell us." Was that her voice? It sounded too high and shaky. Mark gestured them to a pew and they sat, Mark pushing his wife gently down and sitting beside her, clasping her hand tightly with white fingers. Maggie bowed her head, quietly sobbing. Gina sat beside Beth and felt for her hand, her face pale and shaken. Frances sat at the other end, still and tense, her face registering shock rather than the previous suppressed excitement.

Mark's voice was quiet and slow, expressionless. He confined himself to the facts. Melissa had been found dead that morning, her house ransacked. She had been hit over the head and would have died instantly. No-one knew what had been stolen but her jewellery boxes were empty and there was no sign of her iPad or phone. Julian had found her when he went to pick her up. He was in hospital, sedated for shock.

The three women sat, stunned. For a moment Beth's head swam and she saw Mark's lips moving but couldn't hear what he was saying. Out of the corner of her eye she was aware of Frances stuffing her hands into her mouth, eyes wide. Gina sat frozen beside her. For an age it seemed as though they all sat there, no-one moving or speaking, the only sounds Maggie's quiet sobs and Frances's heavy breathing.
Finally Gina gave a shuddering breath and spoke.
"Do they think she disturbed the burglars? Is that it?" Her voice didn't sound like hers either, thought Beth, or maybe she just wasn't hearing clearly. Mark was steadier, calmer.
"It's one line of enquiry. They'll know more when they know the time of death and more about her movements yesterday."
Beth began to sob, tears spilling out of her eyes and pouring down her cheeks. Gina put an arm around her friend, a stunned expression on her beautiful face. Frances continued to sit motionless, her nervous movements stilled for once. Maggie spoke for the first time, looking at them through red-rimmed eyes.
"Come on" her voice shook. "Let's go round to the vicarage and have a cup of tea. We're all in shock."

They made their way silently down the path and over the lawn to the house, walking stiffly, jerkily.
Mark led the way through the kitchen door, ushering them to the large table still cluttered with breakfast dishes. Maggie put the kettle on and Gina went to help, taking out mugs, milk, sugar. Mark stirred his tea, gazing out at the garden.

"The police asked me about Melissa. I told them she's a newcomer; people are only just getting to know her. No-one really knows an awful lot about her, I don't think." He looked round at them, a question in his eyes. Beth shook her head. "No. I mean, we've got to know her a bit, but not her background, family…" She faltered, feeling sick. Had Melissa had family? Would someone even now be receiving a knock on the door, answering it to anonymous faces who brought news that would change their lives for ever?

A flashback to the very same knock on her door, the young policeman looking upset and shocked at the news he had to impart, swept over her.

Mark was talking again. "They're doing house to house enquiries now and want to talk to anyone who knew her, however slightly. I gave them all our names." He looked around again, embarrassed. "I hope that's alright?"

"Of course." Gina squeezed his hand as Frances and Beth nodded agreement numbly.

"Anything, they just need to find out who did this." Gina's voice broke, her face crumpling as the tears came. "The poor woman, she was so full of life, so vibrant. How could this happen?"

Beth was on her feet, wrapping her arms around her weeping friend. She pressed her cheek against Gina's and their tears mingled and hair tangled as they clung to each other and cried.

It was later, much later, when she and Gina were sitting in Gina's kitchen, that she remembered Tom would be waiting for her for their evening walk.

After the vicarage they had gone back to Beth's house to collect Charlie and pack a few overnight things. Neither Gina nor Beth had wanted to be alone and Beth was relieved to leave Bride's Bay, even for just a few hours. She and Gina had both spoken to Carol, remembering with shock after they had reached Gina's that she had had her hospital appointment that morning. How long ago that seemed already.

Carol had heard about Melissa and filled them in quickly about her consultation, her voice thick.

"I had the scan. There's a large polyp in the uterus. It needs to be removed and they'll do a biopsy but fingers' crossed it's benign. The operation will be within two weeks, I should hear in a day or two. Hopefully I can come home the same day or at least the next morning. But I can't believe about Melissa..." she broke off, unable to talk. Beth quickly said goodbye, they'd talk tomorrow, then filled Gina in with the news.

"What we were expecting really" a sigh. "Why does it never rain but it pours?"

There was no answer to that. Gina had opened a bottle of wine and poured them both a large glass and Beth had remembered Tom. Five past seven. He would be waiting for her to knock, Tess sitting patiently by his side. She couldn't face talking and sent a short text, to the point, then wondered if it seemed a bit abrupt. Oh well, she had more important things to worry about than hurting his feelings.

The bottle was emptied and another started before Beth and Gina turned in for the night. Beth was in a spare bedroom at the front of the house. She had left the window slightly open and could hear the waves rolling and splashing onto the shingle beach at the bottom of the garden. There was a thump as Charlie scrambled up next to her. "No Charlie. You can't sleep on my bed here, it's too nice". Charlie rolled his eyes and settled down to sleep.

The next morning the sun shone in a cornflower blue sky, seeming to mock the tragic events of the day before. How could anything be other than normal when the sun was warm, the sea sparkled and all seemed right with the world? Beth and Gina took Charlie for a long walk on the beach then phoned Carol to see if she wanted to meet them at the haven for lunch, Beth aware she was putting off returning to Bride's Bay.

Over lunch Carol gave them more details about her consultation and the forthcoming operation.
She was calmer now but smiled wryly when Gina commented on it, shaking her head.
"I'm not but I'm trying. Poor Ken, he's still being investigated over the burglaries. He's worried about that and me. I can't fall apart. But Ali is. The poor girl came back late last night and stayed at the vicarage, apparently she was in no state to be home on her own. Julian was kept in overnight. She's distraught, according to Maggie."
"And how's Tom taking it, do you know? He was friendly with Melissa, they seemed to get on very well." Gina asked, reminding Beth she needed to contact him again about this evening.
"I don't know, I don't know who's seen him."

Beth and Gina went back to her house after lunch and Beth packed her few overnight bits. Gina was quiet and Beth looked at her in concern. It was no wonder she would be anxious alone in this large house.
"Will you be alright? Did you want me to stay again?"
"No, no. You want to get home." But she looked unhappy and the words

were said half-heartedly.
"Well, I've got things I need to do but I don't really fancy being alone either. Come back with me for tonight?" Gina didn't need much persuading and half an hour later the two women checked the doors were locked and the alarm set and drove the short distance back to Bride's Bay.

Tom did know about Melissa.

She and Gina knocked at his front door on their way to the beach with Charlie and guessed, from one look at his face. His skin was pale under his tan and his eyes were bleak. They walked slowly along the beach, shingle crunching under their feet, gulls screeching overhead. They were quiet as they strolled past the forest of masts at the sailing club and along to Stern Head, finally dropping down to sit near the water's edge, watching Charlie run into the water and snap at the waves as they rolled onto the shingle.

"I just can't take it in." He rubbed his hand over his face, over the sandy gold stubble on his usually smooth shaved chin. He stared unseeingly ahead, hazel eyes hidden behind sunglasses.
"Why did they need to kill her? Why not rob her and go? Or even knock her out. But to smash her head in." Gina, who was sitting next to him on the beach, gave a shocked gasp at his words. She fought for control but her breath came in rasps and small sobs escaped her throat.
"Gina, Gina, I'm sorry. Come here sweetheart." Tom's arm went round her and he pulled her head down onto his shoulder, stroking her hair, gazing over her head out to sea. "I shouldn't have said that."

Beth felt her own eyes fill and tried to swallow the lump in her throat. To distract herself she patted Tess, lying by her side. The beautiful dog gazed up at her with her soft calm eyes. Tom had his arm tightly round Gina's shoulders, his sandy head resting on hers, his large hand wrapped around her smaller ones. Beth felt a rush of envy. What would it be like to be held like that? Comforted and cared for? To give in and let someone else look after you? Gina wasn't resisting and had calmed down in the embrace. But Beth felt excluded, chilled and alone. She hugged her knees and stared grimly at the island over the water, blinking tears away. She was just in shock, frightened and upset. Her emotions were all over the place, like everyone's. And she stifled the thought she could be jealous.

It seemed natural for Tom to walk back to Beth's house with them. Gina and Tom went to sit in the living room and Beth prepared a tray with glasses and a bottle of wine, only for Tom to ask if she had any whisky. Oh dear. She did but she'd had it so long she wondered if it had gone off. Did whisky go off? With reservations, she fetched the bottle and poured him a generous measure.

"Is it alright?" she asked nervously, as she handed Gina a glass of wine and sat down next to her on the sofa. Tom had taken the large but comfy old armchair, stretching his long legs out onto the rug in front. He swallowed and grimaced.
"God Beth, where did you get this from?"
"The Co-op I think. It was on special offer but I've had it a while. Has it gone off?" she asked anxiously.
Tom laughed. "I think it probably always tasted like this! If I'm going to be a regular visitor, I shall bring a decent bottle round to show you the difference."
Not much chance of that, Beth thought, but smiled as he downed more whisky and winked at her.
"It's not that bad, I'm pulling your leg."
But at least the atmosphere had lightened and conversation moved onto various matters, until it inevitably returned to the murder of Melissa.

"Have the police interviewed you yet?" Tom asked Beth, leaning forward. His shirt strained across his back and his neck was thick and strong. She shook her head.
"No, I haven't heard anything, but I've been at Gina's until late this afternoon. Why? Have you been interviewed?"
"This morning. I think because I have - had - been out a few times with her. Not that I could tell them much, but probably as much if not more than anyone else."
"Julian can probably tell them the most" suggested Gina. "How is he anyway, do you know?"
"Home apparently, but not good. He was interviewed while he was in hospital, as he was the one to find her, poor sod."
"They'll be round to me soon then, I expect. And you, Gina." The other woman nodded.

Beth looked at Tom and his bleak expression prompted her to say "I'm so sorry Tom; I know you were quite close to her."
He looked up, startled. "As a friend and fellow newcomer, yes, but there was nothing more between us. We just got on well, we both liked visiting houses, exploring old towns, you know. Melissa always looked at everything with an artist's eye. And she was fun, so lively and cheerful. It's unbelievable. " He shook his head, gulping more whisky.
"I just hope they find the bastard or bastards who did this soon."

He put down his glass and stretched, yawning. He seemed to have aged ten years. "Sorry, I didn't get much sleep last night. I'll be off and leave you in peace. Are you staying here tonight, Gina? You're not driving, are you?" He looked doubtfully at the now empty wine glass.
Gina shook her head. "I'm staying here. We both need the company."
"Good." Tom looked relieved and smiled warmly at her. Lucky Gina, he's made it clear there was nothing between him and Melissa and that he's concerned about her, Beth thought. Where's all this going? But she didn't want to know.

Church was full. People needed to gather together for comfort and security. Plus Mark was giving an address about Melissa and Beth knew, as did everyone else, it would be full of compassion and love. He would try and make some sense of it all; but how on earth could you do that, when an innocent, healthy, vibrant person was cut down and their life ended, in such a sudden violent way?

But Mark did the impossible. The congregation filed silently out of church while the organist played quietly. No rousing recessional hymn today. Beth stayed in the kitchen to help when she saw the extra people crowding into the hall, knowing they were reluctant to leave the fellowship and support they had received, at least for a while.

"Beth, Gina, Carol, can I introduce you to Grace Harris, Melissa's sister."
Maggie stood in front of the serving hatch, a woman by her side. Beth looked up and for a moment felt breathless. At first glance Grace Harris was nothing like her sister; she was a good four inches shorter, plumper and her light brown hair was cut in close layers to her head. But the large eyes looking calmly at Beth were Melissa's; a deep rich brown framed with thick almost black lashes. Her cheekbones were also Melissa's and her

mouth when she smiled a greeting caused Beth's heart to skip a beat. Also Gina's and Carol's, as they admitted later.

Carol left the kitchen to go and talk to Grace, reporting afterwards that the woman had come down on the Saturday morning and had stayed with Maggie and Mark. Of course. She had seen the police and was staying until that evening, going back to London to sort out a few things then returning to Bride's Bay to start the arrangements. Arrangements. What an innocuous word to cover planning a funeral, sorting the house, dealing with the paperwork and officialdom involved with the ending of a life. At least she would have Maggie and Mark to help but Beth's heart ached for her.

CHAPTER 8

Shock. Speculation. Gossip.

Wherever she went, Beth came across shocked faces and huddled conversations. Even the children weren't immune.

Helen came back into the nursery where Beth was supervising the fifteen children drinking their milk and eating their fruit.
"Honestly, Beth. Sue gave all the children a talk in assembly about respecting the poor woman who died and not talking about it, outdoing each other with tales of who had seen what. But what do we get? Everyone in the staff room doing exactly the same thing." She put a pile of folders down with a thump and glared at Beth.
"I suppose it's a coping mechanism" suggested Beth. "You know, talking it through, getting it out of your system? Maybe it's the mind's way of managing horrific events."
"More like a gossip's way of enjoying some excitement." Helen was not to be appeased, snatching a piece of apple as it was about to be used as a missile.
"Joseph! If you don't want it, just leave it on your plate. Don't throw it at Isaac!"
Beth noticed Isaac's smug expression and guessed that he had already hurled the first missile. She sighed. Neither she nor Helen was on their usual form today. At least she could go home in just over an hour. Helen would be there until at least 5 o'clock, Monday being Staff Meeting day.

She was tempted to cry off helping at Tea and Chat, stomach sinking at the thought of more speculation and vicarious shocked excitement. But that wasn't fair on Maggie. Ali wouldn't be there to help today. Nor would Melissa. Lovely sparkling Melissa, who had flirted with the elderly men, commiserated with the unwell, endeared herself to the young mum's through her genuine admiration of their parenting skills and offspring. What an impact she had made in such a short time, Beth realised with a shock. How she would be missed. She had been a breath of fresh air in Bride's Bay.

Even difficult, defensive Frances had blossomed; Melissa recognising the prickly woman's skills with plants, praising her flower arrangements. Tom had told her Melissa had been round to Frances's garden a few times, both women having a strong appreciation of the beauty of nature.

Tom himself had also had an impact on the town. He could even coax a smile from Frances and she was a regular visitor to his garden as well, cutting flowers for church and generally treating his garden as an extension her own. He'd said this ruefully, his plans to change the garden having to proceed slowly and carefully to avoid upsetting Frances. Tom, like Melissa, got along with everyone. He could encourage the shy to chat, the sullen to smile and with his strong frame and muscle was greatly in demand when chairs needed stacking, tables moving or boxes lifted. He was also a natural organiser. Maggie had made noises to Carol that he would be a welcome addition to the PCC but Gina had laughed when told this, saying Tom had anticipated it and had his excuses ready.

He was at Tea and Chat this afternoon, carrying trays of tea around the hall and chatting as he paused by tables. Gina was serving drinks and Beth noticed the glances he made in her direction, though Gina showed no sign of being aware. Beth rinsed dishes and stacked the dishwasher beside her, looking at her friend busily pouring drinks. In her pale blue linen shift dress, her ash blonde hair falling in a silky bob, skin smooth and tanned and her eyes as blue as the sky, she was stunning. Of course Tom would only have eyes for her. And Gina was as lovely inside as out; she deserved some happiness. Beth swallowed hard, giving herself a talking to. Stop wanting what you can't have and be pleased for her.

Gina had gone to speak to someone and Beth came back to the present with a jerk, realising the object of her thoughts was standing in front of her, speaking.
"I said a penny for them." Tom smiled. "Although I actually came over to ask for three more teas and two slices of carrot cake."
If you only knew, thought Beth, forcing a smile and admitting she had been miles away.
"Sorry, no can do with the carrot cake, Angela Harris made it and it always goes first. But I've got a cherry cake or...I think it's a date loaf" looking doubtfully at a heavy, dark cake.
"One of each then, please." Tom was gone, bearing the tray, and Gina returned, a frown marring her smooth skin.

"Alright?" Beth looked at her curiously. Gina sighed, running her fingers through her hair.

"Oh, just the usual gossips. Still suspicious of James and his lads. And Ken, especially as Melissa rented the house through him. Now Julian is in for the wagging tongues. Some of them even think Mark knows more than he is telling. Apparently Melissa met with him a few times and seemed to have something on her mind."

"Mark! That's ridiculous! What could he possibly know?" Beth was indignant and all thoughts of her best friend's potential love life were swept away.

He didn't know anything but that didn't stop the gossip for the rest of the week. Tempers frayed as accusations flew around. Speculation escalated to bursting point as Julian was taken in for questioning and Ken, James and their respective workforces were interviewed again. Grace returned from London to arrange the funeral as soon as the police released the body for burial. She had decided to stay at Melissa's house but spent a lot of time at the vicarage, making plans with Mark and Maggie.

News of Carol's forthcoming operation also provided gossip fodder and she began to feel the strain as she was asked over and over again about it. Ken, never demonstrative or expressive at the best of times, withdrew into himself, hiding away in his study. He was worried about his staff and the effect on them of the investigations; worried about his wife. But he had no vehicle to express his fears and instead became uncommunicative and irritable. Carol, knowing her husband well, accepted this and tried to ease his worry. But the strain told on her and she looked grey and tired.

There was one bright ray in the dismal week. Beth had returned home after the charity shop to a message on the answer phone. Nell had Thursday and Friday off work and wanted to come over.
Delighted, she phoned her back to confirm it was fine, arranging to meet her at the house as soon as she finished work.

Nell was her usual bubbly self. They walked into town and had a leisurely lunch at Mario's then wandered round the shops in the sunshine. Passing by the bakers, Beth popped in and bought some fresh scones, golden and still warm, crammed with plump fruit, then went to buy some clotted cream to go with them. Visitors had started arriving, evidenced by the queue at the ice cream kiosk at the Mermaid Cafe. At Nell's insistence they joined the waiting crowd then strolled home along the sea front, licking the ice creams quickly before they melted.

Nearing Tom's house, Beth caught sight off his sandy red hair over the garden wall. Nell was chatting away, her light voice animated, and he looked up at the sound. Straightening up, wiping his hands down the front of his shorts, he called out a greeting. Beth stopped, turning to her niece.

"Nell, this is a new neighbour, Tom Callow. Tom, my niece Nell."
Tom held out his hand, smiling.
"I recognise you from your photo." Nell looked enquiringly at her aunt and for a moment Beth was confused, before realising he must have seen the photo of her niece on the fireplace on Saturday evening. It was a picture she loved; Nell's graduation, with the young woman proud and happy in her gown and mortar board, the world just waiting for her. He hadn't commented at the time but then conversation had hardly been normal that evening.

"I'm just about to have a break. Care to join me?" Tom picked up the spade and trowel.
"Lovely!" Nell was bounding down the path, Beth following more slowly. Tom led the way round the side of the house and into the back garden, gesturing to a wooden table and chairs under a large apple tree.
"What will it be? Tea, coffee, wine, a soft drink? I've got a nice strawberry and elderflower cordial, courtesy of Waitrose. Especially good with sparkling water and ice."
"Sounds heavenly." Nell smiled her agreement and leant back in her chair, slim tanned legs stretched out in front of her.
"Yes please" Beth agreed, sitting next to her niece and smoothing down the cotton skirt she had worn to work that morning.
"Oh! You beauty!" Nell had spotted Tess, lying in the shade under the table and bent down to stroke her.

Tom was wearing a dark blue Polo shirt and stone coloured shorts, almost down to the knees, with tough brown leather sandals. Beth watched him walk up the steps into the house, at his long straight back, broad shoulders and his strong, tanned legs. His hair shone gold in the sun and lay thick against the collar of his Polo shirt.

Nell sighed contentedly, turning her face up to the sun. He returned after a few minutes with a tray containing glasses and a large jug of cordial, ice chinking.

"This is a pretty garden, and interesting." Nell was looking around, her background in horticulture coming to the fore.
"Unfortunately I can't take the credit. The previous owner made it; he was quite a plantsman, apparently."
"He must have been. Some of these plants are really unusual choices for a town garden, but work well."
Nell was on her feet, wandering around and admiring the different elements.

Eventually she sat down again, smiling at Tom. "I'm jealous! This is a wonderful garden."
"But so is yours – Beth's I mean. She tells me you worked so hard on it, getting it like it is now."
"I did" agreed Nell "or rather, we did. Though to be honest, Aunty Beth did most of the hard work, I just did the pretty, easy bits!"
"Well, you were only a teenager" smiled Beth "and had all your school work to do."

The conversation switched to Nell's job and her university course, then turned to her childhood and education and in Bride's Bay. Any hope she had had that Nell would skip over their early years together and the reason for their move swiftly disappeared when Nell told him all about her mother's death. She talked calmly about the car driven by an eighteen year old who had lost control on an icy road that January morning, hitting Louise's car head on, killing her outright and changing their lives for ever. Tom knew of the death of the young girl's mother, but not all the details, and his eyes were warm with sympathy as he leaned towards Nell, his hands clasped between his knees. Beth couldn't bear to look at him or Nell, fixing her gaze on the birds fluttering around the bird table on the far side of the garden, and so missed the look of sympathy he flashed at her. But Nell was in control, able to talk about it easily, which was a mark of how well the girl had adjusted, Beth thought with some consolation.

The air began to cool and Tom suggested they moved indoors. He had put the cream in the fridge when they had arrived and readily agreed to Nell's suggestion they shared the scones with him. They sat around the kitchen table with a large pot of tea and a plate full of fluffy scones, strawberry jam and clotted cream.

"Mmmm." Nell licked the jam of her fingers." One of the things we Brits do best, like Pimms and roast beef and Yorkshire puddings."
"And apple crumble and custard" joined in Tom. "Beth? What's your secret culinary indulgence?"
"Shepherd's Pie" promptly. "It's such a tasty, satisfying meal, followed by crumble but with ice cream."
"Such sophisticated tastes we all have" Tom laughed, then jumped as Nell grabbed his arm.
"Tom! There's a face, looking in at the window." Her usually slightly high voice rose even higher in fright as
she pointed to the window over the sink on the far side of the room.

He jumped up and strode over to the French doors, stepping over the threshold. Then the women heard a voice Beth recognised and Tom reappeared, his arm under Francis's elbow.
"It's just a neighbour Nell, don't worry." His voice had an edge Beth had never heard before as he ushered the cause for Nell's alarm into the kitchen.
"I'm sorry, I'm sure." Frances's voice had the same tone as Tom's. "I didn't mean to scare anyone. I was just going to cut some foliage. You said it was alright." Tom had calmed down.
"Yes, I did, and it's fine. But you knew I was here, the car's outside. Maybe next time you could knock first?" Frances was wrong footed and annoyed.
"But you might not have been here, just because your car's there. You could have been out walking Tess."

Tom couldn't argue with that and gestured Frances to take a seat, pouring her a cup of tea.
"True. Well, maybe you could just ring the bell on your way in, then anyone will have warning of someone coming round."
This suggestion seemed to meet approval, as did the cup of tea and the last half of a scone, Tom casting a wistful look at it as Frances picked it up. Nell looked at her, opening her mouth to speak.
"I'm sorry, Miss Dobinson. I guess I'm just a bit jumpy, with all the tales Aunty Beth has been telling me."
Back to the murder and burglaries. But Frances didn't seem inclined to

gossip, to Beth's relief.

"Yes, it has been alarming. But I'm sure the police are working hard to solve them. Speculation and panic won't help." Beth didn't often agree with Frances but with these views she concurred wholeheartedly.

Frances went to cut the foliage and Tom tidied up, saying he would follow Beth and Nell down to the beach with Tess later.

"He's rather nice." Nell looked sideways at Beth, speculatively, as they walked home.

"Yes he is" agreed Beth. "He also gets on very well with Gina."

"Oh." Nell looked disappointed, then brightened. "Well, that's nice for Gina." Then added hopefully

"has he got a brother or a friend?"

"Nell!" Beth tapped her niece lightly on the arm as they went indoors to a rapturous welcome from Charlie.

Nell took Charlie for a long walk on the beach on Friday morning while Beth was at work. The fine weather continued so they made some lunch and ate it outside, at the little wrought iron table bought many years before when they had been renovating the garden. Nell had spent the previous evening talking about Will when they had returned from walking Charlie and was talking about him again now.

"So I think maybe I'll head back when you go to flower arranging, Aunty Beth. I want to miss the Friday afternoon traffic."

Yes, and see Will as soon as he finishes work. Beth smiled and agreed but kept the thought to herself.

She left, car windows down and arm waving. It had been a lovely visit, even nicer for being unexpected and it had certainly cheered Beth up.

But not for long.

Beth sensed the atmosphere as soon as she walked into the church. Gina made a face at her from the arrangement she was doing by the font and Carol's back was rigid as she swept some petals from the Lady Chapel. Ali was desultorily soaking some oasis in the little flower room at the side of the church and Frances was darting from one pedestal to another, her movements quick and nervous. No one was talking.

Beth went to the font to see if Gina needed some help, knowing she didn't but feeling intimidated by the atmosphere.

"What's going on?" she whispered.
Gina shrugged. "Ali hasn't said a word. Carol snapped at me and Frances is buzzing around like a bad tempered wasp."
The description was so apt both women smiled and Carol, catching sight of them, put down the broom and joined them.

"I'm sorry Gina, I shouldn't have snapped. I'm just a bit, you know, not myself. I just want Tuesday to be over." "I know." Gina squeezed her arm."And there's no need to apologise. We're all on edge."
She finished the arrangement and the three made their way to the altar, collecting the broom and dustpan full of petals and dry leaves from the Lady Chapel on the way.

Frances had disappeared but her location became obvious a moment later when raised voices came from the flower room.
"For goodness sake Ali! You're wrecking it! Give it to me!"
Ali's low voice could be heard murmuring something, then Frances's, harsh and loud.
"But you shouldn't! How many times have I told you?"
A protest, then a crash and the sound of breaking glass.
"Now look what you've done!" Frances's voice was screeching now, high pitched and furious.
Ali's low voice could be heard, but not what she said. Then crying.

Beth and Gina looked at each other but Carol was already striding down to the flower room.
"Ali! Frances! What on earth is going on?" Her voice trailed off and Beth and Gina looked through the doorway into the small room. There was no space for them but Beth took in at a glance Frances's face, white with fury; then Ali on her knees picking up bits of glass, tears streaming down her face. Scattered around the soaked floor were bits of oasis, crumbs of green against the grey concrete floor.

Carol took charge. "Ali, stop, you'll cut yourself. Beth, take her away and look after her. Gina, take Frances into the Lady Chapel and give her a drink of water. Here."
She stepped over the mess of glass, water and oasis, held a plastic beaker under the tap and passed it to Gina. "I'll tidy this up. Now go" pulling Ali to her feet and pushing her at Beth, then taking Frances by the arm and passing the dazed woman to Gina. Gina didn't look too keen but did as she was told, leading Frances into the church and through into the Lady Chapel

at the side, sitting her down and passing her the beaker of water. Frances was silent now, white and stunned.

She had the easier one to look after, Beth reflected, her arm around Ali as she led the thin woman down the aisle to sit at the end of the front row, as far from Frances as she could manage.

Ali still sobbed quietly, her breath coming in short gasps. She sat down next to the distraught woman, putting her arm round her and making soothing noises. Gradually Ali calmed down and Beth passed her a tissue to wipe her eyes and nose. "I'm sorry" her voice was quiet and Beth had to strain to hear. "I didn't mean to make her cross. I just wasn't concentrating and the oasis started to fall apart and it was new...."

Her voice faltered as tears threatened again and Beth spoke quickly to distract her.
"We've all done that. The amount of times the oasis has fallen apart because I've tried to force stems in, you wouldn't believe." She spoke the truth, but hoped Ali wouldn't mention her transgressions to Frances, knowing she was in charge of the flower arranging budget and resented any waste of money. She could well imagine Frances losing her temper when she saw a pile of new oasis being ruined.

"But the glass?" Beth had a fleeting image of the shards all over the floor of the small room.
Ali shivered. "She grabbed the oasis off me. I lost my balance when she lunged at me for it and put my hand out but I brushed the shelf with the vases on it and one fell off and smashed."
At least she was more in control now and the threatened tears remained at bay. Her voice was also stronger. A moment's silence then she burst out "Vile woman! Who does she think she is, treating people like that? And we're supposed to be friends!"

Beth diplomatically kept quiet. She agreed with Ali but now wasn't the time to say so. But something needed to be done; the flower arrangers were all volunteers and certainly shouldn't be spoken to or attacked like that. Come to think of it, no-one deserved to, even if they were paid. This was one for Mark. Though goodness knows he already had enough on his plate. Ali blew her nose again and stood up.
"I'm going home. I'll go out the side door, to avoid her. But will you tell the others for me, and Mark, that I won't be helping again?"

Beth didn't know what to say so just gave her a hug. Poor woman; Julian under suspicion, the gallery to run and now this.

Gina was in the Lady Chapel with Frances but neither was talking. Frances sat with her head lowered, seemingly in a trance and Gina sat quietly beside her. She looked enquiringly at Beth who motioned with her hand that Ali had gone. Frances lifted her head, aware someone else was in the small side chapel.
She stirred and looked at Beth.
"I'm sorry." Her voice was flat, devoid of any emotion. "I overreacted. I shouldn't have shouted at her like that. I'll apologise." She made to stand but Gina caught her arm.
"Ali's gone home, Frances. Why don't you leave it until another day? Everyone is upset at the moment and saying things they don't mean."
"Oh I meant it." Frances's spirit was returning. "But I shouldn't have lost control like that. I will apologise, but tomorrow like you suggest. Or maybe Sunday, after the service."
She struggled to her feet and turned to Gina.
"Thank you, Gina. And thank Carol for me for tidying up, will you? I'll be off now" and she walked stiffly into the church to collect her bag and leave. The three women left behind sat in a pew and looked at each other.
"My goodness. What a scene." Carol was first to break the silence. "Well, come on girls; let's get these flowers sorted quickly and go back to mine for a cup of tea."

Beth had a quiet weekend and was grateful for it. Gina was going to a concert with Tom on the Sunday evening in Portsmouth and suggested Beth went with them but she had no desire to play gooseberry, quickly inventing an excuse. Tom was visiting friends back in Reading for part of the weekend and so Beth walked Charlie alone on Friday and Saturday.

She sat in their usual place on the shingle, gazing unseeingly at the island, feeling unsettled and fidgety. So many things were wrong, like a jigsaw with all its pieces in the wrong place. A cloud of fear and suspicion hung over the little town. Carol was steady and optimistic on the surface but taut and anxious. Gina was also outwardly calm but Beth knew she was deeply worried about Carol and this episode had brought back all the strain of her husband's terminal illness.

And how did Gina feel about Tom? They had been out several times together; to museums, exhibitions, concerts. They had many interests in common and seemed relaxed in each other's company. She had discovered through Gina that Tom had never been married; he had been engaged but his fiancé had left him for his best friend, while he was doing his PhD. Gina seemed to enjoy his company but Beth had no idea if she was attracted to him and was ready for more than companionship and friendship.

      She sighed. Two months ago life had been so simple. She wished with all her heart this black cloud would roll away and leave them all in peace. And Tom? Did she wish he would go away so the equilibrium would be restored? With a sinking of her heart Beth knew the answer to that had to be yes. If he stayed and got together with Gina, how would she cope seeing them together all the time? How that would hurt. But even if he stayed without getting together with Gina, how would she deal with seeing him every day, knowing there could never be anything between them? She would be devastated if he left. But how much more painful it would be if he stayed. She stood up stiffly and called Charlie. Walking slowly back over the shingle, she finally admitted to herself the simple fact she had been denying. She had fallen in love with Tom and her heart ached so much it was a physical pain.

CHAPTER 9

Melissa's funeral was taking place on June 10th, the day after Carol's operation. Mark was taking it and the choir would sing. Grace had arranged for the Mothers' Union to organise refreshments in the church hall, after the service. Grace herself was doing the eulogy and Beth marvelled that the other woman felt able to do so, when her heart must be breaking. She knew she would never have been able to do the same for Louise, but felt a surge of shame and guilt that she hadn't been able to do that last thing for her only sister. But everyone was different and Beth had had to stay strong for Nell that bleak, January day, when the air had been still and grey, even the birds silent, as though the whole earth mourned the lovely young woman, the mother and sister, who was gone for ever. Beth dreaded Melissa's funeral, then felt guilty for considering her own feelings, when Carol and Ken, and Grace, had so much more to bear.

Carol didn't help at tea and Chat on Monday, Maggie explaining she was getting ready for the operation the next day, so Beth and Gina called round to her house after they had tidied up.

They sat in the conservatory. Carol was packed, her overnight bag in the hall; she hadn't needed time to get ready but couldn't face chatting to everyone, which Beth and Gina had suspected.

"I have to be there at half past seven tomorrow morning. Nothing to eat after seven o'clock tonight. Then I am on the morning theatre list. All being well, I can come home tomorrow evening, unless for some reason they want to keep me in overnight. Then it's a week to ten days wait for the biopsy results. That will be the worst bit." She grimaced, lines of tension around her mouth.

"Just remember the vast majority of results are normal. It's far more likely to be harmless than anything nasty." Gina patted her hand.

"I know" Carol gave them a slightly wobbly smile. "That's what I keep telling myself. But another thing I'm not happy about is that I will miss Melissa's funeral."

"But you can't help that!" explained Beth. "You'll be recovering. No one would expect you to be there."

"No" a sigh "but I would have liked to be there with all of you, to pay my respects."

Gina leaned back in the wicker chair. "We'll tell you all about it. I'm making a flower arrangement for it. Grace was talking about flowers after church yesterday. Of course she's ordered all the formal arrangements and the flowers for the coffin. I said was she having exotic orchids and lilies and so on, Melissa being so vibrant and exotic herself, but she said Melissa preferred simple flowers, freesias, sweet peas, roses, things like that. And her favourite colours were pink and lemon, although she didn't wear them as they didn't suit her. I've got some beautiful lemon and pink peonies in the garden so I said I would do an arrangement as well. She wants to put a photo of Melissa on a side table and we're going to put my arrangement there."

"Oh Gina, that will be lovely." Beth knew the peonies Gina was talking about, also that she would make a stunning arrangement. They talked a bit longer about the funeral then Beth and Gina left, wishing her luck for the next day.

"Get Ken to phone us" reminded Beth. "If he phones one of us, we can call each other."

Beth had been worried she would feel a slight restraint with Tom on their walk that evening but he was so laid back and chatty that she was able to relax and act normally. She filled him in briefly on the scene at flower arranging, but played it down, imagining him cringing at the thought of the arguing women. To her surprise he frowned, taking it seriously.

"Ali worries me" he said, sitting down on the shingle close to her; too close for comfort, but Beth couldn't move away without making it obvious. "She's so tense, like a pressure cooker about to blow. I called into the gallery this morning and she was nervy, brittle. I asked her how Julian was and she just said he'd be in later and turned away. But she looks as if she's about to crack. I've seen students fall apart like that." He was silent, staring out to sea.

"On a happier note, your Nell is a lovely girl, a breath of fresh air."

"Isn't she just!" For a moment Beth forgot Ali, forgot Frances, even forgot the murder and Carol's operation as she thought fondly of her niece who had phoned the night before to say Will had suggested going away for a few days, just to the Cotswolds, before the area became flooded with visitors.

They chatted about universities, courses and job prospects, then walked slowly back up the beach to the main road.

"Let me know how Carol is tomorrow, won't you?"

Beth nodded. "Hopefully I'll know something when we walk the dogs."

She slept badly that night, thinking of Carol lying awake and Grace preparing to bury her sister. She sighed and Charlie beside her opened one eye, sighing too.

It was two o' clock and there had still been no news of Carol. Ken had said he would text when she was back on the ward.

Beth had a sandwich in the garden then, unable to settle, walked along the seafront to the church. Gina's convertible was parked in the car park and she went inside, just in time to see Gina gathering up her bits and pieces. Behind her was a tall arrangement on a black pedestal, a mass of pink, lemon, white and pale green. Informally arranged, spilling ivy down the front, Gina had arranged stunning blowsy peonies, some a delicate lemon, some pearly pink, with lemon and pink alstroemerias and white carnations, frothy white gypsophilla surrounding and separating the pastel blooms. The whole effect was stunning, like an impressionist painting. It managed to combine colour and beauty with peace and grace. The arrangement stood to the side of a small, round table, containing a simple black framed photograph of Melissa. She was standing on a beach, too sandy to be local, in a simple, long flowing white dress, the wind moulding it to her body as she stood sideways, smiling into the camera, dark glossy waves blowing around her beautiful face. She looked carefree and happy. Beth wondered if Grace had taken the photo. It was a moment in time and captured the vitality and beauty of the woman, her very essence.

The two women were silent.

"Gina, it's wonderful." Beth felt her throat closing up and swallowed hard.
"The other flowers are coming in the morning. But I'm happy with these; I think Melissa would have liked them." Beth was in no doubt.
"Come on." She took Gina's arm. Let's go and get a coffee. I think you've deserved one."

They walked round to the seafront to the hotel, both wanting peace and quiet and knowing the coffee shops in the High Street would busy and noisy. Beth placed her phone on the table between them, not wanting to miss a call or text. She ordered the coffees from the bored looking waitress and conversation turned inevitably to the funeral the next day.
"I'll go home first for a quick snack and change, then meet you..."

Her phone began to ring and she snatched it up, glancing at the screen. Ken. She listened carefully, then hung up and looked at Gina, a smile on her face. "All over. Carol's alright and they got home half an hour ago. He couldn't text from the hospital, no signal, but it all went well and she came round from the anaesthetic fine. She's a bit sore but just pleased it's all over. And Ken sounds so relieved."

They had another coffee to celebrate. Beth's phone buzzed with a text coming through. Tom. Crying off from walking Tess with her that evening as he had forgotten he had an electrician calling round at seven.

It was too good an opportunity to miss and she took a deep breath, looking at Gina."He's nice, isn't he? Tom, I mean."
"Very." Gina agreed, sipping her coffee.
"You seem to get on very well together." Even saying the words aloud hurt.
Gina raised perfect brown eyebrows. "Yes, and so do you two."
"Well yes, we enjoy walking the dogs, but we've never been out anywhere, to a concert or exhibition or anything I mean." Gina looked amused.
"Ah. But I have. So, are you saying you would like to go somewhere other than the beach with the dogs?"
"No, no." Beth felt flustered. This wasn't going as she had planned. Gina looked at her curiously.
"So what are you trying to say?" Beth fiddled with the sugar sachet.
"I just thought, you get on so well, you've got so much in common. I just wondered, well, it would be nice for you both, wouldn't? You know, if you got together." Her voice trailed away as Gina remained silent.

"Beth, he's a very nice man, thoughtful, considerate, kind. And extremely pleasant looking. But I'm not looking for another partner. Malcolm was the love of my life. It's nice to have a companion to go to concerts with and so on, but there's nothing else between us. He's never given me the slightest indication he's interested in me that way."

Beth was aware of a flood of relief, starting at her head and flowing through to her toes. She felt almost light headed with it. She had no need to watch her best friend with the man she had stupidly fallen in love with; no need to pretend happiness for the two of them and live with the strain that would have caused her.

Gina was looking at her curiously, a slight frown marring her lovely face. "Beth, why are you asking? Did you really think we were getting close?"

"I didn't know" she confessed. "Like I said, you seem to get on so well, I just thought…" her voice trailed off. "Would it have bothered you?" Gina's blue eyes missed nothing, reading her friend's expression of relief and embarrassment. "Beth, it would have, wouldn't it?"

Beth looked at her friend uncomfortably.

"Oh Gina. I felt so guilty at not being happy for you, if you were getting close to him. But I was so jealous." She swallowed. There. She had admitted it.

"Oh Beth!" The understanding and sympathy on Gina's face was almost her undoing.

"No, don't" Beth flapped her hands in front of her face. "You know I'm being stupid."

"No you're not, of course you're not." Gina caught her hands and squeezed them.

"I am" she insisted miserably. "Even if he liked me, nothing would ever come of it, nothing can come of it, you know that." Gina's blue eyes shone with compassion and Beth had to blink away tears.

"Oh sweetheart, we can't help falling in love."

"No." Beth sighed, wiped a tear away. "I thought I was immune. After…..well, you know, I thought I would never be interested in any man. I didn't want to be interested. Now look at me!" She tried to smile.

Gina didn't know what to say and sat quietly, simply patting her hand.

"Don't give me any sympathy" she blinked hard again. "Come on, let's talk about something else."

So they did.

The church had been full; surprising Beth who had imagined just a handful of local people. Of course, she had chided herself; Melissa had had a life before Bride's Bay, friends and family she knew nothing about.

She had gone home after work to grab a sandwich and change. Tom had arranged to pick her up at half past one, then Frances. She dressed in the outfit she had chosen the night before; a simple dark green skirt that hugged her stomach and hips then swirled slightly over her knees, made of some man made material that fell beautifully and didn't crease. It was the skirt she wore to parent's evenings and committee meetings. With it she wore a simple cream top with a vee neck, embroidery detail around it. Simple pearl studs and low taupe patent court shoes completed the outfit. She looked at herself critically in the long mirror inside her wardrobe door. Her hair had grown and fell in soft waves around her face, from a side parting, golden blonde streaks now outnumbering the darker blonde. Her skin was a light golden brown and her eyes a clear green. Her eyes travelled down, past her sloping shoulders to her chest, to cleavage just visible and the swell of her breasts beneath the cream top. Gazing lower, she frowned. The skirt clung a little too snugly to her tummy. She sucked it in, a bit better. Some Marks and Spencer's industrial knickers to hold it all in were in her underwear drawer, but Beth hated the feeling of confinement and never wore them. Why on earth was she fussing like this anyway? It was Melissa's funeral; she just needed to look smart out of respect. With that thought she picked up her bag and went downstairs, transferring phone, wallet, comb and tissues from her everyday bag to the patent one that matched the shoes. She had bought the matching set for a wedding two years ago and they were fast becoming her hatch, match and despatch set; she mused, then picked up her keys, patted Charlie and went out of the front door to wait for Tom.

He was punctual, jumping out to open the door for her and she slid into the front seat, gathering the folds of skirt around her. Three minutes later he repeated the process for Frances, the other woman dressed in a black skirt, black shoes and white blouse. No one spoke as they drove the short distance to the church, Beth uncomfortable aware of the long leg and muscular thigh close to hers and his capable looking hands on the steering wheel, golden hairs showing against the snowy white of his shirt cuffs. His suit was charcoal grey, good quality wool. No black tie but a pewter coloured silk with abstract black markings on it.

They parked and he ushered the two women ahead of him into the church, a steady stream of people following them. Beth led the way to a pew on the left, twisting along to the end seat, Frances following then Tom. Beth reached across Frances, whispering to keep two seats for Gina and Ken and he nodded, placing his order of service across them. Ken followed shortly with Gina and they whispered greetings, Ken doing thumbs up to Beth in response to her mouthing Carol's name.

The organ was playing quietly and the flowers looked magnificent. Grace had continued with the pink and lemon theme in arrangements either side of the altar; one pedestal being mainly white with splashes of

pearly pink and the other white with a delicate pale lemon.
Gina's arrangement at the side glowed in the gloom of the old church. Mark took his place on the altar, assisted by two servers and motioned for the congregation to stand and the service began.

Three hours later it was all over and Beth was home, changed back into cotton trousers and a T shirt.

It had gone well. Grace had been composed; remaining in control during the service and giving a eulogy that managed to be uplifting and joyful, a celebration of Melissa's vibrant life rather than a tragic sudden goodbye. She introduced Bride's Bay residents to Melissa's cousins, the only family present apart from Grace herself, to close friends from childhood, adolescence, college and working days, to her colleagues in the art world and to acquaintances who had travelled to say their farewells. She gave a short speech before people began to leave, thanking everyone for attending. Beth had been amazed and impressed at her calmness and strength.

Melissa's ex-partner had been there; a shortish man of average build, with cropped dark hair streaked with grey and frameless glasses. But he exuded a power and charisma and Beth could understand his attraction for the lively, colourful Melissa. Grace had caught Gina as she, Tom, Frances and Beth were about to make their farewells and Gina followed her back into the church, signalling to Beth she would be back.

"What was that about?" she queried when Gina reappeared.
"She was just thanking me again for the flowers. She took a photo of them. You know she's a photographer?" Beth nodded her head in agreement. "She usually photographs people, she's quite well known apparently. You know, when someone wants a special studio portrait done. Anyway, she took a picture, while they are at their best."

Tom dropped Frances home first. He got out at Beth's, opening the car door for her. Beth was all for equality but it was nice to have doors held open, an arm shepherding you through a doorway or across the road. Nothing to do with equality really; just consideration and good manners. She looked up at him to thank him for the lifts; her throat catching. Why did men look so good in suits? Especially this one, she thought unhappily; the well-cut suit fitting his tall, broad frame perfectly and the white shirt taut across his muscular chest.

"Well, funeral or no funeral, dogs still need walking" he sighed. "Shall we take them somewhere else this evening, for a change?" Beth nodded, thinking.
"Alver country park? There are some nice trails, though we'd have to keep them on leads."
"Tess is fine with that but I can't imagine Charlie being happy."
"No" Beth pondered. "What about Monkton Common? I can let him off the lead there."
"Sounds good. I'll pick you up at seven." He walked round the car and eased himself into the driver's seat, raising a hand in farewell.

Charlie enjoyed the change of scenery, the common having new scents and places to explore, including rabbit holes. By silent consent they avoided talking about the funeral, or the burglaries. Tom chatted about Grace's work, being familiar with it from an exhibition in Reading, and about places he had enjoyed photographing, discovering he and Beth had visited the same places in Scotland and Wales.
"Have you been to Edinburgh?" Beth asked.
"Yes and before you ask, yes I did go on a Rebus trail, looking up his haunts." Tom grinned at her.
She smiled back. "I've been to the borders, Jedburgh and Moffatt, and the Isle of Arran. But one day I'd like to go to Edinburgh and look at all the places I've read about. And the Highlands."
"Well. Just remember your midge repellent. And waterproofs."
"No umbrella?"
"It would get blown inside out. But you should go, it's one of the most beautiful places I've ever been to. Though this is pretty good too" he added, looking out to sea as they walked back to the car.

Beth showered as soon as she got back in then went to bed early with a mug of tea and her kindle. It had been an emotional day but not as hard as she had expected. Tomorrow she would visit Carol.

Carol was sitting in a cane chair in the conservatory, surrounded by magazines and knitting. Beth dropped a kiss on her cheek and sat down next to her. Ken was in the kitchen making them both a cup of tea. "So, how are you feeling?"
"Fine, honestly, I'm fine. A bit tired still from the anaesthetic and I'm not supposed to lift anything. I'm just glad it's over. Now the wait" grimacing. "But Mr Williams said it all looked alright, apparently they can tell quite a lot by appearances. So fingers crossed and prayers."

Beth had been expecting to fill her friend in on the funeral but Ken had already done so. Carol made no mention of Tom either, so Gina obviously hadn't said anything. Not that she would, reflected Beth. Gina was a private person herself and respected other's privacy. Gina and Carol were the only people who knew about her past and although Carol enjoyed a gossip, she knew the woman would never, ever divulge what she had been told in confidence. They chatted instead about Grace. Maggie had visited Carol that morning, telling her the sister planned to stay in Bride's Bay for a while, taking over Melissa's rental agreement. She intended having a break while she considered her future, apparently tired of apartment living in London.

"She's a nice woman" Carol was saying. "Quieter than Melissa but witty and very intelligent. I hope she stays."
"She won't stay in that house though, not after Melissa..." Beth's voice trailed off.
"No, no" Carol shook her head. "And who knows? A few weeks here and she might be desperate for bright lights and theatres and Cafe Nero!"

Beth walked home, satisfied her friend was alright. It was beginning to rain and she quickened her steps. By the time she reached her front door it was pouring down heavily and was still raining two hours later. No long walk tonight, Charlie, she patted him as he curled around her legs. But he was easily consoled with a few dog biscuits.

It rained all the next day but stopped at tea time and by seven o'clock a watery sun was shining on the rain drenched plants and scattering silver sparkles on the sea.

Tom knocked on her door and they made their way over the road and onto the beach, walking the length then turning back as the shingle was too damp to sit on. He was going to London by train the next morning to meet up with a former colleague, and entertained Beth with tales of his colleague's eccentricity as they strolled along, Tess plodding slowly by his side and Charlie having twice the exercise by running ahead then back the length of the beach.

"So, you see, economics lecturers are not all dry and dusty individuals" he teased, echoing Carol's character assessment, as they walked back along the beach. "What about you? You didn't go to university?"
"No" Beth shook her head. "I didn't have the opportunity. That's why I was determined Nell would go, if she wanted to."

"And she seems to love her work, she's full of it" commented Tom, as they reached the footpath that led to the corner of Beth's road.
"She does" Beth smiled "and Winchester. And her flat. And she's made some good friends" thinking in particular of Will but keeping quiet about him, unsure how public the relationship was.
"You've done a great job raising her."

They had reached Beth's house and Tom walked up the path with her, as she fumbled for her keys and unlocked the front door.
"She's a lovely girl and I'm all she's got. I just want her to be happy."
"She is" Tom looked down at her, her dark blonde head just reaching his shoulder. "And she's an adult now, responsible for her own happiness." Beth looked up at him, smiling wryly. "I know, but I'll always worry about her."

"And what about you?" Tom was standing very close. Beth could see a tangle of gold curly hairs above his polo shirt buttons and his thick neck. She could smell his skin, slightly musky and tangy.
"You deserve to be happy too, Beth. Don't neglect yourself."
"I don't." Beth was struggling to breathe normally, her senses reeling. She fixed her gaze on the polo shirt buttons, dark blue with black thread, apart from one with grey; it must have fallen off and been sewn back on. She felt warm fingers stroking her cheek, soft but firm. Then his face came closer, blotting out the sun.
Warm lips brushed the corner of her mouth, firm and soft at the same time. Then they pressed against hers gently, warm and comforting.

Beth froze, her chest pounding and her lungs struggling for air. She pushed against his chest and gasped as air entered her lungs and the sun shone once again in her eyes.

Tom stepped back, frowning.
"Beth? Beth, I'm sorry, I didn't mean..."
He didn't get to say what he hadn't meant. Beth flapped her arms at him, gabbling an apology.
"Sorry, sorry, it's just been a difficult week. I'm a bit overwrought. Ignore me. And I don't really like people getting so close, physically I mean. I like my own space" She gave a wobbly smile, attempting a laugh.
"Sorry, I didn't realise." Tom stood a couple of steps away, frowning down at her, concern in his warm hazel eyes.
"Why should you?" Beth had regained some control. "I'm sorry, I

overreacted. Just forget it."

She stepped indoors and turned to face him.

"Still friends?" Tom's voice was deep, hesitating.

"Of course." A huge effort to make her voice normal. "Have a good day tomorrow. See you at church."

She couldn't manage any more small talk, turning away to close the door and Tom walked slowly back down the path.

CHAPTER 10

She was safe the next day. Tom wasn't due back until late evening and Frances had offered to walk Tess for him. But her stomach sank at the thought of seeing him at church or on the beach on Sunday evening, any evening come to that. Then she chided herself. She couldn't avoid him for ever. And he had seemed to accept her explanation of liking her own space, hadn't he? He wouldn't make the same mistake again. She would greet him as though nothing had happened and sweep it under the carpet. She was good at that.

In the event it was easy. Tom greeted her after church as though Friday evening had never happened. Then walking on the beach later he recounted his day with his old friend, making her laugh aloud at the old man's antics in the restaurant. She went indoors happily after the walk; it was going to be alright after all. He was obviously content to be friends and wasn't going to act the part of a rejected suitor. And that was all they could ever be. She put the kettle on and stamped down on the pain the thought caused her.

Carol continued to make good progress but the same could not be said of the police enquiries. The studio had yielded no clues, no DNA, nothing. No new evidence had come to light and investigations continued. The gossip and speculation diminished as life continued and people expressed their certainty the burglars must have been from further afield, maybe Portsmouth or Southampton, London even, and poor Melissa had been in the wrong place at the wrong time. She must have returned home and disturbed them. Then been attacked. Maybe they had only meant to knock her out? It had obviously been a burglary gone wrong, a tragedy, but not intended.

Ali still drifted around the town like a ghost and the gallery was more often closed than open, Julian rarely being seen. Robert Salmon served his customers with an even more grim expression than usual; Barbara had lost weight and her bouncy curls were flat, needing trimming. Matthew was still causing rows, according to Sue in the charity shop, who was friendly with Roberta, mother of Hannah Salmon's best friend Amy. It was stalemate; Robert still adamant his son would follow him into the business; Matthew equally determined not to.

James Lamb was busier than ever. The initial shock that he could be involved with the burglaries had worn off and he and Joe were doing estimates and dealing with enquiries. April's son Phil often drank with Joe Lamb and he confirmed the firm was handling as much work as they could and yes, Matthew was as stubborn as his father. The general opinion was that Barbara and Robert would end up losing their son if Robert didn't start listening to the boy. Investigations into Ken's estate agency had also reached a dead end. Ken's solicitor had been forceful and no malpractice had come to light, as everyone had known. Ken had run his agency for over thirty years and had a reputation for integrity, honesty and efficiency. The only cloud hanging over the couple was the wait for the biopsy results.

On the Thursday morning Tom accompanied Gina into Portsmouth for the day. He had expressed an interest in going up the Spinnaker tower and on hearing at Tea and Chat that she planned to go to Waterstones to collect a book she had ordered, had asked if he could keep her company, being a sucker for book shops. They parked at the ferry terminal in Gosport and caught the foot passenger ferry across to Gunwharf Quays, Tom gazing out at the large ferries sailing backwards and forward to the island and even further.

"Do you want to go up the tower now or after shopping?" Gina asked him as they stepped off the ferry, dodging the bikes, and began walking past Portsmouth Harbour station.
"Now?" suggested Tom. "I'm likely to buy a few books then I won't have to carry them up the tower."
Gina laughed. "You won't have to anyway; there is a lift you know."

The queue was short as the school holidays hadn't yet started and Gina and Tom were whisked quickly up to the first viewing platform. She smiled at him as he took his shoes off to walk on the glass platform, gazing at the ground far below. They walked up the stairs to the top viewing platform and stood gazing at the Solent; the Historic Dockyard below them to one side, the island ahead and the coast down to the Witterings and Bognor Regis to the east.
"That's the Mary Rose, in that grey cocoon" Gina pointed to the ground below, then pointed ahead.
"And there are the forts. One of them is a luxury hotel, though I've never been there. If you can't see all three forts because of cloud, you can come back free another day. But there's no need for that today."

The day was warm and sunny, the sky and sea a clear pale blue. Tom sighed contentedly, smiling down at her, his eyes hidden behind his dark sunglasses.

"This is nice. Now, I'll choose a few new books to buy and enjoy, then we can go and have a good lunch. This is exactly my idea of a great day."

"Mine too" Gina smiled back and turned to begin the descent.

"Coffee here, or in town?" she asked, pausing at the level containing the cafe.

"In town? Then we can go to Waterstones and maybe come back to the Quays for lunch?"

They walked along to Commercial Road and had a coffee in Costa before spending a contented hour in the book shop, each coming out with a heavy bag of books. Tom insisted on carrying them as they made their way back to the Quays and entered an Italian restaurant that Gina recommended.

Tom had chosen spaghetti with meatballs and jalapeno peppers; Gina penne pasta with pesto and chicken. They agreed to meet in the middle with the wine colour, sharing a bottle of rose.

"So" Gina regarded Tom with amusement as he sipped his wine and looked around. "I assume you're adjusting quite well to this retirement lark?"

Tom grinned, his hazel eyes crinkling at the corners, the faint lines white against his tanned skin.

"I think you could safely say that. Yes. It's the old cliché, how did I ever have time to work? But it's so true."

Gina smiled. "That's why it's a cliché!" Tom looked at her.

"But then it hasn't been an ordinary, quiet retirement, has it? What with the burglaries and the murder."

"That's true." Gina gazed out of the window at the boats bobbing on the harbour. "You've had quite a baptism of fire here. But you think you've chosen the right area?"

"Oh yes. No doubt about that." Tom wiped his mouth with the linen napkin and put it down. "There's plenty going on, without the crime! And the coastline is lovely, always something to watch, busy in places, quiet in others. And I've made some good friends already."

He frowned and Gina looked at him questioningly. "What?"
"Oh nothing, ignore me." He smiled at her, taking another sip of wine. Gina remained silent, her blue eyes gazing at him curiously and he raised an eyebrow at her and smiled wryly.
"Alright! If you must know, it's Beth."

"Beth?" Gina was startled; she hadn't been expecting him to say that. "What about her?"
"I think I may have ruined a good friendship there." He spoke ruefully, sighing as he replaced his wine glass.
"I think you'd better start at the beginning." Gina was beginning to feel anxious. He sighed again.
"Where to start?" He was quiet for a moment, contemplating. "We get on so well; we have done since we first met. She's so easy to talk to, such good company, kind and funny and interesting. Our walks are so enjoyable and we both seem to enjoy them." He frowned, looking uncomfortable. "But the other evening she just looked a bit forlorn and I wanted to comfort her. I gave her a kiss, just a peck, but she wasn't happy."

He fell silent, recalling her stiffness and her white face. "She really wasn't happy."
Gina fiddled with the stem of her wineglass, finally speaking.
"What did she say?"
"Just that she liked her own space, she didn't like people too close. But I've seen her hug and kiss you and Carol, it's obviously just me."
He stared out of the window, looking unhappy.

Gina was quiet and Tom looked over at her.
"So it is me. She's not interested in me, would never be interested in me, is that what you're saying?"
Gina looked up at him and caught her breath at the bleak expression in his eyes.
"Oh Tom!" She spoke quietly. "You like her, don't you?"
"Yes. But it seems it's not reciprocated." His mouth twisted. Gina struggled to think what to say. She was certainly not going to discuss Beth with him but needed to say something. Before she could, Tom spoke again.
"There's so much I don't know about her. Has she been married? Is she divorced, or widowed?"

This was safer ground; she could just stick to the facts. She shook her head. "No, she lived and worked in Bournemouth. In a hotel at first, then as a nursery nurse when she qualified. She moved here when her sister died and she took over looking after Nell." Keep it simple.
Tom already knew that.
"So has she ever been engaged, ever lived with anyone?"
"No." Gina shook her head, gazing out of the window at the people strolling by, at the huge P&O ferry gliding past.
Tom was frowning.
"But why not?" He wasn't giving up easily. "She's lovely, her personality and her looks. How come she never met anyone?" A thought occurred to him. "Or did she? Was he married?" As he said it he shook his head as though to retract the question. He couldn't imagine Beth having an affair.
Gina shrugged noncommittally. "I suppose she's just been busy bringing up Nell."
This was difficult. She poured herself another glass of wine for something to do as Tom sighed.
"Well, I may like her, but she's not interested in me so that's that. I just hope we can be friends at least."

Gina was in a dilemma. She didn't want to leave it like that, especially knowing how her friend felt about the man opposite, but couldn't say too much. She made a decision, hoping it was the right one.

"Tom, I can't gossip about Beth, you know that, don't you?" He nodded. She took a deep breath.
"Beth does have reasons for not letting people get close, very good reasons. But that's not to say she wouldn't like them to."
"People? Or me in particular?" He was looking at her anxiously.
"You." There, she had said it, and spoke a silent apology to Beth in her head. Tom was silent while he digested her words.
"And these reasons, are they unresolvable?" His clear hazel eyes searched Gina's. She shook her head.
"I don't think so, but it won't be easy."
"Nothing worthwhile ever is. Are you saying I should try?" For the first time during the conversation there was a gleam of hope in his hazel eyes.
"That's up to you. It depends how much you want to."
"Oh I want to. Believe me, I've never wanted anything more."
"Then don't give up." Gina squeezed his hand. "But please, be careful."

He squeezed her hand back, looking into her clear eyes and nodding. "You don't need to worry."
They both stood up to leave the restaurant.

    Tom's first instinct on arriving home was to rush round to Beth's and talk to her. Well, actually to sweep her into his arms first then talk to her, but that wasn't the best idea. He needed to be patient and wait until the time was right. He also needed to think what he was going to say. This was too important to get wrong.

    He hadn't realised he could be such a good actor. He and Beth walked along the beach, stopping to sit in their usual spot, watching Charlie race in and out of the waves. He had to force himself to chat normally; discussing how the alterations were going to his house, asking how Nell was, telling her about the books he had bought in Waterstones. Had to force himself not to stare at her lovely face or her gorgeous soft body. He heard his voice speaking normally but felt like a coiled spring. At least she seemed totally unaware of his tension, listening to his chatter then telling him about school, about the banes of her life Isaac and Joe, and little Ava who had the face of an angel but was the most stubborn child Beth had ever come across. As she chatted easily and smiled he realised to his relief she had obviously put the incident behind her. But however pleased he was that they could still be friends, it wasn't going to be enough for him, not nearly enough.

    Friday morning brought good news. Beth heard her phone go while supervising a group outside on the play equipment but it was break time before she could check the call and phone Carol back. As soon as she answered, Beth knew it was good news.
"Oh Carol, I'm so pleased. What a relief!"
The biopsy results were fine, the polyp was benign and no further treatment was needed. Beth walked to church for flower arranging with a light heart and hugged her friend as soon as she saw her.
"Some good news at last, you must be over the moon."
"Oh I am, believe me, I am."

    There was no Ali. She obviously meant what she had said about not helping anymore, but Frances was already there, bustling around. She had checked Gina's display and topped up the water and was starting on the pink and white pedestal.
"Beth, you do this one. Carol, you do the font and Gina and I will do the

Lady Chapel."
"Yes Frances" Carol saluted the woman behind her back and Beth and Gina stifled their giggles.

The atmosphere that afternoon was light-hearted; due in the main to Carol's news. Beth was so relieved; it really was as though a weight had been lifted. She went about her duties happily and energetically until a glance at Melissa's photo on the small table brought the tragedy sharply back into focus. What a stupid waste of life, and who was responsible for ending it like that?

Tom's opportunity came that evening. He hadn't planned it like that but Beth knocked on the front door with Charlie just as the heavens opened.
"Oh" she gasped. "Where did that come from? I didn't even realise it was cloudy."
He opened the door wide and gestured her through.
"Come in, we'll wait until it passes. Charlie, go on through to Tess" nudging the little dog along with a trainer clad foot. Beth followed him through into the kitchen.
"Coffee?" Tom looked at her, his heart lurching at the sight of her wide green eyes, her lovely mouth.

She nodded and leaned against the kitchen worktop while he made a pot of coffee, watching his economical movements and tall, strong figure in denim jeans and a checked cotton shirt. Her heart ached and she forced herself to look out of the window and admire the garden. Tom followed her gaze as she commented on the display of red and yellow tulips in the border, their petals bright and vibrant against the mellow stone wall, dripping water on to the soil below.

"I have to stop Frances from picking them all, I do want some left in the garden."
He poured the coffee and looked up at the sky; the single black cloud that had been responsible for the downpour had now been joined by several others. "It's not going to stop. Let's take our coffees into the living room and start designing the ark."

"I think someone already did" giggled Beth, following him and sitting down on a large, squashy cream sofa, looking at the water streaming down the large bay windows.

Tom sat in a deep faded red armchair, large enough for two, at right angles to the sofa. He would need large furniture, she reflected, to accommodate his long legs and large frame. She looked around with interest. The room was decorated in cream and deep red; plain cream walls with several pictures, a large mirror over the original fireplace, rich wooden floorboards with an antique rug and deep red cushions on the sofa. Small tables were dotted around, covered with newspapers, magazines and books. The whole effect was warm and cosy, especially when Tom reached over to flick the switch on a table lamp next to him. It was a comfortable room, meant to be relaxed in and enjoyed.

He leaned forward, cradling his mug of coffee, and looked at Beth. His heart seemed to swell and fill his chest as he took in the wave of soft dark blonde hair sweeping across her forehead and falling over her cheek, the skin a soft peachy pink. Her lips were slightly open, perfectly shaped and delicate, and his stomach lurched as he recalled their softness and sweet taste. Her neck was smooth and golden, a tiny pulse beating at the side. She was looking out of the window and he could see her lashes, long and curved, and her slightly arched brows. He knew without seeing them that her eyes were green, as cool and clear as a mountain stream. Her cotton tee-shirt hugged her perfect, full breasts and her legs just reaching the floor were lightly tanned and shapely. He had difficulty swallowing and must have made a sound because Beth looked over at him, catching her breath at his expression.

"Beth." He leaned forward, remembered she wasn't comfortable with him being too close and eased back again. "Beth, the other evening, when I kissed you..."
No no, not that. Please don't talk about that, prayed Beth.
"You were scared. I felt you panicking." He paused, swallowing. "Beth, you've become a dear friend and I wouldn't upset you or hurt you for the world."

Beth felt her heart beginning to pound. She didn't know where to look and gazed down at the rug. She could hear the rain on the windows and the patter of Charlie's feet as he explored the kitchen.

"You said you didn't like people to get too close, to invade your space. But you seem fine with Carol and Gina, and with others. So is it just me?" His voice was anxious.

Beth kept looking down; no idea what to say.
"Please, won't you tell me? I hope I'm a good friend to you too and you can trust me with..." his voice hesitated. With what? He began again. "I hated seeing you upset like that. Beth, can't you tell me why you were so scared?"

She lifted her gaze from the rug and met his eyes, warm, gentle eyes, concern in their hazel depths. Her stomach lurched deep inside her and she was suddenly tired; tired of worrying about his feelings for Gina, and hers for him; tired of looking at him and knowing he was out of reach, tired of secrets. What did it matter if she told him? It couldn't make any difference; it could never work anyway but at least he would understand why and she could put it aside and get on with life.

She clasped her hands together tightly as she looked down again, avoiding his eyes. "I did panic, you're right. And you're right that I'm fine with some other people….." Her voice faltered.
He waited and saw her take a deep breath.
She swallowed then tried again.
"Basically I'm fine with women, it's just men." Her heart was thumping as she squeezed her fingers tightly.

Tom felt a lead weight in his chest, felt sick. He spoke quietly, urgently. "Tell me why, Beth. Please?" This was it. Beth sat stiffly, hands clasped, looking down, her hair falling over her face and took another deep breath.

"Because…..because of something a long time ago. When Louise and I had to move out of our house and into a care home, orphanage, whatever you want to call it." She paused, swallowing hard.
"Why did you go into care?" Tom's throat was aching, his heart racing.
"Because our mother was ill, then she died. There was no one else to live with. Louise and I lived with just our mother; our father left when I was four and Louise two. Mum didn't cope very well."
That was an understatement but she didn't need to go into details.

"When I was ten and Louise was eight Mum was diagnosed with breast cancer. She'd never bothered with her health or anything and by the time it was discovered, it was advanced. Louise and I were taken into care while she had treatment, then we went back home. But near the end we went back into care and she died when we were twelve and ten."

She heard Tom's intake of breath and sensed his stillness. She focussed on the rug, studying every cream strand.

"It wasn't too bad in the home. The staff were nice and tried hard, but they kept changing and we would just get used to one house manager then they'd leave and we'd start all over again. But it was okay. We stayed at our primary schools then went on to secondary. And at least we had each other."

Tom was leaning forward now, but avoiding touching her.
"So what went wrong?" His voice was quiet and strained.

Beth stared unseeingly out of the window.
"They were a nice bunch of children in the home, there were only ten of us and we all got on well. Then when I was fourteen and Louise was twelve, a new boy arrived. He was fifteen but looked older."
This was getting difficult and Beth started fidgeting with her skirt, crumpling the cotton.

"He got friendly with two other boys, a bit younger. He showed off to them and they thought he was wonderful, a real lad. And he kept staring at me. I was the oldest girl in the home and I was quite plump, well, curvy really. He was always looking at my chest and making comments. He started calling me names. The other boys thought it was funny. I tried to keep out of his way but then he started cornering me, squeezing past, touching my chest, that sort of thing. But he made out it was accidental. Then he would apologise and smirk."

"Did you tell anyone?" Tom's voice was hoarse, his throat tight. Beth nodded. "I told the house manager. She said she would have a word with him. And she did, but she came back to me and said he had denied it, he said I was imagining it and his friends backed him up, of course. So after that I made sure I was always as far away from him as possible, and I kept a watch on Louise too. She was developing quickly, like I had. He would look at me and laugh, saying things and making obscene gestures when no-one was looking. I complained about him again but again he denied it and the house manager said just to ignore him."

Beth was calm now, recounting the events on auto pilot. Tom still leaned forward, his hands clenched on his knees, knuckles white. He didn't want to hear any more, he really didn't.

"Then one afternoon one of the younger boys, Gary, came to find me in the living room and said Louise and her friends were playing in the garden house. That was a kind of Wendy house, with curtains and furniture and stuff, in the corner of the garden, that the little kids used. He said she had hurt her leg and was asking for me. I ran out to the garden, over to the house and went in. Louise and her friends weren't in there of course. Jamie had bribed Gary to give me the message. He was in there with his two friends, grinning. He sent the other two out, telling them to stand guard outside."

Tom closed his eyes. His heart was pounding, blood racing to his head, making him dizzy.

"He said I had a nerve, making up things about him, and he was going to give me something to complain about. He slapped my face then pushed me on the floor and stuffed a cloth in my mouth. Then he knelt over me and pulled up my tee-shirt and skirt. He pulled at my underwear. He started to..." Beth couldn't go on.

"Did he rape you?" Tom didn't recognise his voice; it was croaky, rasping, coming from far away.

Beth shook her head. "He tried to, but he couldn't. He kept trying but.... he hurt me, he was so rough...then at last he stopped and hit me again, saying I was frigid and a freak, something wrong with me that I couldn't do it. Then he pulled out a penknife and said if I told anyone about it, he would tell them I had been after him, I had begged for it. He said if I did say anything, I'd better watch Louise very, very carefully. He left and they went off and I lay there in the dark. I couldn't move but I was terrified he would come back. Eventually I got up and went back to our room. Louise was there, as chatty and normal as always. I just wanted to have a bath and go to bed. But I didn't dare leave Louise alone. So I acted as though nothing had happened and I stuck to her like glue all the time. All the time until he left a year later, when he left the home to go to college."

She stared down at the rug, her face white and hands clasped together. She was silent.
"You didn't tell anyone?" Tom was having trouble breathing.
"No. How could I? It would have been my word against his. They hadn't believed me before. And I couldn't risk Louise..." her voice broke. She pushed her hair back from her face with hands that shook.

Tom couldn't bear it. He moved stiffly, like an old man, and squatted down in front of her.

"Beth, oh sweetheart." His voice shook and his head was still spinning.

"No, no." Beth flapped her hands and shrank back. "Don't, don't give me any sympathy."

"Why not?" He tried to breath slowly and calm down, rubbing his hands over his face.

"Because I can't cope with that, with sympathy." She was staring down at her skirt, hands clasped together.

"Why not? What's wrong with someone caring what happened to you?"

Beth shook her head and looked down to where she had begun pleating the material in her skirt with shaking fingers.

"It would start me off crying." She could already feel her eyes stinging, tears pricking at her eyelids.

"So why shouldn't you cry?" He was regaining some control now. His head had steadied and air was getting into his lungs.

"I can't." She shook her head. "If I start, I won't be able to stop. I'll just fall apart."

Tom took a deep breath, looking at her tense white face and agitated hands.

"You should cry, Beth. Don't bottle it up; it doesn't matter if you fall apart." There was a huge lump in his throat and he swallowed hard, opening his arms wide. "Come here, my love. Come to me and let yourself cry. Please?" His throat ached as she looked up at him, eyes swimming.

She leaned forward and that was all the encouragement Tom needed. He wrapped his arms around her and pulled her close against his chest. His arms were strong and warm, his chest solid, and Beth let the tears come as he rocked her back and forth, back and forth, stroking her hair.

"It's all right, my love. You're safe, I've got you." His arms tightened around her. "He'll never hurt you again. No one will hurt you again. Sshh, I'm here. I've got you sweetheart."

Beth's head was against his heart and she was aware of the thump of his heartbeats and the buttons on his polo shirt pressing against her cheek as he held her even tighter, his head pressed against hers, his lips on her hair.

Now she had started crying, she couldn't stop, as she had known. The tears streamed down her cheeks and her chest heaved with sobs.
"I'm sorry" she gulped, her voice shaking.
"No, you've no need to be sorry. Just let go."

She felt him move backwards, taking her with him, then he scooped her up in his arms and moved to sit on the sofa, pulling her across his lap and cradling her against his chest.
"Cry it all out sweetheart. You're safe, it's all over. I've got you, it's alright. Just cry, that's it my love, cry it all out."

He continued rocking her and stroking her hair, his chin resting on her head, arms tightly round her. Beth sobbed and still he held her close to his chest, murmuring, soothing. His shirt was soaked where she lay against it but he didn't move, only held her closer, ever closer, one warm hand smoothing her hair while the other gently rubbed her back.

Eventually the storm of weeping started to ease and her sobs became quieter, the short breaths catching in her throat decreasing until she only gave a small occasional gulp. Tom reached into his pocket and pulled out a handkerchief, gently wiping her eyes then her nose.

"I'm sorry, I've soaked your shirt." Beth's voice wobbled and she went to pull away but Tom's arms pulled her gently back against his chest.
"It doesn't matter, stay here."

Beth leaned against him, her breath still coming in the occasional quiet gasp. His arms were warm and comforting and for the first time for as long as she could remember she felt safe, safe and secure. He carried on stroking her hair, murmuring soothing words, until her breathing was normal and she had stopped trembling. Still he didn't let go, keeping his arms around her, stroking her back. Minutes passed. The tears had stopped and Beth felt calm; tired and drained but calm. She could feel the soft cotton of his Polo shirt under her cheek, rough hair tickled her nose and she could smell the warm, musky scent of his skin. His hands were firm but gentle in her hair and his arms strong, wrapped round her.

She could have stayed there forever, warm and safe, clutching his soft shirt, but eventually she pulled away, sitting up straight next to him and blowing her nose.

Tom eased back, stretching his legs.
"I think we need a drink." He got to his feet, looking down at her swollen eyes and tear stained cheeks. "Go and wash your face, sweetheart, your eyes will be sore."

He helped her up and guided her into the hall, to the cloakroom. Beth soaked her eyes for a couple of minutes then looked in the mirror. Her eyes were red and puffy, her skin blotchy. Her mascara had smudged under her eyes and she wet some toilet paper and rubbed it off, making her eyes even redder. Her hair was all over the place but she didn't have a comb.

When she went back into the living room Tom was sitting on the sofa and had put a small table in front of it with two glasses of wine. He patted the cushion next to him then handed her a glass. It was icy cold, fruity, refreshing and she drank it as if it was water.

"Thank you." Beth put her glass down, keeping her gaze on the small table.
"Beth. I don't know what to say." Tom looked at her, his fingers tense around the wine glass. "I'm just so sorry. So, so sorry."
Beth didn't know what to say either and there was an awkward silence. Tom broke it at last.
"Who else knows?"
"Gina, Carol. Louise knew, before ..." her throat closed up again.
"Nell?" Beth shook her head. "No. She was too young, and now she has a good life, I don't want to upset her..." her voice trailed off. There was another silence. Tom poured more wine, Beth putting her hand over her glass when it was half full.
"That's enough. I got through that last one a bit too quickly." She took another sip. "Anyway, now you know. Not a pretty story." She tried to smile and failed. "But it explains things, doesn't it?"

Tom nodded. "Yes, and I'm glad you told me, I know how difficult it must have been. But I just don't know what to say, or do?" He looked at her enquiringly.
"Nothing, there is nothing." She yawned. "Sorry, what time is it?" Tom glanced at his watch.
"Nearly ten and you're exhausted. But I don't want you to go and be on your own. Will you stay here tonight? The spare room is all ready for guests."

Beth shook her head. "No, I'll be fine, honestly. I know it's been a shock for you but I've lived with it for nearly forty years, remember."
She got to her feet, her head swimming slightly, eyes grainy and sore.

Tom looked unhappy. "But I've made you relive it all. And get so upset telling me."
"You didn't make me tell you. I didn't have to but I wanted you to know why I reacted like I did. And yes I might have got upset but I'm alright now, really I am."

Tom didn't look convinced but saw he wasn't going to persuade her to stay. Reluctantly, he watched her walk into the kitchen to call Charlie and pick up her bag. "Then will you promise me you'll phone if you change your mind or can't settle? Any time in the night? I'll come and get you. Please, I can't bear thinking of you upset, on your own." Beth nodded. "Alright, but I'll be okay. You don't need to come with me" seeing him pick up his keys and nudge Tess awake. "Yes I do. And Tess can do with a walk; it's just the distance she likes, to your house and back."
Beth knew he wouldn't give in and followed him into the hall. "Is it still raining?"
"No, the sky's clear, the stars are out."

He locked the door behind him and walked close beside her, down the road to the corner and across to her house. She let herself and Charlie in, turning to Tom in the doorway.
"Thank you. I can't say I feel better right this minute, I feel a wreck. But I'll be alright in the morning."
He forced himself to simply look down at her tired, pale face. Don't touch her, leave her. But it went against all his instincts.
"Try and get some sleep. But phone me if you want to. Normal walk tomorrow?" Beth nodded and bent down to stroke Tess. "I'll call round to you. Good night."

The door closed and Tom and Tess walked slowly home.

CHAPTER 11

The weekend passed quietly. Beth had tossed and turned that night, as she had known she would; eventually getting up just before three to go downstairs and make a cup of tea. She fell asleep on the sofa, waking four hours later with Charlie nudging her arm. She had done a bit of housework and shopping in the morning, then sat in the garden in the afternoon, falling asleep on the sun lounger and waking up two hours later.

The weather was clear and sunny again that evening and they strolled along the water's edge, Charlie diving in and out of the small waves and even Tess paddling through the shallows. The shingle was just dry enough to sit on and they made their way up the beach to sit down; Tess curling up beside Tom, Charlie bringing Beth a piece of driftwood for her to throw.

She needed to say it. "Tom. What I told you. I don't want it to be the elephant in the room." She looked at him, eyes clear and green again today.
"You mean you don't want it to be something thought about but never mentioned?" There was a question in his hazel eyes. Beth nodded.
"I don't mean I want to talk about it a lot, I don't. Not at all. But Carol and Gina convinced me it's not a guilty secret; at least, not my guilty secret. I don't tell anyone but that's just because it's private. Not because I'm ashamed. Does that make sense?"
"Of course. And of course they're right. You were an innocent victim, not much more than a child."

He paused. "Did you ever have counselling?" She shook her head.
"No, I never wanted to. I just wanted to get on with life, not rake it all up, going over and over it with a stranger. I kept busy, managed it in my own way." By keeping men at bay, ignoring her own needs, Tom thought with sadness, but didn't say it.
"But what I'm trying to say, badly, is that you don't need to be scared of mentioning it, don't think you've put your foot in it if you do say something. Gina hardly ever refers to it, only if I mention it first. But Carol does sometimes. She thinks it's healthier to talk about things, says it's nothing to be ashamed of."
"She's right."
Beth nodded. "I know. But I worry that she will say something in front of

others, like Frances, or April and Sue. Even worse, suppose she said something in front of Nell?" She turned her lovely face towards him, anguish in her green eyes.

He felt a surge of anger towards the boy who had hurt her so much, caused so much damage. He forced himself to take a deep breath to calm down.
"Beth, if it worries you, you should tell Nell. Better to hear it from you than someone else. And she's an adult, she'll cope." Beth didn't look convinced.
"But she'll be devastated." Her mouth was tense and strained, a shadow in her eyes.
"Yes, of course she will. But she's strong, and she's got Will, from what you say. Think about it at least?"
Beth took a shaky breath and nodded. "Maybe. I'm always telling Carol to be careful in front of Nell but perhaps it would be better." Charlie ran up to her then, shaking sea water all over them both and Beth laughed and jumped to her feet.
"Horrid dog! Come on, time for home."

Tom slowly got to his feet, watching her as she brushed the sand off her denim skirt and slipped her feet into her sandals. They walked back in companionable silence; Beth relieved at clearing the air, Tom struggling to cope with the fact he had so much to say but didn't know how to say it.

The days flew by. School was hectic with assessments and reports and planning the summer fete. Church was busy with organising the auction of promises. An increase in day trippers meant longer queues in the shops and crowds to weave through on the pavements and the beach path. When Beth arrived at the charity shop on Wednesday, she had to fight her way through to the back, where Gina was pricing up garments.

But soon both women were called out to the shop to serve and were kept busy until a lull at half past four. Just as they sat down to grab a quick cup of coffee, June Jacobs bustled into the shop, eyes gleaming and jaw open. "You'll never guess."
"No, but I don't suppose we need to." Sue replied, with sarcasm that was wasted on the older women.
"There's been another robbery." Saliva flew from June's mouth and Beth recoiled quickly, her heart thudding.

"Not another death?" She could hardly say the words. Around her were gasps of shock.

"No." June sounded almost disappointed. "But they were caught in the act!" That was obviously almost as exciting as a murder.

"Sit down, June. You must have had a shock." April stood up and urged her to her chair. "Sue, make June a cup of tea, two sugars."

"Well, yes, of course." June blinked, missing the irony in April's comments. She sat down heavily.

"So where? And when?" April queried.

"Highfield Lane, Monkton. The big house at the end, white, kind of farm gates at the entrance. I don't know who lives there."

"The Burwell's." Gina's quiet voice replied.

"Ah. What do they do?" June swivelled to look at Gina, who was standing behind the counter, calm and collected in navy linen trousers and a white top.

"He's an accountant; she's a lawyer in Southampton."

"Well. Whatever they do "June sniffed, envious of high paying, high powered jobs "they were out but the neighbour behind them was sunbathing in her garden. She saw two men climbing through the utility window. Well, my friend said it was the utility window. Her daughter cleans for the house next door and she's been in the house and said it was. So the neighbour calls the police and a few minutes later there's sirens and commotion and they're caught in the act."

She sat back triumphantly, with the air of one who had caught the miscreants personally. Sue handed her a cup of tea.

"So, burglaries solved." She stated with satisfaction before taking a sip and grimacing. "I don't take sugar, dear."

"So who were they? The burglars?" Sue asked.

June shook her head, rigid grey curls unmoving, and bit her lip, unwilling to admit to the limit of her inside knowledge. "I don't know yet." She frowned, mouth turning down, her moment of glory over.

"Well, thank goodness they've been caught." April said briskly. "Now perhaps justice will be done for poor Melissa and we can all get back to normal."

But the two youths arrested for breaking and entering the five houses admitted to four of them, but denied robbing Melissa's. One boy was local, the other from Southampton, and they had no connection to the building firm, the estate agency or any other business in Bride's Bay.

The euphoria at their arrest faded as fast as it had arisen. Grace had been taken to the police station, accompanied by Mark, but had returned distraught. The police had interviewed the youths for twenty four hours and were detaining them on the four burglary charges, but not Melissa's murder. Carol filled Gina and Beth in as they sat at their usual table in the window on Thursday evening. It was her first evening out since her operation and she looked well.

"Maggie said Grace is so upset. She had thought, like all of us, that the police had caught whoever killed Melissa. But it seems not. The investigation into her death is still ongoing. They think someone else was responsible for it." Carol looked at them unhappily.

The three women were silent. Beth pushed her food around her plate, trying to quell her anxiety. A killer was still walking free. Or killers. The other two obviously felt the same as Gina pushed her plate away and poured more wine.

Carol tried to think logically. "But that means there must be two gangs robbing houses. How do we go from no break-ins around here to two gangs?" No one had the answer to that.
"And if there are two gangs" Carol continued, slowly "one of them wasn't violent, but the other is."
Out of the corner of her eye, Beth saw Gina suppressing a shiver.
"Gina, you can always stay with me, if you want?" Gina smiled at her gratefully.
"No, I'll be alright, but thank you. But you're welcome at mine?" She raised her perfect brows.
Beth also declined. But she wondered if later that night she would wish she had accepted.

Gina had an appointment next day and had told the two women she wouldn't be at flower arranging. "Can you check my arrangement for me? The peonies will be over by now, maybe the gypsophilla, but the rest should be fine" she had asked, as they were leaving Waves on Thursday evening.
"Of course" Beth nodded. "I'll see what I've got in the garden to replace them, or pick something up at Maisie's Blooms."

A quick hunt of her garden at lunchtime had provided some alliums in a delicate violet colour with white tips. She picked a bunch, also some greenery, and walked to church in plenty of time, planning to call into the gallery for a get well card for a colleague on the way. But the gallery was shut, a notice stuck to the inside window reading "Closed until further notice." She hesitated, wondering whether to call into Bryn Cards and Gifts but deciding to look in Emma's Gift shop the next day. She had a better selection.

She was a few minutes early for flower arranging but went in, putting her offerings down on the floor by Gina's arrangement and going into the flower room to gather a rubbish bag and secateurs. Gina had been right, the peonies were over, their soft petals wrinkled and brown at the edges. She pulled them out and dropped them into the bag, scattering papery brown crumbs on the floor. The gypsophilla also sprayed tiny specks of dry dust around her as she worked and she pulled their stems out too. The aquilegias and carnations were still pretty, but then carnations lasted for weeks in the cool. The ivy tumbling down was also still green and glossy. It wasn't too bad, she considered. She only needed to place the alliums in the gaps left by the peonies and add a bit more greenery between them.

Trimming an allium stem, she pushed it into the bare patch of oasis between the carnations. It wouldn't sink in and the stem bent and broke. Bother. This was always the problem, she thought, I waste as many flower stems as I use. Frances would be horrified. The thought of the other woman's scorn spurned her on to quickly dispose of the ruined stem and trim another one. She tried again and again it jammed and broke. Beth pushed the flowers away from the oasis and peered into the arrangement. All she could see was a patch of green oasis. She tried another stem in a different gap but that one resisted the oasis too, snapping near the base. Frances would be here any minute and she was running out of alliums.

She prodded and poked frantically in the arrangement, breaking bits of oasis off in her haste. If Frances saw that she would really be in trouble, remembering Frances's white faced fury with Ali. In a panic she pressed the oasis. Maybe it was too dry, which was why the stems wouldn't go in? But no, it was wet. She pressed again then halted. The oasis was rough and damp but under the broken, crumbled part she could feel something hard and smooth.

She scrabbled around, breaking off more bits of oasis, feeling more and more of the smooth, wet object. Putting her fingers around the damp, clammy surface she pulled it out. She was just holding it up, staring at it in horror, as Carol and Frances walked in and stared at her, wide eyed.

Carol reacted first. "Beth, Beth, what is it? What have you got?" The three women stared at the clear plastic bag, dripping with water, and at the contents.

Frances was white faced, eyes wide. "Don't open it. It's a chisel or something. And it's all…" Her voice shook as she stared at the object in Beth's hand in horror. Beth slumped down on a pew, holding the plastic bag at arm's length. Her hand shook as she looked down at the transparent bag, smeared with red, and at the hammer inside it.
"Beth, it's covered in blood." Frances's voice shook. Beth felt a wave of nausea, her chest burning as bile rose into her throat.

Carol had run to find Mark and Frances sat down heavily next to Beth. Neither woman spoke. Beth held her arm out as far as she could, her arm soon beginning to tremble with the effort. After what seemed hours Mark rushed in, skidding to a halt in front of her. "Beth, Beth my dear. Give it to me."
She needed no encouragement. Maggie appeared behind him and put her arm around her shoulders. "Come with me, Beth. I've phoned the police. Mark will deal with this. You too, Frances."

Shepherding the two women in front of her, she led them outside and round into the vicarage kitchen, where Carol was already making a pot of tea. How many times was she going to drink tea for shock? Beth thought hysterically.

Frances sat opposite her, her face almost transparent with horror. "What was it? What was it doing there? Why was it so bloody?" She looked at the others in confusion.
"Let's wait for the police." Carol replied calmly, picking up Frances's cold hand . She's bearing up better than Frances and me, Beth thought, trying to control her own shaking hands as she picked up her cup.

Police seemed to be everywhere. Questions and more questions. Beth answered in a daze. Frances left but Beth had to remain, going through it all again.

At last they seemed satisfied and said she could go for now. Go? Beth didn't think she could go anywhere. Her legs wouldn't move. No-one had said anything. But she knew. She had known from the moment she pulled the bag out of the arrangement and saw the red and brown smears. She had found the weapon that had killed Melissa.

Maggie urged Beth to stay for the night but she went with Carol. Maggie had enough to do and Carol wasn't going to let Beth go home alone. The police had warned them not to mention the discovery so Carol had sent a text to Tom from Beth's phone, explaining she wouldn't be walking that evening. Then Ken had gone round to collect Charlie and his food and bowl for the night. The police had called round again in the early evening with more questions. Then Ken had taken her to the station to sign her statement. They hadn't got back until nearly midnight. She hadn't expected to sleep but the drama of the week caught up with her and, after drinking the warm milk Carol had made her and snuggling under the soft duvet, Charlie by her side, she had felt her eyes closing and knew nothing more until the sun streaming through the thin curtains woke her in the morning.

"Oh my God. Beth!" Tom looked at her in horror as they made their way down the shingle to the water's edge the following evening. He sat down abruptly.

The police had phoned that afternoon to say they were certain it was the murder weapon and were just waiting for DNA test results to confirm it. But all indications suggested it was.

"Are you alright? What a shock, you must be..." His face turned to hers was shocked and worried.
"I'm fine, really." Beth interrupted. "Honestly. It was a shock finding it but I'm okay now. I stayed at Carol's last night. And now at least they might get further with the investigation. They've been talking to Gina today."
Tom raised his brows in query.
"She did the arrangement" explained Beth. "The one especially for Melissa's funeral. The one I" she faltered "the one I found the hammer in."

Yesterday had been a nightmare; questions, statements, checking statements. And she knew Gina had been through it all today. But she was alright, she reflected, just relieved that the murder weapon had been found and the police could act on it. She would have preferred someone else to have found it, obviously, but at least it was found.

Tom looked at her in amazement but realized she was telling the truth. Her face was so transparent; it was only too obvious when she was happy, scared, upset.

"But let's not talk about it. Tell me how Tess got on."

Tom had taken Tess to the vets the day before, worried about the dog's sight. One dog ailment led to talk of another and canine talk occupied them for half an hour, until they made their way back up the beach.

"Come in for a drink?" They had stopped at Tom's gate. Beth shrugged, nodding.

"Why not? Sunday tomorrow, a lie-in. Well, for as long as Charlie lets me, anyway."

She followed him into the kitchen as he opened the doors into the garden, the sweet scent of honeysuckle and roses drifting in. She leaned against the worktop as he took a bottle of wine out of the fridge and opened it. She was wearing a mint green cotton dress, the colour causing her tanned skin to glow and her eyes to shine a clear green with gold flecks. The dress was fitted at the waist, emphasising the soft curves of her chest and hips. The walk had been breezy and her hair tumbled around her face. Tom felt a tug at his heart and concentrated on pouring the wine to distract him from the urge to smooth back her hair and stroke that warm, scented skin.

He handed her a glass and motioned her to sit on the sofa by the open doors. It was smaller than the one in the living room and she was intensely aware of Tom's long, muscular jeans-clad leg close to hers, his tanned, golden haired arm stretching along the back of the sofa behind her. She shifted into the corner of the sofa, her knee the only part making contact.

But the icy cold drink relaxed her and she leant back with a sigh. "What a week. I keep thinking it can't get any worse and then it does. And Bride's Bay used to be so quiet and dull."

"I'm sure it will be again, once all this is over." Tom sipped his drink and looked at her.

"Did you think about telling Nell?" Beth nodded.

"Yes. And I will. But I'll wait until after her trip to the Cotswolds. She's so looking forward to it. And if she and Will are still an item after that, well, that will make it a bit easier." She looked down at her drink. "And I told Gina and Carol that you know" she added quietly.

"What did they say?"
"That it was better to be honest, no reason to keep it a secret, nothing to be ashamed of, all those things." "They're right. But you know that."
"I haven't told Carol I'm going to tell Nell yet; I feel a bit awkward, I don't want her thinking it's because I'm worried she will blab."
"Just say now Nell is an adult you think it's right that she should know." Beth nodded.
"Yes, I will. But I am worried about how she will take it. Nell, I mean."
"She's bound to be shocked and upset. She loves you and will be hurt for you. But she's a sensible girl, she'll be alright."
"I hope so." Beth sounded unconvinced. "Still, at least it will make her realise why I resist all her matchmaking efforts and she might stop."

Tom's eyebrows raised in query. She began to explain, smiling ruefully. "She always wants me to get out more, join social groups, meet people, by which she means men! She never believes me when I say I'm perfectly happy as I am." She paused. "When she was growing up she and her friends used to try and match-make me with their divorced dads. Some of their efforts weren't very subtle!
So at least it will make her realise why I've always resisted. And when she asks about old boyfriends, that sort of thing, it's difficult, so it will stop all of that. I don't like lying to her." She fell silent.

Tom looked at her. "What do you say when she asks?"
Beth shrugged. "I just say there was never anyone serious, I never met anyone special."
"And did you tell boyfriends about ..." he hesitated "about what happened?"
She looked at him, a surprised look in her beautiful green eyes.
"There weren't any boyfriends. How could there be? That's what I meant about lying. I made up a few boyfriends; I was very vague about them. But I hated being dishonest, having to remember what I'd said, and keeping secrets from her. So actually it will be a relief to tell her the truth."
Tom was amazed. "You never went out with anyone? Had no boyfriends, relationships?"
He couldn't believe what he was hearing, putting his glass down and leaning forward.

She shook her head. "I did go out with a couple of boys, well, three, in my teens. Just the one date with each of them. But it was never going to work, so I never saw them after the first date."

He rubbed his forehead to try and clear it. "And did you tell them, what happened I mean?"

She shook her head. "There was no point. I knew it would never work. As soon as they tried to touch me, kiss me, I panicked. I froze, and felt faint and sick. Well, you know. I just had to get away from them. I made excuses and they just gave me looks as though I was strange, weird. After those three dates I couldn't bear the thought of going through it again and I realised all I had to do was avoid dates, stay single. If I was asked out, I said I already had a boyfriend. It was easy. Easier to say that than have them realise I'm frigid, have something wrong with me. Better than being embarrassed and humiliated."

"No!" He couldn't help himself, bursting out with the denial. "Beth, no, that's not right. It wasn't you, it was him. There was nothing wrong with you. You weren't much more than a child and he terrified you, hurt you, but that doesn't mean there's something wrong with you. It was him, but he blamed you." He knew he was repeating himself, saying it badly. But he desperately needed to convince her.

Beth shrugged. "Well, it doesn't matter if he was right or not. The end result was the same. I couldn't bear being touched; I couldn't have a physical relationship. And I've got used to that, it's fine."

She felt a sharp stab as she said the last words, knowing they might have been true once but now caused her heart to ache for something that could never be. But he must never, ever know. Or even suspect.

"But Beth, that means you've denied yourself so much; love, romance, children, a home..." his voice faltered. She shook her head. "No I haven't. I've got a home, I love my little cottage. And a family in Nell, I've brought her up for the past ten years and she's like a daughter to me. And I've got good friends, Charlie. I live in a lovely part of the world with a job I love, no money worries, my health. Lots of people don't have those things."

Tom's head was still reeling with everything she had said.
"But did you never meet someone special, someone you wanted to be with? Didn't you ever fall in love?"
"No" she stated adamantly. "It could never work so I couldn't take the risk. I never let myself start to like anyone like that."

He didn't know what to say. He felt so angry and frustrated thinking of the lonely way she had lived but stifled his feelings, forcing himself to breathe slowly and calm down. He wanted desperately to tell her it wasn't too late; there was still time in her life for love and romance. He longed to convince her there was nothing wrong with her, that she had been misled into thinking there was, had been scarred emotionally. But he knew she wouldn't believe him. And even if she did, why should he think she would care? She wasn't interested in him romantically, whatever Gina had said. She saw him as a friend, a neighbour, nothing more. He felt totally helpless; his whole body aching with love for her that would never be returned.

She must have sensed his discomfort because she swallowed the last of her drink and stood up.
"Anyway, time we left. And like I said, I will tell Nell, as soon as she's back. Come on Charlie boy, time for home." She got up and carried her glass over to the sink, Tom watching her rigid back under the cotton dress.
"Thank you for the drink. Are you going tomorrow?" She was trying hard to talk normally, only the paleness of her face showing tension.

Tom nodded, his tongue sticking to the roof of his mouth.
"Yes. I've got a meeting with Ken before the service." He was mentally kicking himself for not knowing the right words to say, or the right actions. He was always so in control, on an even keel, but now he felt so helpless.
"Okay. Well, see you tomorrow then." She managed a smile and opened the front door. The sun had almost gone down but the evening was still warm. The breeze had dropped and only small ripples scattered the surface of the pink tinted sea. .

He watched her walk down the path, Charlie trotting at her side, so independent and self-contained, and his heart ached.

CHAPTER 12

Tom walked slowly back into the kitchen and poured himself another glass of wine, sitting with it at the kitchen table. Tess gazed up at him with her big soft eyes, cloudy with age. His chest was heavy; he felt useless and overwhelmed. What was he going to do? Gina had implied Beth wanted him to get closer but she had given him no indication of that. So how on earth did you get someone to fall in love with you? He couldn't imagine her ever believing there was nothing wrong with her; the belief was too firmly entrenched. Besides, her fear of anything physical was so great, remembering the fear in her eyes at the simple kiss. He couldn't imagine her ever trusting him enough to give him a chance to love and care for her. His life had always been planned, organised, had worked out exactly as he wanted but now he was out of his depth. Running his fingers through his hair, he realised had absolutely no idea what to do, apart from continue with their friendship and gradually gain her trust. Then maybe that friendship would turn to love. He had never felt like this about anyone before, not even Delia. And instead of rejoicing in the greatest happiness in his life, the greatest joy, he felt bleak and helpless.

He didn't sleep much that night, tossing and turning. He watched the hours ticking by, imagining her lying in her own bed; alone, always alone. Finally, he fell asleep.

He awoke two hours later needing the toilet, with a dry mouth, head pounding and heart heavy. For a moment he was dazed, wondering why. Then he remembered and groaned as he swung long legs out of bed and staggered to the bathroom. Only five fifty. But he wasn't going to get any more sleep. Washing quickly and dressing, he went slowly downstairs. He would take Tess for a walk on the beach.

The sky was a pale blue, streaked with pink and apricot. A slight breeze blew and wisps of snowy white cloud drifted across. It was going to be a beautiful day. He sat on the shingle and gazed out to sea, already boats bobbed over by the island and a ferry steamed across from Portsmouth.

What could he do? He could phone Gina and talk to her about it. She would be calm, rational; she would listen and advise. Or would she? She wouldn't gossip about Beth, and she wouldn't tell him what to do. Besides, she had enough to worry her at the moment. Plus this was between him and Beth. He had to sort it out with her, not through a third party. And he would sort it. What had Gina said when he had asked her if the reasons for Beth's distance were resolvable? She had said it depended how much he wanted to resolve them. Well, he certainly wanted to; he had never in his life wanted anything more. Her voice echoed in his head "Then don't give up." Staring bleakly at the island across the water, he had a sudden urge to get away for a couple of days, think things through and work out how best to tackle this. And maybe absence would make the heart grow fonder; maybe she would miss him while he was away and begin to have some feelings for him. It was worth a try.

He stood up and stretched, his head clearer and mind calmer. It would be alright. He wasn't giving up.

Gossip and speculation reached fever point again. The strong police presence in the little town fuelled the unease. An incident centre was set up in a hall for interviews, with teams working all day. It seemed unreal. Beth was questioned again, also Gina, Maggie, Carol, Frances and Ali and the other flower arrangers. Mark and the church wardens were interviewed several times. Who had access to the church? Were the doors kept locked? Who had keys? Where were the keys kept? Who would know that? On and on and on. Gina looked shattered; her lovely face drawn with worry and exhaustion, another victim of lack of sleep.

The fact the murder weapon was found in her flower arrangement had hit her hard and she found it difficult to face people. Carol took matters into her own hands one day, worry about Gina making her unusually reckless. She text Beth on the Wednesday evening, asking her to go round the following afternoon for coffee and a chat; mutual support, as she put it. Now her health scare was over and Ken's agency in the clear, she could worry about others and support them, something she was very good at.

Beth arrived a few minutes late and walked into the conservatory to see Ali, Francis, Gina and Grace already seated. She looked at Gina enquiringly and the other woman raised her eyebrows, shrugging. The only seat left was by Ali so Beth sank down next to her, smiling. Carol came in, carrying a tray with glasses and a large jug of pink coloured water with bits of fruit and ice cubes floating on the top.

"Non-alcoholic cocktails" she informed them, setting the tray down on the cane table next to various bowls of nibbles. "Although the alcohol is over there" nodding to a pine cupboard "if anyone wants to add a little something to theirs." Beth could have done with a large splash of gin but resisted, seeing to her regret that no one else was taking Carol up on the offer.

"Now" Carol announced, sitting down opposite Beth and Ali, looking around the group at the curious faces.
"I thought it might be a good idea to get our heads together, clear the air a bit. Just to see if we can come up with any way that hammer could have got there."

Carol had no problem with plain speaking, Beth thought with amusement.
"But, surely that's a matter for the police?" Grace looked puzzled. "I mean, don't get me wrong Carol, I'm very grateful you want to help, but they're investigating, shouldn't we just leave it to them?"
Gina and Francis were nodding agreement. Ali didn't say anything, sitting like a rabbit caught in a car's headlamps.
"Yes, of course" Carol agreed. "But we are here all the time, we know who goes in and out of church, we'd notice a stranger going in, poking around. Wouldn't we?" There were more nods of agreement.
"Plus we know it wasn't there on Tuesday the 9th, because Gina did the arrangement that day. But it was there on Friday the 26th. So who had anything to do with the arrangement between those two dates? Can we pin it down more?" She gazed around at the bemused faces.

Frances spoke up. "I checked the flowers the week after the funeral, that would be the Friday the19th?
I only topped up the water, the flowers were fine; but I would swear they hadn't been touched since Gina arranged them." Carol was busy scribbling notes on a pad of paper, then looked up at Frances.
"But you didn't need to move any? So you wouldn't necessarily have seen anything under the oasis?"
Frances shook her head. "No. But you wouldn't see anything under the oasis anyway, unless you pulled it all out completely. Even if you change the flowers, you just pull the dead ones out and push the new ones in."
Beth nodded agreement. "Yes, that's right. I only found it because the flowers wouldn't go in properly and kept breaking." She cast a guilty look at Frances, anticipating a reprimand.
Carol nodded. "Okay. So, it wasn't there on 19th but it was on 26th. So we're narrowing it down."

"Haven't the police already asked all of this?" Grace spoke quietly, trying not to sound negative but feeling it would all have been investigated already. The women looked at each other.

"They asked when I did the arrangement" Gina confirmed.

"And they obviously know when I found the hammer" Beth added. "But Frances, do they know you checked them on the Friday before?" Frances shook her head.

"I wouldn't have thought so. At least, they didn't mention checking them to me"

The other women all nodded agreement.

"So they don't know the dates we do" Carol said slowly. "We ought to tell them." She looked around.

"But we're not telling them much, are we?" Gina commented. "Only that Frances checked them in between me doing the arrangement and Beth finding the hammer. And she didn't notice anything anyway." She looked apologetically at Frances. "Sorry Frances, I don't mean to sound negative." To her surprise the touchy woman gave her a smile.

"We can't make things up just to give them more information, Gina."

Carol was still writing. "Well, Ken and I will tell them about Frances checking them on the 19th anyway. Every bit of information could be useful. You'd have noticed at least if the arrangement had been messed with, wouldn't you?" she appealed to Frances, who nodded agreement. "So it does narrow it down to the week between the 19th and 26th at least. Did any of you see anyone else in the church that week, anyone messing with the arrangement?"

They were all certain they hadn't. Ali swallowed, speaking for the first time. "But Carol, there would have been loads of people there that week. There was the Sunday service and evensong. Plus the early morning prayer services every day. There was even a funeral on the Tuesday. The church is always open, anyone could have gone in at any time."

"I know" Carol admitted defeat. "I just thought someone might have seen something, or someone."

"It was a good idea." Grace smiled at the disappointed looking woman. "But so many people go in and out, and so many have stopped to admire the arrangements."

"But it would have taken time to take all the flowers out" said Gina slowly. "Then put the oasis back with the flowers in the same arrangement."

"Couldn't they have just picked up the whole piece of oasis?" asked Grace. Gina frowned.

"I don't think so. The flowers would all have fallen; they'd break, even fall out. Beth, did the arrangement look any different on the 26th?" Beth thought back, shaking her head.

"No, it still looked perfect, just like you'd done it. But quite a few flowers had gone over and needed removing."

No one could think of anything else and Carol topped up the glasses.

"Well, all we've managed to do is reduce the time to that week" she sighed. "But thank you all for coming. And you're right, Grace. Let's just hope and pray the police solve it soon."

Ali, Grace and Frances all left together but Carol gestured to Beth and Gina to stay seated.

She escorted the other three round the side of the house to the front gate then returned and sank down in her chair again, disappointment all over her face.

"Well, that was a waste of time. I'm adding rum to my punch. Anyone else?" Gina shook her head but Beth nodded, holding out her glass.

"Still, I hope it's cleared the air a bit and they're a bit easier on you now, Gina."

"Well, it's only really Frances. Poor Ali doesn't say anything. But Frances looks at me as though I must have put it there as I did the arrangement."

"She always looks disapproving. I feel guilty every time she looks at me, I'm always sure I've made some sort of flower arranging faux pas." Beth swigged at the large glass of punch and sighed. "That's better."

Carol looked at her curiously. "Not like you to hit the bottle, Beth. Are you alright?"

"I'm fine. Just tired. School's busy, the shops are busy, all this hanging over us. It's enough to turn anyone to drink." She kept her voice light. She had no intention of telling her friends about the scene with Tom, the scenes plural, come to that.

She knew they would both listen sympathetically and be upset for her. They wouldn't offer advice; well, Carol might, but Beth didn't want advice. Neither woman could fully understand her difficulty, although she knew Gina would come the closest. If Carol knew she had fallen for Tom she would both be so pleased for her; she had given up trying to match make but Beth knew she longed for both her and Gina to meet eligible men. Even though Gina was aware of how she felt for him, Beth couldn't talk about it to her, there was no point. Nothing could ever happen and that was that.

She hadn't spoken to Tom since the Saturday evening. He had been at church on Sunday but had left without staying for coffee, texting in the afternoon to say he was going to be away for a few days. She was relieved and devastated at the same time. Her head told her this was the way it was and to stop thinking about him. But her heart ached and she found herself crying for what could never be.

One person who was looking better these days was Barbara Salmon. Beth called in for some mince on the way home from Carol's and was surprised and relieved to see the pretty woman bustling about happily. "Beth, nice to see you. How are you?" Beth smiled, stated she was fine. Lied. She was getting good at this. "You're looking good, Barbara. Are things a bit better?" she asked cautiously, not wanting to pry.
But Barbara beamed back at her. "Oh Beth, yes, you wouldn't believe. They say it's an ill wind..."
Beth looked at her enquiringly.

Barbara leaned over the counter, conspiratorially. "Robert and Matthew. Robert was so relieved when it came out James Lamb had nothing to do with the burglaries, or those lads who work with him. He met up with James and they had a long talk about Matthew. James told him he thought he should let Matthew have a go at an apprenticeship as a builder, just for a year, see how it goes. He said Matthew would probably hate working out in all weathers, the early starts and low pay. And if he did hate it, he could leave whenever he wanted. Robert saw the sense in that. He still wants him to work in the business but has agreed he can give the building a try after his exams, see how he gets on. Of course he's hoping he will hate it and leave."
She laughed and Beth saw the relief on her face. For a moment her own spirits lifted.

"Oh Barbara, that's wonderful. What does Matthew say?"
"He's over the moon. He says he'll work so hard, make a go of it, that it will all work out. I told him, Dad's meeting you half way here; letting you

have a go, so don't go in all guns blazing that you will never be a butcher. Go along with him that you're just trying it out for a year. If it turns out it is what he wants to do for ever, then hopefully after a year Robert will accept that."

"That sounds perfect."

"And Hannah has made Robert's day. She said if Matthew isn't going to work for him, maybe she will, then the business will be hers one day and she'll make a fortune." Beth laughed.

"So what happened to the nail bar or human rights lawyer?"

"Well, she's not planning on actually doing any butchering, she says she will just pay others to do it and enjoy all the profits! So she'll just spend money at the nail bar instead of working in it!"

Beth laughed. "That's one feisty girl you've got there!" Barbara smiled back, making a face.

"I wonder who she gets that from?"

The charity shop was busy again the next day but Gina and Beth spent most of their time pricing goods in the back room. Beth was aware of Gina looking at her curiously from time to time. Unwilling to answer any awkward questions, she kept the conversation going for most of the afternoon; chatting about school, about Nell, about Charlie, anything but Tom. If Gina realised one subject was being omitted from Beth's prattle, she was too thoughtful to comment on it. Sue Carter had no such compunction however, turning to Beth as she handed round mugs of tea. "I haven't seen Tom this week, Beth. He wasn't at Tea and Chat on Monday either. Is he alright?"

"He's gone away for a few days. I don't know where he's gone, or when he'll be back."

She answered calmly, trying to look nonchalant. But even saying the words caused a stab of pain. How she missed him, and how she had no right to, she thought bleakly.

But walking home along the seafront after the usual Thursday evening meal with Gina and Carol, her stomach lurched with pleasure as she saw the dark grey estate parked on his drive. The front windows were open to the scented night air, throwing out a warm pool of light. Just keep busy, she told herself, keep busy and don't think.

Flower arranging was on Beth's mind the next morning, as soon as she woke and realised it was Friday. Fortunately three and four years olds were not party to the thoughts going through their nursery nurse's head, and she was distracted from the morbid images by their demands and actions. Now and then the memory of pulling that plastic bag, stained and heavy with blood soaked contents, crashed into her head.

She really didn't want to go back into the church that afternoon to see the pedestal and recall its gruesome contents. But Grace had phoned the night before, asking if she and Carol would like to go round for a cup of tea after flower arranging. She would just concentrate on that.

But in the event it was fine. Frances was already there, standing beside three empty pedestals with their bare black metal supports and shiny black tops.

"I thought we needed a fresh start." She nodded towards them. "I've cleared them all out, given them a good wash and polish. The oasis is soaking. And I've brought all fresh flowers." She pointed to a table nearby, covered in bright blooms and fresh green foliage. "I hope Gina doesn't mind though? I did her arrangement as well."

As usual the woman's speech was staccato, her actions jerky. But there was a question in her voice when she mentioned Gina's arrangements and Beth felt a flood of warmth towards the woman. She usually rode rough shod over anyone's feelings. But it had been thoughtful to remove all traces of last week's nightmare and have a fresh start. Frances had never been close to any of the women, with the possible exception of Ali, but Beth felt a new respect for her. Maybe she wasn't so prickly after all, just shy.

Beth shook her head. "Of course she won't mind. And what beautiful flowers."
She looked appreciatively at the piles of stocks, pinks, aquilegias, alliums, choisya, lilies, ivy and ferns.
Frances looked gratified. "Well, I bought the lilies. And those" nodding to the pinks "are from Tom's garden but the rest are from mine. I grew the aquilegias from seed."
"Oh Frances!" Beth clapped her hand to her head. "I've got a load of yoghurt pots for you. I took some into school today for the children but I kept a pile behind for you, I meant to bring them."

Beth had two boxes of recycling in her back garden; one collected by the council weekly, the other she recycled herself, taking the items to school for

junk modelling. But she always kept some plastic pots back for Frances, knowing she made use of them for her seedlings.
"It doesn't matter, bring them on Sunday." Frances turned away as Gina and Carol walked through the door. "Gina, I hope you don't mind...."

The afternoon passed peacefully. By four o'clock the church boasted new arrangements in blues, purples and white by the altar, by the font and in the Lady Chapel. Frances stood back, a pleased expression on her face. "There. Can't beat fresh flowers." Gina straightened from sweeping the floor, agreeing.
"Do you know, St Andrew's in Ramsfield have started using faux flowers? They say it's so much cheaper.
Plus they don't have the man power to do fresh flowers every week. They just use fresh for celebrations and special occasions." Frances sniffed.
"That will never happen here." Gina and Beth exchanged a smile. How true, while Frances was around.

Carol caught Beth's and Gina's arms as they walked out into the warm sunshine, blinking after the gloom of the church. "Are you both coming to Grace's for a cup of tea?" Gina shook her head.
"I can't. I told her I'd have liked to but Robert is phoning in a bit. He and Emma are off to New York for a few days tomorrow, they've got to be at the airport at some unearthly hour so they're staying the night there. He's phoning before they set off to the hotel."
"Aaah" Carol looked pleased. "That's nice. Is it serious then, him and Emma, do you think?" she asked hopefully. "It would be lovely if it was. You like her, don't you?"
Gina laughed. "Carol, they're going on holiday for a few days. That's all."
"There are nice jewellery shops in New York." Carol wasn't giving up.
"I'm sure there are. Maybe he'll bring me a nice piece back." Gina replied with a smile, deliberately misunderstanding.

Beth laughed. "Give up Carol. Perhaps Nell and Robert will both settle down one day and provide us with babies to dote on, but for now we make do with yours!" And they did. Carol's grandchildren, four year old Florence and seven month old Noah were gorgeous and Beth and Gina had seen them regularly since they had been born, enjoying watching them grow up.

Florence was a serious, dark eyed, dark haired little girl, quiet and reserved until she got to know people. Her baby brother Noah was a blue eyed red head with a cheeky smile, into everything, just as his mother and uncle had been, according to their proud granny.

She and Carol walked down the road, crossing over to Melissa's house; Grace's now, for a while.
Grace opened the front door, welcoming them with a wide smile so like her sister's.
"Come in, come in. I'm glad you could make it. Let's go through to the kitchen. Or the garden?"
"The garden" Carol said promptly. "Let's make the most of the weather. It could be raining tomorrow."

She and Beth wandered around the garden then settled down at a small table on the patio. Grace had placed a tea tray with cups and saucers, milk jug and teapot on it. A moment later she reappeared with a plate containing a luscious looking coffee and walnut cake.
"Now" she started pouring tea. "How are you two?"
Carol was the first to answer. "We're fine, thank you. But what about you? How are you? Any developments?"
No polite small talk for Carol, thought Beth in amusement, straight to the nitty gritty. Grace shook her head. "Not as far as I know. They still don't know if it was a bungled burglary, poor Melissa disturbing them and getting.... well, you know. Or if it was deliberate."

Carol looked shocked. "You mean, they meant to kill her? It was planned?" Beth was as stunned as her friend.
Grace shrugged. "They're thinking of the hammer. It could be it was taken to use to break in with, but they didn't force their way in, a key had been used. So why take a hammer to break in if you have a key? Which makes them think they took it with them intending to..." her voice faltered. "I keep saying "them" but the police have no idea if it was a gang or one person. Nothing was found, not even a hair. They'd cleaned up after themselves thoroughly." Her lovely face was strained and she angrily rubbed her eyes.

"How did they have a key?" Beth asked, in an attempt to distract the woman opposite from thoughts of the murder scene. Grace rummaged in her pocket for a tissue, wiping her face before answering.
"It was a spare one, it was kept under a loose brick on the wall; you know the wall with the steps leading to the lawn?"

She looked more composed now.

"So someone would have to have known it was kept there." Beth felt sick. "That means someone local."

"Did you know the Thomson's kept a spare key there?" Carol asked Beth. She shook her head.

"Nor did I." Beth could almost see the wheels turning in her friend's head as she thought about it.

"Well, someone did. But as I say, they don't know whether it was used to gain entry for robbery or...not. The fact Melissa was out that evening suggests they thought the house would be empty. Maybe she did come back earlier than they expected and disturbed them.... but that still doesn't really explain the hammer. And they could have just run off, no need to..." She gulped and picked up her cup, taking a swallow to collect herself. "So now the police keep asking if she had any enemies, if there could be anyone with a grudge. They're going into everyone in her past, Neville, ex boyfriends, but I can't think of anyone who disliked her." She looked up at the two women, eyes swimming with tears.

"She was lovely, inside and out. No one ever had any cause to hate her enough to want to... sorry."

Carol patted her hand. "We know. She endeared herself to everyone here the moment she arrived."

Well, not quite, thought Beth; remembering Ali's furious white face when she had seen Julian gazing admiringly after Melissa. And Maggie had made a few barbed comments about the amount of Mark's time she took up. That surprising scene in the church kitchen flashed through her head. Even Carol had complained to her once that Melissa was always in Ken's office, asking about property to buy in the area if she decided to settle there when her lease was up. But resenting her effect on men was one thing, being jealous at the attention she received from one's husband was a normal human reaction. But no-one would murder her because of it, surely?

With a lurch of her stomach Beth thought of the rumour that had been circulating in the town that week. Ali had gone to stay with her sister for a while, saying she needed a break after all the shocking events. No-one was surprised, knowing her to be highly strung and nervy. But Julian had also disappeared. The gallery was closed, blinds pulled down. Rose Evans had said he was selling it, though if he was; it wasn't through Ken's agency.

Could Ali have been driven to attacking Melissa, overcome by jealousy and anger? Immediately Beth scolded herself. No, no, it was ridiculous. She felt ashamed of herself for even thinking about her friends and neighbours like that.

Grace obviously wanted to change the subject and Beth asked her about her immediate plans.

"I'm going to stay for now. The police said I could use the studio again so I've cleared Melissa's art things out into a spare bedroom and closed the door on them, for now. I've bought a sofa and some chairs and stuff and made it back into a living room. I'll show you in a bit. Mark and some friends of his helped; they pulled up the vinyl and got rid of it." She shivered violently. "It's still a bit bare in there and I don't use it much. But I like Bride's Bay and I can work here. I'm making a bedroom into a dark room and will think about some work, sometime." Her voice trailed off then she shook herself, continuing. "So I plan to stay for a couple of months and think what I want to do. I might go back to London, but I'm a bit tired of the noise and crowds there. Plus I can get there easily from here when I need to. And I've enjoyed being by the sea, in a small town. Melissa thought it was right for her, so maybe it will be right for me. Who knows?" She looked at them with a shrug and a smile.

"Well, if you decide to stay, we will all be very pleased. But in the meantime, anything you need, you know where we are. And if you are looking for things to do…"
"Carol" warned Beth. "I know, I'm just saying" indignantly "and sometimes it's better to keep busy."

Conversation became more general and at last Beth and Carol stood up to leave.
"Come and look at the living room before you go." Grace carried the tea things back into the kitchen then led the way down the hall and into the old studio.
"Grace! This is lovely!" Beth looked around in delight.

Grace evidently had the same talent for style as Melissa had shown. The living room was now cosy and welcoming. A large duck egg blue sofa stood on the parquet floor together with two wingback chairs in a cream, taupe and duck egg blue tartan, arranged around a low oak coffee table. A console table stood against the wall with a vase of flowers on it and piles of magazines.

A small light oak dining table and four chairs stood at the other end of the room. Billowing cream curtains framed the windows. There were no pictures or ornaments but Grace had placed a large vase of roses on the table and photographs on the fireplaces.

Beth walked over to look at them. They were all Grace's own work; a couple of landscapes, a seascape and a photo of a floral arrangement. She looked closer. "That's the one Gina did for Melissa's funeral, isn't it?"
Grace walked over to stand beside her, nodding. "Yes, I loved it. And Melissa would have too. It seemed right to have it in here; a kind of memorial to her, without meaning to sound morbid."
"It does" agreed Beth, gazing at the pastel pinks and lemons, contrasting with the vibrant greens.

She looked around again. "You've certainly made it homely."
Grace shrugged. "It's a beautiful room, lovely proportions and original features. Hard to get it wrong, really."
"Don't be so modest" Carol laughed. "It's stunning. And we hope you stay here, even if not in this house.
But remember what I said, if you need anything or want to get involved in anything..."
"Carol!" Beth grabbed her arm and pulled her back into the hall, opening the front door.
"Thanks for the tea and cake, Grace. See you on Sunday?"
Grace agreed and waved goodbye as the two women walked down the path.

Beth walked home along the seafront, reflecting on the conversation. How awful to think Melissa may have been targeted. She shivered, feeling vulnerable and scared. She wished Tom was there, solid and reassuring beside her. But no, she told herself, don't think about Tom. Forget him. Think about anything but him; think of Nell, school, Charlie, holidays.

The school holidays were looming and Beth had no plans. She would talk to Gina about it; see if she fancied going away for a few days. Knowing how nervous her friend had been with all the burglaries, she guessed she would jump at the chance. It was a good idea. They could get away from Monkton and Bride's Bay; away from crime and suspicion, away from unhappy friends and arguments, away from Tom. Then she could forget about him when he was miles away.

But the thought of being away from him, from his kind hazel eyes and lopsided smile, the thick floppy hair she longed to push out of his eyes, his tall, muscular body and warm voice, hit her like a bullet.
A pain swept through her, a physical ache. It was too late. She already knew what it felt like to be held tightly in his arms. She knew the smell of him, the sound of his deep voice, the feel of his fingers stroking her hair. How was she ever going to forget that?

CHAPTER 13

Beth woke up early on Saturday morning. The sun streamed through the window. What was she going to do today?

She needed some shopping but didn't want to do it locally; there was too much chance of bumping into Tom. She knew his Saturday morning routine was to stroll into town, potter around the shops and have a coffee in one of the coffee shops or at the hotel. She knew what she would do. She would put Charlie in the car and drive out to Portchester. She could take Charlie for a good walk then do a bit of shopping. Maybe have a pub lunch somewhere. Then this afternoon she would do some gardening.

She dressed quickly and ran lightly downstairs, feeling better for having planned her day. She sat at the kitchen table, gazing out into the garden, absentmindedly eating toast and marmalade and sipping her tea. Yes, the vegetable patch would definitely go. She would replace it with another border. Maybe seasonal bulbs? It would keep her occupied planning it, then planting it up. And maybe she would look at evening classes for September. Working with young children was fun, exhausting, rewarding, but not exactly intellectually stimulating. Or perhaps she would join the reading group at the library?

Thinking of books reminded her she still had Tom's Ian Rankin. She had finished it but hadn't given it back. She hated it herself when she lent someone a book and it wasn't returned. Would he be annoyed? But no, Tom rarely, if ever, seemed annoyed. The only time she could recall him even sounding irritated had been the day Nell had been startled when Frances had appeared in his garden. Her throat ached as an image of his warm, open face came into her head. He was calm, calm and reassuring. Reliable, honest, kind and considerate. And attractive.

She sighed and put the cup down as she thought of his arms around her, his hands stroking her hair. Why was life so unfair?
Why couldn't she be a normal, ordinary woman? And why did this have to happen now? She had always known she would stay single and had been happy with her life; content with her job, enjoying the companionship of her friends. Now she was aching for something she could never have.

She sighed again and stood up to tidy away the dishes. It was time to stop moping and get on with the day. Get on with life. She locked the back door and gathered together the things she needed, then called to Charlie. He seemed to approve, jumping happily into the car and settling down on the back seat.

The morning went as planned. Traffic was light and they arrived in Portchester in just under half an hour. She parked in the town centre then set off to walk down to the castle and the church, Charlie trotting happily alongside despite being on a lead. They went to the castle first, strolling around the grounds and she admired, as ever, the amazing view over Portsmouth and the Solent. Today the sky was a deep blue, as blue as any she had seen in the Mediterranean. The forts stood out, grey and invincible, and the Spinnaker tower soared into the cloudless sky, a white sail proud and strong. Sailing boats and ships were scattered on the sparkling waters of the Solent, like toys on a boating pond. A large car ferry ploughed its way to France, toy figures standing on its decks. Across the water she could see the buildings, trees, chimneys, spires of the island.

She remembered Tom asking her which church he could see, leaning into her to point it out. She could still feel his hands on her shoulders, burning her skin through her top, his warm breath on her cheek; feel his solid chest against her back. Tears filled her eyes and she angrily brushed them away, telling herself fiercely to look at something else. She turned to gaze down the coast, at the buildings she recognised as being part of Bride's Bay. Down there somewhere was her little cottage, her garden, the church and school, her friends and neighbours, her life. All going on without her. And it was home. No matter how painful it would be, living near Tom and loving him so much, she wouldn't move, couldn't move. Somehow she would have to find the strength to cope. She looked over the velvety emerald grass to St Mary's church and had a sudden yearning to go into the old, stone building, to sit where hundreds, thousands of people had sat before; in joy, pain, fear, love.

She was just one more person, no different. She walked slowly over to the graveyard and down the path to the church entrance, tying Charlie's lead up while she went into the cool dark of the old building. As usual, the peace and quiet acted like a balm on her troubled thoughts and she sat for a moment, eyes closed, praying for the courage to accept what she couldn't have, and the strength to cope with it. She could have stayed there longer but thought of Charlie waiting patiently outside. Or probably impatiently.

Getting stiffly to her feet, she walked slowly outside, her heart still aching but feeling calmer and more resigned to her life.

She strolled back into the town centre, admiring the beautiful old houses on the way, then enjoyed mooching around several shops; buying wool at the haberdashery, planning to crochet a throw for Nell's flat; then calling into the deli to treat herself to some cheeses, cold meats and olives. She had even remembered to take a cool bag with a freezer pack in it, to keep the delicacies she bought chilled until she got home. Shopping finished, she loaded the bags and Charlie into the car and drove out of the car park, heading for home, an eye out for a pub to stop at for lunch on the way.

She found one after ten minutes, a pub she had been to with Gina and Carol, knowing it had a large, dog friendly garden. Strolling to a table on the edge of the garden, she sat down in the shade of a parasol, Charlie panting at her feet. Taking a bottle of water and a small dish out of her bag, she poured Charlie a drink and placed it on the grass. The dog sorted, she studied the menu, ordering a brie and bacon panini and large lime and soda from the pretty young waitress then sat back to enjoy the peace of the pub garden. It was early for lunch and only two other tables were taken; a young couple with a sleeping baby in a buggy at one and an elderly couple at the other.

Beth gazed at the couple. The elderly man was hovering over the woman; he was small and slight with light brown wispy hair, dressed in greyish trousers with a belt and a checked shirt. She was looking up at him, laughing; thick hair haloing her head in white waves, her figure stout in a pale blue summer dress, feet comfortably shod in sturdy cream sandals. Beth felt a sharp stab of envy. The way he hovered protectively, the expression on her lined face as she smiled up at him, both spoke of mutual love and respect. It was such an ordinary scene, just an ordinary couple out for a pub lunch in the sunshine. But one she would never know; growing old with a soulmate, knowing the other as well as yourself, sharing a life and a history. Growing old with Tom. Her throat closed on an aching lump and she looked away.

Just like she had never known the beginning of a shared life, she thought, gazing now at the young couple. They were poring over something on the table between them, the menu? Long blonde hair touched short, dark, crisp waves.

The baby in the buggy was chubby legged, chubby cheeked, legs spread froglike, feet bare, stomach rising and falling in a navy and white striped short sleeved bodysuit. Beth could see fair fuzzy hair, full pouting lips. She had spent plenty of time with toddlers, primary age children, even teens when she had taken on Nell. And of course she remembered Nell as a baby; a blonde angel, soft curls and big blue eyes. But she had never held her own child. She had never sat in the quiet of the night cradling the heavy weight of a sleeping baby, inhaling that milky smell, cuddling the warm soft body, feeling and hearing baby breaths, gazing down at perfect pink lips, kissing a soft downy head. Her arms seemed to ache for the child she had never borne, never held.

She jumped as the waitress appeared at her side, her footsteps silent on the grass. Her panini had arrived, stopping her reverie. Just as well. Regrets would get her nowhere. Her life was as it was, stop regretting what you haven't had, hankering after what you'll never have, she chided herself, cutting into the panini and watching the cheese ooze out, hot and delicious. Count your blessings. This introspection wasn't like her, this sadness deep inside, a yearning for something impossible. But she had never been in love before. And it hurt. Who was it who had said "Tis better to have loved and lost than never to have loved at all?" But she hadn't loved and lost. How could you lose something you had never had? But she had loved. And she wished with all her heart she hadn't. Whoever had said it, they were wrong. She had been fine before, settled and content. Now she was hurting. Hurting and unhappy. She finished the panini and drink and gathered up Charlie's bowl, tipping the left over water on the grass. The elderly couple had gone but the young couple still sat, eating and drinking, while the baby continued to sleep, shaded by a parasol, under the warm sun.

She drove home, putting music on as a distraction. The CD that played was Lana Del Ray. No, not right for her mood, not right at all. She changed it for Amy Macdonald. That was better. Except Amy MacDonald made her think of Scotland, and Tom talking about Rebus. Was everything going to remind her of Tom? Crossly she pressed the button, changing the CD to Train and forcing herself to think about Nell, school, holidays, anything but Tom, as she drove home.

She was in a better mood by the time she pulled up outside her cottage and went indoors, checking the doormat for letters and the phone for messages. There was nothing.

She went into the living room, immediately feeling the heat that had built up within the old cottage walls and raised the sash window slightly. Then went into the kitchen and flung open one of the French doors into the garden. She would take a cool drink outside with her and do some gardening, keep busy, burn off some of the calories from all that cheese in the panini.

The garden was half in shade, half in sun. She began at the end in shadow and spent a happy forty minutes weeding the vegetable plot and picking some carrots for the next day. Then moved to the trellis and tidied up the clematis and winter jasmine that smothered it, trimming parts and threading stems through the lattice.

Charlie lay on the grass watching her as she pottered. She should have changed, she thought ruefully, brushing bits of green off her skirt, glancing at her watch. Only quarter to four. Now what? She could refill her glass, sit on the swing and relax, but was reluctant to do that, knowing she would probably nod off then wouldn't sleep that night. And it was hard to count her blessings at night; when a lack of distractions let thoughts and memories flood her head. Where could she go? Yes, she knew. She would walk round to Frances's with the yoghurt pots. If she wasn't in, she would carry on to the local corner shop, buy a gardening magazine and take it home to read. Charlie panted in the shade, looking as though he would prefer to stay put stretched out on the lawn, but followed her into the kitchen to have his lead put on. They walked down the road and turned into Frances's road, parallel to Beth's, and she knocked at the door. Frances was in. She looked surprised to see Beth but invited her inside, through the narrow hall and into the kitchen.

"You needn't have made a special trip. They could have waited until tomorrow."
"I was passing anyway. So I thought I would bring them, call in on the off chance you were here."
Beth stood at the window, gazing out at Frances's garden. It wasn't as long as hers but was a riot of colour.

"Well, now you're here, do you want a drink?" The question was asked awkwardly. Frances wasn't used to people calling round, having many acquaintances but few friends. Beth thought of Ali. Quiet, nervy Ali. And was she still a friend after the scene between the two women?

While Gina, Beth and Carol chatted at flower arranging, helping each other, Ali and Frances had usually worked together; at least, Frances had arranged and Ali had assisted. Until the row, at least. She had also seen the two women in town, having coffee together and had heard them mention visits to each other's houses. Two kindred spirits in some ways; both women reserved, defensive, easily offended. Though Frances had no qualms about upsetting others while Ali avoided confrontation; never offered an inflammatory remark or contentious opinion, or any opinion at all, come to that. But Ali also loved her garden; having a large plot behind their small Edwardian house on the sea front. Beth had never seen it but had heard Carol and Frances talk about it.
"Thank you, that would be nice, tea, coffee, I don't mind." Beth smiled her thanks.

There was nowhere to sit in the kitchen and Frances gestured back to the hall. "Do you want to go and sit in the front room?"
"Shall we sit outside? It's too nice to be indoors."
Frances opened the kitchen door and Beth stepped through, onto a small paved patio with a wrought iron table and two chairs. She gasped.
"Frances, this is beautiful!" Frances looked gratified.
"I like it. I like plants" she stated unnecessarily.

She disappeared back indoors to make the drinks and Beth gazed around the garden. A winding gravel path led under an arch, disappearing behind a large choisya. Further down a pear tree drooped over a smaller gravel area and the path reappeared, winding past a small pond and finishing at a rustic wooden bench with a backdrop of evergreen honeysuckle. Clematis, passionfruit, ivy and climbing roses clad the fences either side of the garden and informal borders scattered the ground, crammed full of nicotiana, aquilegias, glorious fuschias dancing and spilling onto the crumbly earth beneath them. Teracotta pots jostled for space on the patio and the whole effect was one of colour and beauty.

"Thank you." Beth picked up her mug, bone china with flowers. Of course. "It must be a lot of work."
"A lot of love" the woman corrected. "It's my life." The words, stated so simply, made Beth catch her breath. She had always felt a bit sorry for the difficult, defensive woman, imagining her to be lonely, bored.
But she realised in a flash she wasn't unhappy, or bored. She was perfectly fulfilled and content; her hobby giving her pleasure and satisfaction.

Beth felt a stab of envy; how lovely to have such an all-consuming passion, something that gave so much joy.

She finished her tea then strolled along the gravel path; under the arch smothered in roses and clematis, round to the pear tree with its delicate glossy leaves. A small greenhouse was visible behind, it's staging crammed full of small pots and Beth could imagine the heavy humid air behind the glass. She continued along to the pond full of water lilies, the flash of orange beneath as goldfish darted and hid; then strolled back up to the table and chairs. And all around her in the borders were delicate flowers; soft orange poppies, violet alliums, pink and lemon aquilegias. She paused to admire them. Where had she seen those before?

"These aquilegias, Frances, what sort are they? They're beautiful." Frances glanced over.
"They're called Swan Pink Yellow. Pretty, aren't they? I grew them from seed."
Beth frowned. "I've seen them somewhere."
Frances shrugged. "I got the seeds from Bob Emery. I expect others did too. Tom's got them; maybe that's where you've seen them. They'll be in a lot of gardens round here."

Beth picked up her bag and smiled down at Frances, still seated. "You put me to shame. And you've inspired me to go and think about my garden. I think I've got a bit lazy, I always go for labour saving plants these days. But I think I'll do a bit of research and choose more flowers."
"Well, any help you want just ask." Frances stood up and walked her through the house to the front door.
Beth turned to her "Thanks for the coffee, Frances; it's been lovely to see your garden."

Charlie followed her down the path and they made their way home. Now there was just the evening to get through. What was on television, she wondered. Or she could start googling some new plants.

There was nothing on television. Nothing she wanted to watch on the main channels, as she thought of them. Nothing on the others either, just repeats; Murder She Wrote, Rosemary and Thyme, Lewis.
She wasn't in the mood for a crime. She had seen them all before, was bound to know who had done it.

And it wasn't even half past five yet. There was a lot of time to get through before she could go to bed. She wasn't going to walk Charlie again tonight. He had walked as much as even he wanted to today. Plus her mood was too introspective to risk seeing Tom. She had text him to explain they had been out all day; she would walk as normal again tomorrow. He had replied briefly; no worries, he would see her at church.

She got her laptop out and started googling plants. So many to choose from, this wasn't going to be easy. Maybe she would just go to the garden centre instead. Or talk to Nell about it. What had Frances said that aquilegia was called? Something about swans, and colours. Swan Pink Lemon, that was it. She tapped it in. Swan Pink Yellow, not Lemon. She looked at the image of the flower, frowning. Where had she seen it? It wasn't in a garden. It was somewhere else. Somewhere with other flowers.

She jerked her head up. She had it. They had been in Gina's arrangement for Melissa. Peonies, gypsophila, carnations, ivy and aquilegias, the same pinky yellow aquilegias as in the picture on the screen.
She had seen them when she was checking for dead flowers; they had still been quite fresh. But something was wrong. What was it? She sat back, frowning, trying to tease out the muddle of thoughts in her head. She closed her eyes and imagined the arrangement. She could see the black pedestal stand, the ivy tumbling over the edges, the white froth of lacy gypsophila. She saw the cream and pink and lemon in the delicate petals of the peonies, the carnations, the….

Her eyes snapped open. She knew what it was. Of course she did. The photo she had seen at Grace's yesterday; there were no aquilegias in the arrangement. The peonies were there, and the carnations, the gypsophila billowing around them, the ivy trailing down. But between the blowsy pink and lemon peonies, huddled next to the lemony cream carnations and the delicate gypsophila, were alstromerias. Alstromerias, not aquilegias. She was certain of it.

Beth sat back, thoughts whirling through her head. It didn't make sense. She must be wrong. There was one way to make sure. She walked to the worktop and picked up the phone. Gina would tell her. Dialling the familiar number, she leant back against the counter, thoughts and ideas spinning like angry bees around a honey pot. There was no answer; just five rings and the answer phone cutting in then Gina's quiet voice stating she was unavailable, please leave a message.....

Damn. Now what? Grace! She could tell her what was in the photo. She scrabbled through her handbag, searching for her diary. Why did everything always sink to the bottom? Finally locating it she thumbed through the pages at the back for Melissa's number.

Grace was there. "Beth, hello. How are you?" she replied in answer to Beth's greeting, sounding surprised to hear from her.
"Fine, thanks" Beth replied hurriedly. "Grace, you know the photograph on your fireplace? The one of Gina's flower arrangement for Melissa?"
"Yes?" There was a query in Grace's voice. Beth took a deep breath.
"Could you do me a favour?"
"If I can."
"Could you look at it and tell me something?" Beth felt slightly ridiculous asking.
"Sure, I'll go now."

Beth heard footsteps as she walked over the wooden floor into the living room.
"Okay. I'm looking at it. What do you want to know?" Grace sounded curious now.
"Can you tell me what flowers are in it?" Beth felt really stupid now. Grace would think she was mad; she had seen the arrangement itself for two weeks and the photo only yesterday.
"Of course. There are peonies, carnations, alstromerias..."
Beth interrupted her excitedly.
"Alstromerias? Are you sure? Not aquilegias?"
"Of course I'm sure!" Grace gave a laugh. "Beth, I photograph flowers all the time, at weddings. I know my alstromerias from my aquilegias. What is all this?"

"I'm not sure" Beth said slowly. "But thank you Grace, I'll talk to you again soon."
"Beth..." But Beth had cut the connection and sat down, head in her hands. What did it all mean? Why had the flowers been changed? And when? And who by?

She sat still, a kaleidoscope of ideas and images flashing into her head. She was watching a roundabout in her head, spinning round and round; glimpses of different faces stared at her as they spun past. At last she stood up stiffly, like an old woman. It couldn't be, surely it couldn't. But it was the face she kept coming back to.

Picking up her car keys, she patted Charlie's small head and out of habit went to pick up his lead. No, she wouldn't take him; he could stay home. She put the lead back on the side and left the house like a sleepwalker. Driving on autopilot, she found herself on the other side of town, turning into Addison Close. Across the road, in Addison Crescent, was the photograph causing all the problems. For a moment she was tempted to go and see it again for herself. But there was no need, she already knew enough. Slowing down, she indicated and parked outside Carol's.

Carol answered the door, smiling a greeting which faded as soon as she saw Beth's expression.
"Beth? Beth love, what on earth is the matter? She took Beth's arm, leading her through to the kitchen and sat her down on a chair, taking her cold hands in hers.

It sounded ridiculous. Beth knew how crazy it sounded but Carol sat quietly, gazing intently at her friend's face, rubbing her hands. At last she spoke.
"I don't know, Beth. It sounds implausible but..." she frowned. "I don't know what to think. But I do think you need to tell the police. They need to know, then it's up to them."
"I will. But will you come with me?"
"Of course I will. No, we will, Ken as well. He'll be home in an hour or so. It can wait until then. We'll come round to you and pick you up, then go on to the police station."
"But what if I'm wrong? And I expect I am. I'll look stupid. And I could be causing so much trouble….."

Carol squeezed her fingers. "It won't matter. It's better to get it checked out. The police will check it out. Now, would you rather stay here until Ken gets back?" Beth shook her head, getting to her feet.
"No, I need to get back for Charlie. He had a long walk this morning, so I'm not taking him on the beach tonight. But I need to feed him before we go. We might be a while at the station."
"Tom would feed him for you. Why don't you phone him?"
Beth shivered, seeing his warm eyes, hearing his deep voice, and felt an ache deep inside.
"No, it's alright. By the time I've fed him, I expect Ken will be back. I'll wait for you."

Was it really still Saturday? And only six o'clock? How long ago it seemed that she had set off for Portchester, not just eight hours. The elderly couple in the pub garden, the young family, had that really been just a few hours ago? Beth drove home in a daze, parked the car, got out and locked it. She walked up the path and unlocked the front door, calling out to Charlie as she walked through the hall.

CHAPTER 14

Charlie didn't come to greet her. She could see down the hallway, into the kitchen. There was no sign of him there; not in his basket or on his blanket on the sofa. And one of the kitchen doors out onto the garden was swinging open. Beth frowned. Surely she hadn't left it open? She never did that when she went out. She always checked it. Always locked it. Had she left in such a hurry she hadn't locked it or checked it? She couldn't remember. It was the sort of thing you did automatically, having no memory of actually doing it; like turning off the gas, unplugging the iron, driving the same route somewhere. How many times had she arrived at Gina's and had no recollection of actually driving there? It wasn't a matter for concern. Everyone did it. It usually just meant you were preoccupied with other thoughts. And she certainly had been, when she had gone haring off to Carol's. The only thought in her head had been to share her suspicions with her friend. But if somehow she had forgotten to lock the door, it would still be closed, wouldn't it? There were two French doors into the garden; one was always held back with a bolt, only unlocked when she wanted to open both doors. The other door was locked with a key. Could she have left it open, could it have been blown open? No, it wasn't windy, wasn't even breezy. And where was Charlie?

She went into the kitchen, stepping out into the garden and calling him. There was no response. She called again.

She gazed around the garden but no black bundle of hair bounded out from under any shrubs.
The garden was silent, still. So, he wasn't in the kitchen and he wasn't outside. The garden was secure; there was no way he could have escaped. James Lamb had fitted a side gate to keep the little dog safe, at the same time as he had fitted the dog flap. Little rascal, he was probably asleep on her bed. He was exhausted from the long walk that morning; though it was surprising he hadn't padded downstairs when he heard her open the front door, head on one side, tongue hanging out. She turned to go back into the kitchen, holding on to the door frame as she climbed the step, and froze.

A figure stood in the doorway leading to the hall. A dark figure standing still, face a blur of white.
The light was behind Beth and the figure in shadow. Beth's heart lurched. Her mouth was dry, chest thumping as her brain registered a slight figure,

grey all over, from head to feet, clothes, hair. Apart from the white face. The breath swept back into her lungs as she realised who it was.

"Frances!" She gasped. "You scared me! What are you doing here? How did you get in?"
There was no answer. The woman stood still, eyes steely grey and cold, staring at Beth. Then spoke quietly.
"Sit down, Beth."

Beth stood in the doorway, frozen with fear; two simultaneous thoughts racing through her head.
She was right and she was terrified. A third thought swept over her…turn; turn round, into the garden, run round the side of the house. Get away. Even as the thought screamed through her head and she started to move her frozen muscles, the other woman moved swiftly and silently across the room, grabbing her arm, gripping it tightly to pull her to the table and push her heavily down onto a chair. Beth's spine slammed against the seat back and her head snapped back then forwards again, like a puppet. Her upper arm burnt from the other woman's grip.

"Sit!" Frances hissed. She had thrown something onto the sofa behind Beth. Now she picked up a pile of brown rags and yanked one of them round Beth's middle, round again, then again, then round her arms, tighter, ever tighter. Beth realised they were being knotted behind her back, behind the chair. Tights. They were nylon tights. And she was being bound to the chair with them, arms pinned to her back, twisted awkwardly up behind her, wrenching her shoulders from their sockets. Now Frances was scrabbling on her knees and Beth felt her ankles pulled apart and tights being wound round and round her ankles and the chair legs. Round and round, rubbing her bare ankles against the hard wood. Frances was breathing heavily. Eventually she stood up. "There. You're not going anywhere now, are you Beth?"

"Frances" Beth's voice was shaking. Her head was swimming with fear, vomit rising in her throat. "Frances, what are you doing? Why? Please. Please don't."
The other woman sat at the end of the table, sideways onto Beth. Her face loomed close to Beth's and she felt faint at the expression in her eyes as she spat out the words.
"Because you know, don't you? You saw. You know what I did."

Beth swallowed bile, feeling it burn her throat. Blackness was filling her head; the room was spinning around her, Frances's white face floating close, then fading.

She nodded, her heart pounding, trying to leap from her chest. She forced herself to breathe, clear the darkness from her head. Talk to her. Isn't that what you were meant to do? Keep them talking, calm them down? Her mouth was dry, her tongue stuck to the roof of her mouth as she forced the words past numb lips.
"I think you killed Melissa. I think you made it look like a burglary and you killed her. You changed the flowers to hide the...the hammer."

Frances clapped her hands. "Well done, Beth. The police are stumbling around, haven't a clue, but you've worked it all out yourself. So clever, Beth!"
"Not really." Beth swallowed vomit and forced herself to breathe slowly. "I might have worked out what you did, how you did it, but I don't know why."
Frances's face still rolled in towards Beth, then receded, like the waves on the beach. She stared at Beth, pale blue eyes watery and blurred, terrifying in their lack of focus and expression. Beth faltered.
"Why did you kill her, Frances? What had she done to you?"

"What had she done?" Frances jerked, her head snapping forward, eyes focussed again. She leaned towards Beth and breathed in her face. "You ask what had she done?" Her voice rose, saliva sprayed into Beth's face and she cringed back, closing her eyes, lightheaded and dizzy. This wasn't calming Frances down. She was losing control, eyes wild, teeth bared, breathing heavily. She spat out the words. "I'll tell you what she did. She ruined this town, poisoned it, contaminated it. She was scum, scum and dirt. With her pretty face and pretty clothes; tossing her hair, smiling, laughing. Chatting up all the men, laughing at the women, pretending to be oh so friendly and all the time looking down on them, despising them. Helping with everything, offering paintings, as she's so talented, clever, beautiful Melissa! And everyone thinking oh lovely Melissa, sweet Melissa, aren't we lucky she moved here? No!"

She slammed her fist down in front of Beth and she jumped, keeping her eyes shut tight to avoid seeing the venom in the other woman's eyes.

"Ali wasn't lucky, was she? When that tart started making eyes at her husband, charming him, flirting with him. All over him in her short skirts and low tops. Then she pretended to be so sweet and friendly to Ali when really she was laughing at her for not being able to keep her own husband interested. And no-one saw what she was up to! Except me."

There was the sound of heavy breathing. Beth half opened her eyes to see the woman next to her staring out into the garden, eyes glazed again.

"Maggie wasn't lucky either, was she? She didn't want Melissa here. She could see what the bitch was up to as well. And Mark, stupid man, always at the whore's house, telling everyone how wonderful she was, giving us her paintings. She's so kind and generous. Oh yes, generous with her body. "

Frances was gasping now, spitting the words out with such venom that Beth had to force down another wave of vomit.

"Even your precious Carol complained about her." Beth's eyes snapped open. No. Carol had never complained about Melissa, had always said what a breath of fresh air she was. Frances continued to stare ahead, her arms wrapped around her thin body.

"You didn't hear her moaning to me how Ken was late again, showing that bitch around areas he thought she might like to live. Always pestering him in his office, tossing her hair, flaunting herself in those trashy clothes. She was evil, pure evil, and none of you could see it. You were all too stupid to see she was laughing at us, ridiculing us."

Beth forced the dizziness away and tried to think clearly. What should she say? If she argued with the woman, she would tip her over the edge. If she agreed with her, what then? But Frances wasn't waiting for her to say anything.

"Then she had the nerve to try and tell me how to arrange my flowers. Me! I've arranged those flowers for nearly thirty years! Oh Frances, have you ever thought of doing some modern arrangements, something simple but effective, one bloom, one leaf type of thing? I've got some photos, I'll show you. These pedestal arrangements are quite old fashioned, aren't they Frances?"

Frances did a sickening impression of Melissa's light, amused voice. She was staring not at Beth but out into the garden, sitting back in her chair with blank eyes, reliving the many slights and criticisms.

"But she always made it sound as though she was helping me, not laughing at me. She even Mark told she had some good ideas to share with me and he said weren't we so lucky to have her? Have her!"

She spat out the words, swinging round to Beth again. "They could all have had her. She was anyone's. And she didn't care who it was. And poor Ali, watching her. Listening to her with her own husband."

The phone rang, making both women jump.

"Just leave it. Whoever is phoning can leave a message." Frances's face loomed close to Beth's again. The phone rang, six rings, then Beth heard her own voice leaving a message, then a familiar voice, agitated and urgent. Carol.

"Beth! Beth? Are you there? Oh bother. If you're out with Charlie, phone me as soon as you get back."

Frances looked at her. "Lucky for Carol her husband has more sense than to get taken in by a tart!
But Julian, stupid, stupid Julian. With a lovely wife like Ali. But he took that evil bitch all over the place, Portsmouth, Southampton, Romsey. Dressing himself up, ignoring poor Ali, neglecting her for that…that whore. And Mark, all excited, like a silly schoolboy. Oh he says, Melissa says why don't we have an autumn flower show? Isn't that a wonderful idea? Clever Melissa! I've suggested that year after year but no, it's too close to the summer fete. Until she suggests it! And telling Tom he shouldn't let me have free rein of his garden for my flowers. His garden, not hers! But she says I shouldn't be able to wander around freely. But she can wander around Ali's house! Oh yes, wander anywhere. Make herself comfortable in Ali's bedroom, in Ali's bed, with Ali's husband. Julian, stupid man, brains in his trousers. And now Ali has gone. My one friend."

Frances's face crumpled and her eyes filled with tears. Beth's armpits and shoulders were burning where they were twisted backwards. She sat as still as possible to ease the pressure on her ankles but the position was causing her calf muscles to cramp, making her feel sick again. She looked at the woman sitting opposite her, at her grey face, at the tears rolling down her cheeks. She seemed to be shrinking; chin shaking, arms wrapped tightly around her.

"Frances." She forced herself to speak gently. "Frances, this has really upset you. You're not well. Why don't you untie me and I'll make you a nice cup of tea and we can phone Doctor Clarke. She'll look after you."

Frances stared at her, eyes glazed and watery. She looked puzzled.

"Am I ill? If I am, that woman has made me ill. I was fine before. Everything was fine. I was so happy in my lovely little town. I've lived here all my life, you know, I was born here. It was my parents' house before. My father made the garden; he set it out as it is now. I played in it as a little girl, I loved it so much. I even had my own little part to grow things in. Daddy used to help me. He said I had his green fingers. He made me a swing on the apple tree. I would swing and swing and watch him gardening. And I was happy. So happy. Then after he and Mummy had gone, I still had my garden, his garden. And I kept it just the same. I looked after it so well. For Daddy. So he would be pleased and proud of me. And I was so happy. I grew flowers for church. And I had my friend Ali. It was all so good. Until she came."

Tears poured down her cheeks. "Until she came" she repeated bitterly. "Like a serpent in the Garden of Eden, changing everything."

She was rocking now, backwards and forwards, hitting her arms on the table, her grey head sinking lower and lower. Beth fought back nausea; the pain in her shoulders and calves was making her head spin, turning black at the edges.

Frances looked up at Beth. "She had to go, you know. I knew, as soon as Maggie told me she wanted to join the flower arranging group. I couldn't have that, Beth. She would have poisoned that as well. She would have taken over and everyone would have said oh clever Melissa! Look at that! When you think of the boring arrangements poor Frances did. I couldn't have that, Beth. My flower arranging was the best thing in my life. Everyone knew me because of it. I grow everything in my garden for my flower arranging. There's nothing else in my life, nothing else worth living for. I couldn't let her take it from me, could I?" Glazed grey eyes stared at Beth, their expression chilling Beth to the core. "I couldn't, could I?"

She was mad, thought Beth dully. And none of us realised. And now it's too late.

Beth had to say it, had to hear her admit it. "So you killed her."

Frances rocked backwards and forwards, nodding. She looked at Beth, surprised she should ask.
"Of course. She was poison. Evil. Someone had to get rid of her. I couldn't let her do any more damage, break up any more marriages, make my life not worth living. I was waiting for her, just like I was waiting for you. I knew she was going out that afternoon so I went to her house. I let myself in and waited for her to get back. She came in and went to the kitchen. I was in her studio; I knew she would go in there sometime. And she did. I was sitting on her chair, waiting for her. And she was just like you. She stared at me. How did you get in Frances? she said. What are you doing here? She wasn't even scared, not like you. She just looked at me, tossing her hair, tapping her foot, bold as brass! The cold bitch! I told her I had something I wanted to show her. I pointed to a book on the table. She started saying I had no right entering her house like that, but she bent over to look at it and I hit her. I hit her. Again and again until I knew she was dead."

There was silence. Beth put her head down to stop passing out.

"There was so much blood. I hadn't realised there would be so much. And it was so red, so red."
She was quiet, staring out into the garden. Then shook herself. "I put the hammer in a plastic bag then I left." "How did you get into her house, Frances?" Beth's mouth was so dry it seemed too big for her mouth. Frances looked at her in surprise. "The spare key, of course. Just like I used yours. I thought you might have moved it, with all the burglaries. But it was still there. The Thomas's kept theirs under a loose brick in the wall by the washing line. Melissa didn't even know it was there! But I did, I used to water their plants for them when they went away. Why on earth did they lend their house to her? To an evil bitch like her?"
She was shaking, flecks of saliva flying out of her mouth.
"And the hammer? How did that end up in Gina's flowers?"

"I put it in my kitchen, under the sink. I hid it but I knew it was there, I could smell the blood on it every time I went into the kitchen." Frances hugged her arms and rocked. "So I had to get rid of it. I was going to bury it in the garden but then I thought, no, I can't put that in Daddy's lovely garden. It would contaminate the soil, contaminate all the plants. It would poison them, kill them. It had that evil woman's blood on it.

I couldn't have it amongst all our beautiful flowers. How could I have her blood in the soil? Our beautiful flowers growing out of her bloodied soil?" She shuddered and moaned.

Beth could hardly see her now. She tried to focus but only saw black; black spots enlarging then shrinking. She felt sick and dizzy. "So ... so you took it to church?" Her voice sounded far away and there was a thundering in her ears.

Frances nodded, her face crumpling. "I wasn't going to leave it there, I was going to go and throw it in the sea. But I called into the church first to check on the flowers, I knew the main pedestal needed freshening up. Mark came in and started chatting. He told me to go round to the vicarage for a cup of tea after I'd finished. I couldn't take it round there. They were free of her now I'd got rid of her, I couldn't take her evil blood back into their lovely home, could I?" She was silent.

"Then I thought, put it under the oasis. No-one will ever find it there. I could go back the next day and remove it, throw it in the sea. So I lifted the oasis and flowers out to put the bag with the hammer underneath it. It just fitted. I tried to put the oasis back but the alstromerias were fragile, so delicate, and some of them broke. I panicked and tried to stick them back in but I just broke more."

The woman was calmer now, reliving it. "I couldn't be long; Mark might have come back in at any time. So I threw them away, got the aquilegias I had brought for the pedestal and replaced them, in the holes I had pulled the alstromerias from. Then I put the whole lot back. It looked perfect. No one would ever have guessed what was under them."

She smiled, calm and dreamy, then looked at Beth, expression hardening.
"Why did you have to get there before me that Friday? Why did you have to find it?" Beth shook her head. "Someone would have found it, Frances."
"Not if I had thrown it in the sea." She gazed out of the window, eyes swollen from weeping, nose red and dripping.
"Untie me Frances. Please? Then we'll call the doctor and get you some help."
"What?" Frances jerked awake. "I can't untie you. You know too much."
"But I want to help you, see you get treatment...." Beth's voice trailed off at the puzzled expression on Frances's face.

"I don't need treatment, Beth. I'm fine. She was the one who was sick. But I did the right thing; I got rid of her for you all. I'm sorry I have to get rid of you too though. I like you Beth, you've always been friendly, you've never laughed at me. And your little dog, he's a sweet thing – was a sweet thing."

Beth froze. "Frances" her voice shook, tears springing to her eyes. "Frances, what have you done with Charlie? Where is he?"
"He's in the front room. It's better you don't see him. But he didn't suffer, Beth, honestly. I was very quick."

Everything spun and shifted. Beth heard a moan leave her lips, low and desperate.
"Oh Frances, why Charlie? He didn't do anything."
"Well, nor did you Beth" Frances sounded surprised. "But I have to kill you, don't I? You know. I can't have you knowing. You'll tell the police then they'll come for me. And I can't leave my little house, or my beautiful garden, can I? Who would look after it? What would Daddy have said? But I am sorry about Charlie. He wouldn't have wanted to live without you though, would he? I'll miss you, you're a good person. And Tom will miss you; I've seen the way he looks at you. That whore was after him too, but at least he had more sense, he only had eyes for you. And he's kind; he lets me share his garden."

She rocked again, hugging her knees, smiling to herself.

Tears were streaming down Beth's face. All she could do was beg. "Frances, please don't do this. Please. Let me get you some help. You don't know what you're doing."
"Oh but I do. It's all planned. But I will try and make it painless for you. I'll stand behind you and you won't see me. It will be over so quickly, you won't feel a thing. Just like Melissa. She didn't make a sound, she just fell down. Like you will. Now, shall we get it over with?"

She stood up and walked behind Beth to the sofa and picked up the hammer.

CHAPTER 15

Carol had watched Beth leave with misgivings. Supposing her friend decided to go back to Frances's house and challenge her? But she wouldn't do that, would she? Beth wasn't the bravest woman on the planet. Plus she had said she needed to get back for Charlie. She sat at the kitchen table, fretting, watching the clock and willing Ken to come home.

Fifteen minutes later she couldn't stand it any longer. She needed to speak to Beth. She picked up the phone and dialled the familiar number. Pick up, Beth, she prayed, pick up. The phone rang and rang until the answer phone cut in. Swallowing down her panic, she left a message.

Where was Ken? Why was he always late when she needed him? She paced the floor, wondering desperately what to do. Tom! She would phone Tom, get him to go round. He could get there in seconds. She leafed quickly through her diary for his number, dialling it with shaking fingers. Please be there. Please, please be there. He answered on the first ring.

"Oh Tom, thank God. Listen, can you go round to Beth's? Check she's alright for me? No, there's no time to explain. Just go, PLEASE. And we'll be there as soon as we can." Tom had put down the phone while she was still speaking. She couldn't wait any longer for Ken. She phoned his office and told him he was needed at home now.

Tom grabbed his house keys, slammed the front door behind him and ran down the path, down to the corner of the road and across to Beth's house. Her car was outside, the front window slightly open. Everything looked normal. What on earth was upsetting Carol? She had sounded desperate. He walked down the front path and raised his hand to ring the bell, looking through the living room window and froze, heart thudding. Charlie lay asleep on the sheepskin rug in front of the fireplace. Charlie often lay asleep on the sheepskin rug. But not with his head in a large pool of blood.

Tom felt his chest being squeezed and his heart was pounding so fast he thought he was having a heart attack. Sweat started pouring down his face, wetting his back and armpits. What should he do? He pushed at the front door quietly but it was locked. Go round the side? But if Beth was in the kitchen with ...his mind refused to frame the words...they would see him as soon as he turned the corner.

Had she got home and disturbed a burglar? He could feel his heart hammering and limbs shaking. He had to get in. He stared at the window. Could he fit through? He had to. Did it open all the way? He knew these old sash windows often stuck. Please don't stick. Please. The words pounded through his head in rhythm with his heartbeat. He pushed the frame up quietly, willing it not to squeak. He eased it up as far as it would go and immediately it started to slide down again. Pushing it back up, he shoved his head and shoulders through, plugging the gap. He felt his back and sides scraping along the wooden frame and knew he had broken the skin, but he was in. Partly, at least.

    The sofa was under the window and he lowered himself onto it, arms and chest, pulling one leg up under his stomach and sliding it through, scraping the skin, until his knee was on the sofa. He knelt on one leg and his arms, bending the other leg and pulling it through. If a passer-by saw him, they would phone the police. Please, he prayed, someone see him. He was sprawled on the sofa, arms on the floor and legs over the back. Quietly he edged forward, straightening his arms and pulling his legs into a standing position then straightened up. He avoided looking at the little dog, sprawled out on a patch of dark red.

    Creeping to the door, he opened it a fraction, willing it not to make a noise. He could hear voices and quiet sobbing. Beth! At least that meant she was alive! He felt faint with relief and shook his head to clear it, legs trembling. He tried to peer through the door jamb but could only see the hall way. Pulling the door open a fraction more, he positioned his body to peer round the doorway. Beth sat with her back to him, bound to a chair. He couldn't see anyone else in the room but could hear a voice. He heard Beth's quiet sobs again then a figure appeared behind her. Frances. With horror he saw the hammer in her hand.

    A firework seemed to explode in his head and he flew down the hall, lunging at Frances as she raised the hammer. He threw his weight against her and they crashed to the floor, Frances's head cracking against the table leg, the hammer flying from her hand and spinning across the tiled floor. There was a loud bang as it hit the skirting board. Tom lay on top of the woman; his weight pinning her down, his hand forcing her head onto the floor. He gasped, trying to suck air into his lungs. Beth was staring down at them, her eyes glazed. Tom pushed his weight down harder, pulling Frances's arms behind her so they were under his chest.

Her legs thrashed and he pressed harder with his knees to prevent her kicking and wriggling free. He needed to restrain her, tie her up. Looking around desperately, he spotted Charlie's lead on the worktop. With one hand round her wrists, he grabbed the lead with the other and pulled it down, then tied it round and round her wrists, binding them as tightly as he could. He leaned back on his feet, keeping his knees on her legs, and unbuckled his belt, pulling it off and wrapping it round her ankles. It was too big; she would wriggle out of it. He frantically unravelled it, tying it in a knot instead, then another knot, pulling it so tight she could never break free. Finally he stood and looked at the woman trussed up on the floor. She was screaming and swearing; throwing herself around the floor, smashing her body into the hard tiles. He stepped over her to the other side of Beth. She looked up at him, eyes sightless with terror, and he caught her as she fainted.

"Beth, Beth." A voice was calling her name. She tried to open her eyes, opened them a bit more but couldn't see anything, only blue. She tried to focus and realised the blue was material, soft cotton.
"Beth, open your eyes, look at me." The voice was urgent.

She tried again, forcing her eyes to stay open, moving her head carefully to search for the voice. Tom was kneeling beside her, one arm wrapped tightly round her while the other held a phone to his ear.
Was he talking to her or someone on the other end of the phone?
"Now" he was saying. "Police and ambulance." She closed her eyes again and drifted away against the warm soft cotton.

Then the room was full of people. Carol, crying, calling her name. Ken's deep voice. And others she didn't recognise. She could hear heavy footsteps, rustling, breathing. Now she was lying on the sofa and Carol was beside her, stroking her hair, saying she was alright. Images flashed into her head and she struggled to sit up.

"Beth, wait, take it slowly." Carol's arm was round her as she straightened up and looked around her kitchen. No Frances. Where was she? But a big man dressed all in green was kneeling in front of her, saying her name, asking if she could hear him. Yes of course she could. What did he think? He was shouting in her ear. She couldn't be bothered answering. She looked at the figures shifting in her vision. Another figure in green moved to stand in front of her, blocking her view. It wasn't a nice shade of green, it was too dark. And it was creased, creased and crumpled.

Why hadn't he ironed it?

The one kneeling was shining a torch in her eyes, holding her wrist, fixing something on her finger. Then a band was wrapped around her arm, pumping up then collapsing. Carol was still crying.

"Would you like some water?" The green man was leaning over her, holding a glass of water to her lips. She drank thirstily, asked for more. Other people were moving around her kitchen. Who were they? What were they doing there? Everyone was talking. Looking at her. Why? What had she done? Ken was talking to one of them and Carol still cried. She wished she would stop, her head ached. But Tom. Where was Tom? She didn't want all these people, she wanted Tom.

Carol was still beside her, holding the water now. Beth clutched at her. "Carol, where's Tom? I want Tom." Her voice rose, anguished.

And he was there. Pushing Carol and the green men aside as he fell on his knees in front of her and pulled her into his arms.

Finally the kitchen cleared of uniforms. The paramedics had left first, offering to take Beth to hospital but she had refused. They left with instructions to phone the local GP or the out of hour's doctor to get some sedatives, but Beth didn't want to take anything. The police had left, stating they would be back in the morning but would contact Tom first. Frances had been taken away; where to, Beth had no idea and didn't care. Her first conscious thought had been Charlie and they had told her only that he had been hurt and the vet had taken him for the night. Ken had investigated as soon as he and Carol had arrived and had felt a faint pulse, phoning the vet to get there as soon as she could. The vet had been noncommittal; Charlie could pull through but it was a serious head wound. But Beth had been satisfied the little dog was alright and had calmed down. Now only Ken and Carol remained, sitting at the table while Tom sat on the sofa, his arm tightly around Beth.

"You'll come back to ours for the night, Beth?" Carol asked, her hands still trembling as she nursed a glass of water. Before she could answer, Tom had shaken his head.
"I'm taking her back to mine, Carol. But thanks. Could you drive us back though? Beth's not up to walking."
"Of course." Ken stood up. He locked the French doors and handed the keys to Tom while Carol rinsed the glasses. Tom helped Beth to her feet.
"Come on. Let's go."

They drove the hundred metres to Tom's and he unlocked the front door, urging Beth through. "Upstairs for you. Bed and sleep, the best cure for shock."

Beth wearily climbed the stairs, Tom's hand under her elbow. He nudged her into the bathroom. Opening the bathroom cabinet he took out a new toothbrush and handed it to her, then disappeared onto the landing to get her a towel.

"I'll go and get your room ready. Don't lock the door." He left her and went into the spare bedroom, switching on the bedside lamp and turning the duvet down, then went to his own bedroom to find a tee-shirt she could wear. He returned to sit on the spare bed and wait for her to come back in.

Her face was still white but her eyes were more focussed. She sat on the bed and he stood up, handing her the tee-shirt. "The best I can manage for a nightie. Now, do you need any help?"

Beth shook her head. "No, thank you." She kicked her sandals off and started to unbutton her blouse, but the tiny buttons were fiddly and her hands were shaking.

"Beth, let me help." Tom hunkered down in front of her and gently began to undo them, sliding the blouse off her shoulders. She didn't resist. He reached behind her and unfastened her bra, slipping the straps down and pulling it away. Picking up the tee-shirt he dropped it over her head, gently pulling her arms through, tugging it down over her stomach and hips. Then he pulled her to her feet and felt under the tee-shirt for her skirt fastening, unclipping it and sliding it down to her feet. Finally he scooped her up and lay her down on the bed, pulling the duvet over her.

"Now, try and sleep. You're safe. I'll leave the doors open so just call me if you want me." He clicked off the lamp. Her eyes were closed before he had even left the room.

Tom poured himself a whisky and sat downstairs with it, stroking Tess. He felt himself slowly begin to unwind, the tension gradually seeping out of his body. Tess gazed up at him calmly, her eyes milky and gentle. Putting the glass in the sink, he patted the dog goodnight and went upstairs. He washed quickly and found a pair of pyjamas. He didn't usually wear any but needed some tonight, in case he had to go into Beth, if she woke up, called out. He looked down at the bed. His room was only across the landing but suppose he didn't hear her? He needed to be closer. Picking up a pillow, he switched the light off and walked out to the landing.

The light was still on and he decided to leave it, didn't want Beth waking up in pitch black. Creeping through the doorway into the spare room, he sat down in the armchair in the corner, pulling the dressing table stool towards him as a footrest. He pushed the pillow behind his head and settled down, looking at the figure in the bed. Beth lay fast asleep, curled up on her side, hair spread out on the pillow, breathing regular and even.
He sat in silence, watching the sleeping figure until his eyelids became heavy, closed, and he slept.

Until just after 3 o'clock.

His eyes snapped open. A noise had woken him; moaning and muttering, bedding rustling as someone tossed and turned. He straightened, instantly alert. Beth was sitting up, gasping.
"Beth, Beth, it's alright." He was on his feet, hurrying to sit on the bed in front of her, grabbing her shoulders. "You're alright. You're at my house."

Her breath was coming in short gasps and she looked at him, wide-eyed. Then memories flooded back and she gave another cry; falling forward onto his chest, clutching at his pyjama top. His arms went round her, holding her close and tight, his hand pressing her head to his shoulder, his lips on her hair.
"Tom, oh Tom." Her voice shook.
"It's alright sweetheart, it's alright." He rocked her gently, smoothing her hair, murmuring in her ear.
"Frances." She pulled back and looked at him wide eyed. "She killed Melissa. She was going to kill me. And Charlie..." Her voice broke and her chest heaved as she fought for breath and was overcome by a storm of weeping, gasping and sobbing, tears streaming. Tom pulled her back to him, pressing her head against his chest, wrapping his arms round her so tightly she couldn't move.

"It's over my love. It's all over. She's gone and you're safe." With a stab he remembered saying those words before. He squeezed her even closer, kissing her hair. "It's finished Beth, and you're alright. And Charlie, she didn't kill him sweetheart, he was knocked out. He's at the vets. And he's a fighter, he'll pull through."
He hoped desperately what he said was true, but if it wasn't, well, they'd deal with that when the time came.

He rocked her back and forth, making soothing noises in her ear, repetitive calming sounds as to a hurt child.

At last her sobs quietened and the trembling eased. She lay exhausted against him, still clutching his top, her breathing almost normal with just an occasional hiccup. Then she eased her hold on him and leaned back, wiping her cheeks with a shaky hand. Tom reached past her to the box of tissues, took a handful and gently wiped her cheeks and nose. "Don't think about it anymore, my love. Try to put it out of your mind." It was a stupid thing to say, how could she? But he couldn't think of anything else to comfort her. "Would you like a drink? A cup of tea? Something stronger?" Beth shook her head, hiccupped.
"No. Just hold me. Please?"

He lay down on top of the duvet and pulled her into his arms. She rested against him, head on his chest, her hand on his shoulder. Her hair smelt of soap, something light and tangy. He stroked it gently.

Gradually her breathing slowed and he felt her relaxing in his arms. His left arm was going numb, his shoulder trapped under her head. He shifted slightly to ease it and she stirred, clutching his shoulder. "Don't leave me, please. Don't go." A lump filled his throat and he tightened his arms.
"I'm not going anywhere, my love."

At some point in the night he eased her away from him, climbed under the duvet, then pulled her close to him again.

He woke later and twisted his head to look at the clock. Seven twenty. Beth still lay tucked under his left arm, head on his shoulder, her cheek resting against his chest. Her arm was flung round his waist, his right arm was around her back, her skin warm and soft. She looked peaceful, skin smooth and relaxed in sleep.

He thought back to the events of the night before. He would never forget that moment when he had looked round the doorway and seen Beth tied and bound to the chair, her face white and eyes dark with terror. Then Frances appearing, the hammer in her hand. He fought back a wave of nausea. Then thought of Beth crying, shaking, in shock. So many tears in her life. So much fear. So much unhappiness. He felt his eyes stinging and an overwhelming sense of helplessness. But she was here, safe, in his arms. Alive.
Melissa was gone. But Beth was alive and he felt his whole body ache with the need to protect her, love her, make her happy.

He stayed still for a few more minutes then gently moved his left arm, easing it out from under her, resting her head against the pillow. Then moved his right arm, pulling away, gently placing her arm on the duvet, until he was able to sit up on the edge of the bed. Much as he wanted to stay there, hold her until she woke, he didn't want her to wake up with him in her bed, not remembering why and panicking.

He had a shower and shaved then went downstairs to let Tess out into the garden, with an apology.
He wasn't going to leave the house to walk her this morning. He made a pot of coffee and some toast then sat down at the kitchen table. The Sunday paper had been pushed through the front door and he sat reading it, sipping coffee, but not taking any of it in. He was just waiting for a sound from upstairs.

Beth woke up just before half past nine and for a split second wondered where she was. Then she remembered. She swung her legs out of bed and stood up slowly, imagining her legs would be shaky, but they were fine. Padding to the bathroom, she washed her face and brushed her teeth, looking around for a brush or comb and spotting Tom's. She used that, he wouldn't mind. Then she went downstairs, into the kitchen.

Tom had heard the toilet flush, the water running, and looked up with a smile. She walked into the kitchen, feet bare, his tee-shirt down to her knees, sleeves almost to her elbows, but looking beautiful.
He swallowed a lump in his throat, just about managing to speak.
"Hi. How are you?" Beth sat down next to him, pushing the hair out of her eyes and managing a smile. "I'm alright."
"Coffee? Tea? What would you like to eat?" She shook her head.
"Nothing to eat thanks, but coffee would be nice." She looked out of the window, feet resting on the bottom rung of the wooden chair. The sun shone and the sky was blue. How could everything look so normal? Tom got up to pour her coffee, popped more bread in the toaster, then put a plate of hot buttered toast on the table.

"Dig in." He had already had breakfast but took another piece, hoping the hot buttery smell might tempt her to eat some. It did, and she ate three of the slices to his one. He poured them both more coffee, surreptitiously looking at her to see how she really was; if she was pale, still in shock. But her colour was good and her hand holding the mug of coffee was steady.

"Carol phoned earlier. She wanted to know if you needed some things from your house. I said I expected you needed underwear, a clean top, that sort of thing. So she and Ken went round and she's brought a bag round for you" indicating a holdall by the door.

"That was good of her. What time was that? I didn't hear the phone, or the door."

"She phoned at half eight. She said she couldn't wait any longer to see how you were. I answered the phone as soon as it rang, I didn't want it waking you. And I thought it might be the police. She and Ken went round straight away so you would have clean clothes for when you woke up."

Beth felt a lump in her throat. What good friends she had. "Have the police phoned yet?"

He shook his head. "Not yet, but they will, to tell us if they will be coming here or if we go there."

"What do you think will happen?"

"They'll ask us loads of questions, we make our statements, sign them. That's all, I think, but I don't really know."

"And …and Frances?" Beth stumbled over the name. "Where do you think she is? What will happen to her?" Tom put his large warm hand over hers, squeezing it gently.

"She'll be in custody. They will be interviewing her; I expect she's having mental health assessments as well. But you won't see her, don't worry about that."

"Tom, do you think she was mad? She was so…so calm at times then so weird. She seemed to think everything she was doing was normal, right…" her voice trailed off as her hands round the mug started trembling. Tom shuffled his chair closer and put his arm tightly round her shoulders. "Sshh, don't think any more about it. Wait until the police talk to us."

She nodded then stared at him, wide eyed. "Tom! Charlie! I haven't even thought about Charlie!"

"The vet will phone us as well, tell us how he's doing." He swallowed a lump in his throat. Please God let the little dog pull through.

The phone rang twice while Beth was in the shower. Gina first, anxious, upset, wanting to know how she could help, asking Tom to let her know when it was a good time to call round. Then the police. They were requested to go to the station to make their statements and sign them. There was no call from the vet. Was that good or bad?

They drove to the police station and Beth was taken to an interview room. Tom had asked to stay with her but had been refused, told to wait in the reception area. After half an hour he was also taken to be interviewed and sign his statement. Then it was back to the reception area. Still no Beth. A uniformed constable said she was still being interviewed. Time passed. Tom drank a hot, watery drink without noticing what it was. He sat fidgeting, then paced up and down, thoughts racing, heart thumping. Just as he thought he couldn't take any more he saw a uniformed officer accompanying Beth along the corridor back to reception, Beth pale but composed. She looked up at him and shook her head but reached for his hand.

They drove home in silence. Tom was desperate to ask her how it had gone, what had happened, but waited for her to begin the conversation. At least she was calm, outwardly at least, showing no sign of tears or shakiness.

As they stepped into the hall the answer phone was flashing and Tom pressed it without thinking. His stomach lurched as the voice began and he realised it was the vet. Surely she wouldn't phone with bad news? Please, no. She didn't. Charlie was conscious, eating and drinking, he would be fine. She was keeping him in another night for observation but all being well Beth could collect him the next day.

They had been standing close together in the hallway, frozen, staring at the phone as they listened to the message. When it finished Beth looked up at Tom. "Oh thank God" she whispered, relief in her eyes. The phone rang again, startling them both. Carol. What was happening? Could she and Ken call round?

What was left of the afternoon passed with phone calls and the visit from Carol and Ken. Then Gina. They didn't hold a post mortem on the events of the previous evening; Tom had been ready to intervene to prevent it but Carol had already filled Gina in and the three really just wanted to see how Beth was. The phone kept ringing and Tom fielded anxious calls from various people, eventually unplugging it from the wall. The police had his mobile number and anyone else could wait until tomorrow. Beth had already switched her mobile off, unwilling to talk to anyone. Tom had said she needed to ask for a few days off work. At first Beth had resisted but, with additional pressure from Carol and Gina, she gave in and phoned the head teacher.

Tom began the conversation, explaining briefly the events of the weekend, then Beth spoke to her head, agreeing to stay home until at least Thursday, promising to see the doctor if necessary. He had also phoned Nell, calming her down then passing her to Beth. Nell had wanted to jump straight in her car and drive down but Beth persuaded her to wait until the next day. Nell eventually agreed, reluctantly, to go into work the next day and ask for some time off, saying she would see Beth the following evening.

Carol, Ken and Gina left, promising to call again the next day. They seemed to assume she would still be at Tom's, not seeming in the least surprised. Carol had brought round a cooked chicken and some potato salad, stating she hadn't known what Beth and Tom would have had to eat that day. They had in fact been given some sandwiches at the police station but neither had eaten much.

Tom made a simple salad and opened a bottle of white wine and they sat at the kitchen table, realising how hungry they were as soon as they began eating. By the time they had finished and tidied away, the sun was setting. He made a pot of coffee and carried the tray through to the living room, placing it on a small table by the sofa, then sat down on the sofa next to Beth who was looking out of the window, at the darkening sky and the lights appearing on the island, at the small tents being set up at the water's edge as the evening fishermen arrived.

He looked at her, his hazel eyes anxious.
"How are you feeling? Are you alright?" Beth looked up at him, nodding.
"Yes. I'm fine. I just can't believe how much has happened in twenty four hours. Already it seems unreal, like a dream….or a nightmare." She grimaced. He placed his hand over hers, gently stroking the palm.
"It was, a nightmare I mean. But it's over now." She looked at his hand, so warm and strong, hers hidden beneath his long fingers.
"Tom. If you hadn't come when you did…."
"Sshh, stop there." She felt pressure on her fingers. "I did come, and you're alright." He swallowed hard, an image of Frances standing over Beth with a hammer in her hand, flooding his head. "Don't think about it, sweetheart."

"Yes, you did. And I can't thank you enough for that or for the time since then either..." She kept her gaze on his hand, seeing the long fingers, short clipped nails, the golden hairs. What lovely hands he had, so strong but gentle.

"Beth, no, there's no need for gratitude" he said quietly. "I just thank God you're alright, you're safe." His voice cracked.
"Beth, I know this isn't the right time, but I need to say it. I love you, so so much, and if anything had happened to you…" He couldn't continue, there was a huge lump in his throat.

He felt her fingers tense, her whole body go rigid. He closed his eyes as he realised what he had done, frightening her off. This was the end of his dreams. So stupid of him, stupid, stupid, stupid, the word pounded in his head.

There was silence then he felt and heard her breath come in a gasp. Opening his eyes, his heart missed a beat at the look on her face.

"Beth? Beth, why are you looking at me like that?" He looked into her eyes, registering with disbelief what he was seeing.
"Beth, do you…" He stumbled over the words. "Could you ever have feelings for me?"
She was looking at him, lips slightly apart, eyes glowing with joy and he saw her swallow before she said the words he most wanted to hear.
"I do already…"She swallowed again. "I love you too."

He felt a huge wave of relief and joy sweep over his whole body as he let go of her hand and pulled her into his arms, pressing his cheek against hers.
"Beth, oh my sweet love. Do you really mean it?" His heart was hammering, his breathing shaky.
"Yes, oh yes." Trembling, she reached her arms up around his neck and felt his thick, soft hair, as she had dreamed of doing so many times, inhaling the tangy, musky scent of his skin, feeling rough stubble against her cheek. Her heart raced and her lungs felt as though they were punching their way out of her chest. He held her tightly, his cheek still against hers, his arms warm and strong as he held her close, kissed her hair, shuddering with joy and relief.

They stayed like that until their heartrates slowed; Beth pulling back slightly to look up at him. He smiled down at her, stroking her cheek with trembling fingers and sighed shakily.

"You have no idea how I've longed for this. How I've wished and prayed for it." His voice still felt dry and hoarse.
"I can't believe you love me." Her voice sounded uncertain, nervous.

"Oh my darling girl, I fell in love with you as soon as I met you. You were so beautiful, so soft and lovely; I just wanted to sweep you up in my arms and never let you go."

Beth looked at him, her beautiful eyes wide and disbelieving. "I had no idea. I thought you liked Gina."

"I did …do…like Gina. But as a friend. But you, as soon as I saw you, I fell head over heels; I knew you were the love of my life." His voice trailed off, he swallowed and tried again. "But when I found out what had happened, and you were so adamant there would never be anyone for you, I just felt sick, hopeless. But I knew I could never give up. I just had to wait and hope that one day, you might start to feel something for me, might one day love me as much as I love you. Oh my beautiful girl, I love you so much." His voice shook and Beth felt him trembling.

"I love you too." She tightened her arms round his neck, pressing her face into his neck and closing her eyes. "But…" she faltered "but suppose I can't, can't do anything physical…" her voice trailed off.

His arms tightened as he spoke quietly into her ear.

"Sssh, it will be fine, you'll be fine. I know you're scared, but we'll take it very, very slowly, we won't do anything you don't like. We've all the time in the world and it will be alright."

"But … suppose it isn't, and I can't… we can't have a physical relationship. Suppose there is something wrong with me? It wouldn't be fair on you." Her voice was muffled against his chest. From pure joy she had gone to feeling sick with dread

"Beth, look at me." He loosened his arms and pulled back, cupping her face gently, searching her eyes and seeing the fear and worry in their green depths.

"There is nothing wrong with you. Believe me, sweetheart. You weren't much more than a child and you were frightened, hurt, but there's nothing wrong with you. He blamed you but it wasn't you. Please my darling, just believe me." His eyes were anxious, strained, desperate for her to believe him. "And I know it's left you scared, but we can deal with that."

She looked down at the buttons on his shirt.
" I want to believe you." Then, so quietly he could hardly hear.

"But Tom, I have no idea what to do. I've no experience." She kept her gaze on his strong neck, on the sandy hair revealed by his shirt collar.

He felt her swallow and tightened his arms around her again, pressing his lips against her soft, sweet smelling hair.

"It doesn't matter, Beth. We'll take it very slowly, one step at a time. There's no rush. And you don't need a gold medal you know. Not everyone has loads of experience."
"But not many women in their mid-50' have none." Her voice was muffled and embarrassed.
"Maybe not. But you don't need to worry." He put his fingers under her chin again, lifting her face until she was looking at him.
"Or be embarrassed. It will all happen naturally. And I will never, ever hurt you, you know that. Please, just trust me; believe me that it will be alright."
"I want to. Oh Tom, I really want to." Her lovely eyes looked up at him for reassurance and he put his hands back on either side of her face, kissing each eyelid tenderly.
"Then just stop worrying, sweetheart, we're going to be fine." His voice shook.

He leaned back, pulling her round so she was lying across his lap, her arms round his neck as he held her close and stroked her hair.
"Just love me, Beth. Love and trust me." He rocked her gently, kissing the top of her head, holding her closer and closer.

"I do." She moved her head and gazed up at him, seeing the love in his eyes and felt she had come home. A wave of joy swept her from head to toe and she ran her fingers through his hair, revelling in the softness. She smiled up at him and Tom saw the shadows begin to melt away and a look of love, hope and happiness shine in her eyes.

He gave a sigh of relief and leaned back, pulling her with him, gently kissing her forehead as he tightened his arms and swore he would always keep her happy and safe.

EPILOGUE

It was the following Saturday. Beth had stayed at Tom's on Sunday night then he had taken her to collect Charlie on the Monday morning. The little dog looked none the worse for his adventure, except for a shaved and stitched patch behind his ear. Nell arrived in the evening, nearly suffocating Beth with hugs.

Tom stayed for dinner. Beth had made Nell's favourite pasta dish and she served it up as they sat around the kitchen table. She had expected to see her aunt looking shaken and pale but she was relaxed and glowing, her blonde streaked hair tumbling around her face, eyes shining. She wore jeans and a tee-shirt, the simple clothes showing off her curves, skin golden brown against the white top. Catching Tom's expression as he looked at Beth she caught her breath. So that was how it was, she smiled to herself. After dinner they sat in the living room with a glass of wine, Charlie curled up on Beth's lap. She couldn't bear to have the little dog out of her sight and he seemed content with the extra fuss she made of him. Tom sat opposite the two women, long legs crossed, his smile affectionate as they listened to Nell's chatter. The phone rang and Beth went into the hall to answer it, handing Charlie to Nell.

She looked at Tom anxiously.
"How is Aunty Beth really, Tom? She seems fine but it must have been a terrible ordeal."
"Better for seeing you." He smiled across into her worried blue eyes.
 "And yes it was, of course it was. But honestly Nell, she's alright. It was terrible, but it's over and she's going to be okay."
Nell looked at him, a question in her eyes. He leaned forward, squeezing her arm.
"I'll make sure she's okay." Nell nodded, grinning at him.

Beth came back into the room and the conversation became general, Nell planning what they would do that week.
"I can't do too much" protested Beth. "I'm supposed to be off sick, remember?"
"Then I prescribe lots of long walks on the beach, lots of fresh air" declared Nell. "And lots of relaxing in the garden, doing nothing. I shall thoroughly spoil you for once."
"Well, I'm not going to argue with that!" Beth smiled at her niece.

"Breakfast in bed?"
Nell snorted. "Do you really think Charlie will let you get away with that?" The little dog heard his name and opened one eye, wagging his tail.
"No" laughed Beth, picking the little dog up and hugging him. Tom felt a pull at his heart as he looked at her, so soft and lovely, and she loved him. His heart swelled and he felt his eyes fill; how lucky he was.

She stayed off work for the rest of the week; her shoulders still aching from where they had been twisted back and her ankles bruised from the tight binding. Nell stayed then went home on Saturday morning, torn between wanting to stay with Beth and seeing Will.

"Go!" Beth had laughed. "I'll be fine. I'm out this evening anyway, then church tomorrow. Then it's back to work. And I've got Carol and Ken, and Gina."
"And Tom." Her niece gave her a sideways look.
"And Tom" agreed Beth, feeling a bubble of happiness.
Nell hugged her. "I'm glad. He's so nice."
They had talked about Tom in the week, Beth playing it down, insisting it was early days. But Nell wasn't fooled, knowing this was serious for both her aunt and Tom.
"Now you go home. Go and see Will, have a good weekend."

Now it was Saturday evening and Carol, Gina and Beth sat at their usual table in the window overlooking the sea at Waves. Ken and Tom were with them.
"So we don't know if she was mad or bad?" Carol asked, blunt and to the point as ever.
Beth hadn't been keen on discussing the matter but knew it was inevitable and was keen to get it over with, then change the subject. Tom shook his head.
"Mad, I would say, or rather mentally ill. I can't see her standing trial. But that's for the powers that be to decide."
"Where is she now? Gina asked quietly.
"In a psychiatric unit while they assess her."

The five were silent, each thinking their own thoughts.
"And to think none of us realised. She lived amongst us all these years and we didn't have an inkling what was going through her head." Carol marvelled. "How can that be?"
"I suppose we see what people want us to see" Gina said quietly. "People

put on a front, an act. And you never really know what goes on behind closed doors."

The discussion continued and Beth gazed out of the window. The island was clear this evening, she could see Carisbrooke Castle and Osborne House as though they were postcards or photographs. It was a warm sunny evening and the visitors were out in force, strolling along the beach path and sitting on the beach. The jet skiers were out playing, small yachts tacked back and forth and a large cruise ship was making its slow, stately way out of Southampton.

She remembered sitting at this same table with Melissa, the evening she had met her. It seemed so long ago. Was it really less than three months ago that she had moved to Bride's Bay? And how much had happened in the little town since. The weeks of fear and suspicion over the burglaries, the gossip and upset. The break-up of a marriage. The worry over Carol's health. The violent loss of a beautiful, vibrant woman who had brought colour and life to the small town for a few short weeks. Finally the sad, shocking realisation that someone they thought they knew so well should turn out to be so evil, or so ill. Whichever it was, thought Beth; it was devastating, life changing. But life would go on. And Melissa Harris hadn't been the only newcomer to bring change to the little town. She looked over at Tom, laughing at something Ken was saying, and her heart leapt. He was so good looking, so solid and dependable, and so special. He looked up and caught her watching him, then smiled at her with so much love that her eyes filled.

"Beth, are you listening?" Carol poked her arm. "I asked you..." Back to the present. Back to the meal and the wine, and conversation about grandchildren, the auction of promises, the school fete, the tourists, the unwanted new supermarket. Back to normal.

They walked out to the car park together. Gina climbed into her little sports car, roof down, waving as she drove away. Carol and Ken turned out of the car park to walk the short distance back to their house.

Tom opened the passenger door and looked down at her before she climbed in, eyes warm and gentle. "Alright?" Beth nodded, smiling back into his eyes, and climbed in.
And maybe, just maybe, it would be.

Printed in Poland
by Amazon Fulfillment
Poland Sp. z o.o., Wrocław